DELILAH

Recovered

Barbara—
Thank you for inspiring
me to write again!
XOXO
Amelia

DELILAH

Recovered

Amelia Estelle Dellos

atmosphere press

To Eric for saving me
To Alena for making me better

"All battles are first won or lost, in the mind."

— JOAN OF ARC

One

"Fair is foul, and foul is fair."

Dee's grip tightened around her leather-bound journal, her hands slick with sweat as she tried to steady her breathing. She traced the gold embossed "D" on the cover. Her journal was the only thing she owned that was expensive that she couldn't justify the cost of other than she had to have it. Each page held her secrets along with the mundane details of her life, from steps walked to ounces of water consumed. For a moment, she forgot she was sitting in his mansion.

"Tell me, Delilah, what is the one thing you want most?" Samuel asked, shifting his body toward her.

Usually, men like Samuel ignored Dee. Of course, he was handsome, the kind of handsome that always gets his way. Somewhere in his mid-thirties, Samuel carried himself with a maturity far beyond his years. Dee could feel his heavy gaze on her. She studied her shoes to steady herself.

"Look at me," Samuel said.

His tone was sharp, demanding. Her head snapped up. Dee wanted to say she wanted the job working for his company. She needed this job. It had finally come down to paying her rent or getting evicted. When their eyes met, he repeated his question in a slow husky growl. His steely gray eyes knocked the breath out of her lungs. Dee had to force herself to hold his hard gaze.

"A family," she said, before she could stop herself.

When Dee said it, she wanted nothing more than to take those words back and swallow them up whole. Before he could react, the door swung open, and Mrs. Fairfax entered carrying the tea tray. She was his assistant, a portly white-haired woman, dressed in a prim blouse with a rounded collar buttoned up to her neck, a simple black skirt, and black Oxfords. It struck Dee that Mrs. Fairfax appeared less like an executive assistant and more like a nanny.

When Samuel stood and turned toward Mrs. Fairfax, his face softened.

"Don't strain yourself," Samuel said, taking the heavy tray from her and setting it down on the desk.

"Now, there's a good boy." Mrs. Fairfax patted his arm.

Dee could feel the sincere affection between them. It surprised Dee to see this warm side of the otherwise cold-hearted mogul. Before she left, Mrs. Fairfax turned around and gave Dee an encouraging smile.

Samuel placed the tea strainer over her teacup in a few swift movements, filled it with tea, poured the hot water over it, and then flipped over the small hourglass timer. Her eyes traveled around the midnight blue room, examining the rows and rows of vintage books lining the walls. A massive dark oak desk with thick snakes carved into it formed the centerpiece. At a glance, out of the corner of her eye, the intertwined snakes appeared to slither up and down the desk legs. The desk featured a round stone tablet with a hole the size of a ring in the middle. Dee squinted her eyes to read the words etched into it.

"Good and evil shall pass through these doors." The words caused the tiny hairs on her arms to stand at attention.

Dee turned around, and her eyes settled on the fireplace. Tiny, scarlet-colored stains covered the swords and daggers hanging over the mantel, with a magical alphabet made up of half-moons, arrows, and crosses carved into each knife handle. The blades' symbols matched the engraved seals on the weathered wooden front door, which had greeted her when she arrived. Despite her nerves, Dee counted the seals. She couldn't help herself. There were forty-nine.

She stood up and walked over to the daggers. Gently, she ran her index finger over the letters. Dee picked up a small sword. It had an etching of a dragon and a serpent on the handle. Dried blood dotted the blade. Holding it in her hand, Dee had a vision of a man's hand pressing the edge against a woman's neck, drawing a stream of blood, along with the sensation of the knife-edge pressing into her own neck.

"My mother collects them."

His voice brought her back to the moment, and the dagger slipped from her hands. She froze. She watched him catch the knife in one swift motion before the razor-sharp blade almost sliced open her leg. The knifepoint left a tiny tear in her pant leg. Her shaky hand landed on her neck. Dee rubbed it, then checked her fingers for blood.

Samuel placed the dagger back on the wall.

"Please, sit down."

His hand rested on the small of her back as he led her back to her chair. The heat of his touch radiated down her spine.

Dee tried to settle into the overstuffed chocolate-colored leather chair. Chicago in July. Each summer, the city grid turned into a steam room, and by the time Dee had finally made it to her job interview, she could feel the large beads of sweat seeping through her off-season, navy-blue outlet mall suit.

He glanced at his watch, again. Samuel's vintage Cartier with a worn alligator strap peeked out from his crisp white button-down shirt, open at the collar. Studying up for her interview, Dee had found an article in a men's magazine about Samuel and his antique watch collection.

Samuel reached out and handed her a cup of tea. He sat on a rich velvet couch framed in wood and gold leaf.

"I love high tea," she said.

Samuel sighed, pinching the bridge of his nose between his thumb and index finger.

"You mean afternoon tea. High tea is taken in the early evening, whereas afternoon tea occurs"—Samuel paused for effect— "in the afternoon."

Heading into this interview, Dee already knew Samuel embodied the old world, across-the-pond rich. She'd got the complete picture from her internet research—Cambridge educated, dated a string of socialites, and friends with royalty. Dee didn't need to see his gothic horror movie mansion or get schooled on tea services to remind her she was out of her league. The bus ride from her fun-sized studio apartment to the Gold Coast framed by Lake Michigan and ornate mansions gave her ample time to work herself into a tizzy. Dee had tried in vain to concentrate on the shiny neighborhood. The sidewalks rolled along, one after the other, all lined with the promise of a juicy steak or an expensive designer purse. Despite the scenery, she kept calculating her overdue rent. It didn't matter how many times she added the numbers; Dee owed more than she had.

This interview isn't going well, Dee thought as she set her teacup down on a small end table.

The library's walls featured museum-quality artwork. One painting caught Dee's attention. Samson, a beast of a man, sleeping soundly like a child with his head on a woman's lap. His herculean body draped over Delilah's luscious crimson skirt. The vivid silky color drew her into the haunting scene. Dee couldn't help herself. She had to get closer to the painting. The rich fabric painted like confection candy drew her to it. Dee wanted so badly to touch it. Tilting her head, she could see herself in the woman's profile, her dark almond-shaped eyes, and her thick wavy hair.

"*Samson & Delilah* by Rubens." Samuel answered the question Dee hadn't asked. "This painting holds a special place for me. You know the story, of course."

Standing so close to him, with not one strand of his caramel-colored hair out of place, Dee took note of Samuel's singular flaw—a nasty scar, puckered and red, that crept up out of his shirt on the left side of his neck and ended at the edge of his cheek.

"The mighty warrior, Samson, falls prey to the deceitful Delilah and loses his strength," Dee said. Her eyes focused on Delilah's creamy skin and voluptuous curves in contrast to Samson's golden skin and hard angles.

"Delilah was bribed to entrap him, to find out the secret of his strength. Samson proclaimed his love for her over and over. Delilah wouldn't accept it unless he confided in her," Samuel said.

"Until finally, Samson told her the key to his power."

Dee paused.

"His hair."

"And in this painting, Delilah's final betrayal, she holds him as if he were a sleeping babe while a servant cuts his hair, rendering him helpless," Samuel said.

"And who betrayed you, Mr. Solomon?" Dee asked, pointing at his scar.

Ignoring her question, his hand flew to his neck.

"You may call me Samuel."

For a moment, they admired the painting until Samuel broke the silence.

"Isn't your given name Delilah?"

"Yes," Dee said.

"Yet, you go by the Dee?"

"The name, Delilah, it seems... I don't know how to explain it..."

She paused and waited for Samuel to fill in the blank. He didn't. Instead, he waited for her to continue. It wasn't in her nature to let a conversation breathe; she had a compulsive need to fill in the pockets of silence.

"It doesn't suit me."

"How so?" he asked.

"It's too big for me."

"Maybe someday you'll grow into it."

Didn't he know that she was an orphan, raised by her guardian, Ms. Tabitha Anthea Masterson, from Sandwich, Illinois? A small-town boasting weekend antique summer fairs and a tenacious tornado alley. All she had was an accounting degree from an average Midwestern university. Both the unimpressive companies she had worked for since graduation had gone belly up despite her best efforts to get their books in order.

A flood of cortisol rushed through her veins, signaling to her brain that her next panic attack was well on its way. To try and stop it, Dee counted backward from four. A trick she used to distract her anxiety. Silently Dee counted *4,3,2,1* because she knew deep down that she wasn't qualified for this job. He only hired Ivy League graduates. When the recruiter had contacted Dee about the position, she was shocked.

"Why am I here?" she asked.

"To interview for an accounting position," he said, leading

her once again back to the chair.

"What will you do for my company?" he asked as he sat down and folded his hands on top of his lap, waiting for her response.

Dee knew she'd have to steady her voice before answering his question. Dee made the mistake of making eye contact. Her mind went blank like a fuzzy television.

"Anytime now."

She watched as he drummed his fingers on his knee. Then he checked his watch.

"Micro-investments."

The word tumbled out, and the high pitch of her voice rang in her ears.

"Sorry?"

"Micro-investments in third-world countries."

Dee swallowed hard and attempted to level out her pitch and talk at a slower pace.

"Micro-investments would be the way to go for MILLO."

Samuel nodded, encouraging her to continue.

"They're low risk because the investments are small with an opportunity for high yields," Dee said.

Samuel remained silent with his head tilted, staring at an unseen horizon. He seemed bored, and Dee wanted to impress him. For her, it wasn't just about the job either; she wanted his approval.

"Plus, you'd also help people in underdeveloped nations by injecting much-needed capital, resources, and work into their economy."

His face broke out into a wicked smile, showcasing a set of unnaturally stark white teeth.

"Ms. Smith, you misunderstand my intentions entirely. I want to take over the world, not save it."

Sinking into the chair, Dee hoped it would open up and swallow her and put an end to whatever this was. Samuel studied her for a long moment.

"I get this strange feeling you and I have met before," Samuel said.

"You shop at Target?"

"You should know I, more than anyone, appreciate a good deal," he said with a teasing smile. "I am rendered helpless by the five-dollar bin."

The air in the room shifted, charged and heavy, like before a summer storm.

"What do you think happens when you die?" he asked.

Dee gazed around the room. The walls closed in on her. She couldn't take it anymore and pulled off her suit jacket. It didn't matter at this point. Dee knew she wasn't going to land this job.

"You're dead," she said.

"Do you believe in reincarnation?"

"No, I don't."

"What if we knew each other in another lifetime, and this life is a continuation of our previous life?"

"Like one endless stream with no beginning or end?"

She took a sip of her tea, while willing her hand to stop shaking.

"Yes, exactly, one life bleeding into the other, starting in a different era, but with the same trials to bear and overcome," Samuel said.

"And this question has what to do with accounting?"

Her hand shook, and she spilled tea on the table when she set her cup down. She tried to sop it up with her hand.

"It has absolutely nothing to do with accounting, Ms. Smith. No afterlife then?"

Samuel drank his tea, waiting for her answer.

"It's easier to believe in something, right? Gives our lives meaning. For me, though, it doesn't add up. Heaven is a fairytale concocted to give people hope," she said.

"Just darkness, then?"

"Yes."

"I'm not a big fan of darkness."

"Is this a psychological test?"

She couldn't figure out where he was going with this line of questions.

"Delilah, what if there's more to this world than we can even begin to comprehend with our five senses?"

He placed his teacup down and folded his hands on his lap.

"Like a sixth sense?"

"Not even a sense, but magic. What did Shakespeare say, 'There are more things in heaven and earth, Horatio, than are dreamt of in your philosophy.'"

"You believe in ghosts, fairies, and little green men?" Dee asked, shaking her head in disbelief.

"Nope, only fairies."

He leaned back into his chair and smiled at her.

"He wants the ring. Guard it with your life," said a woman's voice.

"Is there someone else in here?"

Her head spun around, searching the room for the person who issued the warning.

"No."

"I heard a woman's voice," Dee said.

She looked down at her leg and noticed the tear in her pants had transformed into the size of a nickel. A nervous tick, Dee hadn't realized she had been working at it with her index finger during the interview. Her vision blurred. Adrenaline flooded her body, and her panic attack went from a low idle in the background to all systems go.

Dee stood up. Her legs wobbled. Samuel's two strong arms reached out and steadied her.

"What did this voice say?"

Peering into Samuel's eyes, and for the first time since she arrived, Dee saw something that shocked her—fear. Dee's panic spun out of her control. She felt like a wounded animal seeking shelter. She had one thought on repeat.

I gotta get out now. I gotta get out now. I gotta get out now. I gotta get out now. I gotta get out now. I gotta get out now.

"I need to go home. Now," Dee said.

"Of course."

He guided her to the door. She stopped to pick up her backpack and almost tipped over. Again, his hand reached out to steady her.

"May I escort you home?"

Dee hated feeling helpless.

"I will make it on my own."

She pulled her arm away from his hold and walked out the door.

Two

"Not all who wander are lost."

Dee caught sight of herself in the rearview mirror, and it was a sight to behold. Her mascara and eyeliner had now formed a dark rim around her violet eyes. Her cheeks, which usually had a rosy blush, were haunted, ashen. Her hair had sprung loose from the ponytail holder.

"Where are you going to watch it?" her Lyft driver asked.

Dee took her index fingers and tried to wipe away the excess make-up under her eyes while at the same time concentrating on her breathing, gently reminding herself to breathe in and to breathe out. "Watch what?"

"Watch what? Are you serious, my lady? The Triple Moon! It hasn't appeared in like three hundred years or something," he replied.

Dee had no idea what he was saying. He slammed on the

brakes, and a string of expletives came pouring from his mouth. She fished around the back seat, trying to find the seat belt under the bright red seat covers. Dee held onto the headrest to steady herself. The car jerked forward, and she noticed the seat covers were embroidered with an image of a sun with a face in the middle.

He turned around and smiled. "Sorry about these lunatic city drivers. Hey, do I know you?"

Dee looked at him. He was striking with his sun-kissed olive skin with wet, jet-black hair and onyx eyes to match.

"We have never met," she replied as she focused intently on her journal, with her pen in her hand, attempting to will their conversation to end. She started writing; writing in her journal always made her feel better.

———————————————————————————————————————

July 18 @ 3:33 pm - in a Lyft
State of Mind - Frazzled & Freaked Out

Samuel Solomon, the third, is a third-degree ass. Did I get the job? That's probably, a real hard no. Nearly passing out and running out of the interview like a crazy person, not the best look when trying to land the biggest job of my life.

And what was up with the fairy and magic and sixth-sense stuff???
It was all bananas with a capital B. Right?
Who asks that stuff in an interview?

14

Was it even an interview???

IDK

Maybe I'll show up on a reality TV show about the worst job interviews ever. I'm probably already a meme. "Woman who runs out of job interview like her hair is on fire." I can see my hair with the Photoshopped red flames.

Oh, God. I'm so screwed.

I'm going to have to move back home...like a little country mouse, who can't make it in the big city.

Good grief. Was there a vibe between us?

No. I'm making that up. That was so in my head. I was having a vibe with me, myself, and I because even though Samuel is extremely arrogant, he's also extremely handsome and rich. He doesn't date unemployed accountants. I doubt he dates employed accountants... unless there's a supermodel/CPA/Influencer/Mogul out there.

"I'm Mahai Symeon Nicolae Andri, at your service," he proclaimed. "I'm a wanderer."

She stuffed her journal into her bag. "And I'm an accountant."

Mahai had a deep baritone laugh. "Ah, my lady makes a good joke."

Dee surveyed the car for the first time. There was a bobblehead of a saint bobbing up and down on the dashboard. It read "Sarah the Black" underneath it. It was a room on wheels with the floorboards carpeted in oriental rugs, and it smelled like a head shop.

"So, the Triple Moon, are you going to the lake?"

"I want to get home," Dee replied, watching the traffic come to a standstill.

"You know what they say about this moon? The last time it appeared in the sky was on the night the last witch was burned alive. And after the light of this moon, a descendant of Joan of Arc will lead the witches out of the shadows once more."

"Lead the witches out of the shadows," she repeated.

"Only if you believe that kind of stuff," he said as he winked at her and popped a piece of gum into his mouth.

"Would you like a piece? It's black licorice," he said as he showed her the package of Black Jack gum.

Dee knew it was rush hour, and the traffic was not going to move anytime soon.

"You know what? I'm good. I think I can walk from here."

Mahai shrugged. "It's of no consequence to me."

Dee gathered her backpack and tried to open the door, but it was jammed.

Mahai mumbled something under his breath. "Try it now."

The door flew open, and Dee tumbled out into the street. The moment she slammed the door shut; the traffic began to move. She watched the beat-up black Land Rover as it took off.

Dee walked the rest of the way home. Even though she was

bone tired, she didn't want to take the L subway. Her nerves were frayed, and she wondered if the day was, in fact, a fever dream.

"More like a nightmare," she said out loud.

All she wanted was a cold shower and her bed. It was so muggy that steam was rising from the asphalt, and her clothes were sticking to her body. She felt a drop of water land on her forehead and looked up. She stopped and watched as dark clouds tumbled across the sky.

Of course, I forgot my umbrella, she thought as the sky opened up on her. It was at that moment Dee realized she was at St. Mary's of the Angels. Relieved, she let out the breath she was holding. There was something about this church. In its orbit, she always felt safe and protected. She could see the stark white angels standing sentry around the rooftop from across the city. She ran to the stairs, taking shelter under the massive white Ionic columns. She pulled out her phone to check the weather app to find out how long the storm would last. Her phone was dead.

The sky turned black as white-hot lightning battered the church's roof severing the angel's wings from its body. The mammoth ivory stone statue came crashing down into the side of the church, rocking the building like an earthquake before landing in the middle of the street.

Dee turned toward the door. When she put her hand on the door handle, she felt a hand around her neck. A man wearing a balaclava mask grabbed Dee and held a gleaming crescent-shaped silver knife to her throat.

"I've got her," he shouted over the crack of thunder.

Another dark figure came up behind her and pulled at her right arm, shining a flashlight on a small spiral birthmark on the inside of Dee's forearm.

"It's her," said the woman.

As he pressed the knife into her throat, Dee made eye

contact with her captor: his eyes were mismatched, one blue and the other brown.

Suddenly, Dee had a vision. She saw a young boy with warm golden skin and curly chocolate-colored hair kneeling with his head down as a man with a cruel jaw towered over him with a whip. When the whip came down and cracked against his back, his head shot up, and his eyes filled with terror.

The woman screamed. "Wolf, execute her now."

Behind the man in black, Dee saw another man, dressed in a white T-shirt with a thin leather harness running over his shoulders, jeans, and construction boots, emerge from the shattered angel statue. On his heels was a formation of women dressed in charcoal turtlenecks, leggings, and knee-high boots with tight ponytails on top of their heads.

The woman in black turned around. "Not the fucking fairies."

Dee took her moment and kicked her captor with all her might in the groin. The man in the white T-shirt extended his arm and, with an invisible force, pinned the man in black against the wall.

"Aros, we have no quarrel with the Grigori," the man in black screamed in labored breaths over the rain and lightning.

In a flash, the fairies descended upon Dee's assailants, surrounding them like a swarm of furious flies, ready to rip them into pieces. Dee was caught in the vortex, unable to breathe, unable to run. Her last moment of consciousness was a fairy seizing her, launching her through the air, before she heard an unholy hollow crack as her skull landed on the pavement.

Three

"Evil is a voluntary act."

Later that night, in an uncomfortable silence, Wolf and his partner, Joanna, entered what appeared to be an abandoned candy factory. The chipped crumbling facade housed a state-of-the-art headquarters and training facility for a centuries-old secret organization, the Sect of the Silver Hammer, founded in the 1300s to exterminate witches.

"All our training, and you hesitated," Joanna said as they entered the sub-armory.

Wolf began to remove his wet gear. "I looked into her eyes."

Joanna pushed Wolf against his locker with her elbow pressing into his throat, making it difficult for him to breathe.

"You had her," she hissed.

Joanna was the toughest soldier he knew, and he'd served

Delta Force in the Army Special Services.

She released him and slapped him on the back. "I won't tell your old man."

They changed out of their special operations gear and into sweats embellished with the Sect's crest— a silver hammer in a circle with words "Thou Shalt Not Suffer a Witch to Live" written in Latin underneath it. They walked through a series of polished cement hallways, stretching through the bowels of the building. When they entered the leader of the Sect's office, they found Gart Jacob Zandt staring at a painting of Joan of Arc.

Gart pointed at the painting. "Evil comes in many faces. See hers, a simple young peasant girl. She was a nobody from nowhere. What did she do before we killed her? She used her powers to lead an army of thousands of men to win a war."

Gart spun around. His salt and pepper hair still cropped close to his head, showcasing an angry throbbing vein on his forehead. He took one long stride and was nose to nose with Wolf.

"Tonight, you had one simple mission. It was to execute another nobody from nowhere before she could wreak havoc on our world, before she could start another war, the war of good versus evil," said Gart.

"Sir, we had her, but we were ambushed," Joanna attempted to explain.

Gart turned his attention to Joanna. "My two best soldiers, soldiers I trained, no less, bested by a mute fallen angel and a flock of fanny-pack wearing fairies."

Gart took a step back and crossed his imposing arms across his broad chest. "Now, because of you two, war has been set into motion, and there's no guarantee we're going to win it."

Wolf met Gart's steely gaze. "Father, we—"

"You don't deserve to call me father, you hear me?" Gart

spat as he cracked Wolf across the face. The force of the blow brought Wolf to his knees. Gart walked away, leaving Wolf alone.

After his father's reprimand, Wolf was in the gym, pounding the punching bag until his knuckles bled. The sweat was cascading down his muscled back like tears over the large red scars covering it. Each mark on Wolf's back was a testament to the shame he had brought to the Zandt name.

Every night, no matter how late, Wolf made sure to visit the chapel to pray. No matter how tired, he would climb a hundred narrow steps, never stopping until he reached the stained-glass image of the tree of life with a massive flaming sword guarding it, backlit by an eternal flame at the top.

There was a small wooden altar with a crucifix hanging overhead. Both were made in the 1500s for Heinrich Krammer, the clergyman who wrote *The Malleus Maleficarum*, or *The Hammer of the Witches*. The original book rested on top of the altar. It had been used for centuries by generations of witch hunters to hunt, test, and torture witches.

The chapel floor was crafted out of rough, uneven cobblestones held together by grainy cement which cut into his knees when he kneeled to pray. Wolf would always begin with the Lord's Prayer. He always got tripped up on the passage, "Forgive us our trespasses as we forgive those who trespass against us." He said these words every night before bed, but he was never taught to forgive. Gart had only tried to plant hate in Wolf's heart.

Before rejoining the Sect, Wolf had spent most of his adult life in the military deployed in active war zones. After four tours in the Middle East, he saw honest soldiers refuse mercy and corrupt soldiers give mercy. He knew if Joanna had had the knife to Delilah's neck, she would be dead. But he couldn't kill her. Even though he had failed his father, failed the Sect, he had no regrets for showing Delilah mercy tonight, Wolf thought as he drifted off into a restless sleep.

What seemed like hours later, Wolf woke up from a dream in which he had found himself running at breakneck speed through the forest, drenched in perspiration. It was dark, with only the moon to light his path. Although he couldn't see anyone following him, he knew he was the prey. He patted his legs and pockets. No gun. No blade. In the distance, he heard a wolf howl in pain, and as he turned his head toward the sound, he tripped over a fallen branch. Face down in the dirt and shrubs, Wolf struggled to pull himself up. Suddenly, someone seized his leg, dragging him through the forest, the ground scraping away bits and pieces of his skin as he clawed at the earth, trying to break free.

His captor released Wolf next to a blazing fire. As he turned over, he flinched at the wild violet eyes gazing down on him. Delilah.

A wicked smile broke across her face. "Will you deliver me from evil?"

Wolf jerked awake. He was still on the chapel floor, his thighs covered in blood.

Four

"I am sent to comfort the poor and needy."

When Dee regained consciousness, it was an endless void filled with darkness. Then agony, as a searing pain radiated up and down her entire body. The throbbing in her head was on a continual loop, bursting open and shattering into a million tiny shards. Her eyelids were two lead weights pressing down into her skull. She tried in vain to open them. The panic consumed her. When she realized she couldn't move her frozen body, her heart began drumming against her chest.

Suddenly, she was moving, not by her own accord, but on a cart. She could hear the faint sound of wheels, like a wonky shopping cart underneath her. She pushed open her eyes, catching bits and pieces of the light before they slammed shut again.

Flick.

Am I dead?
Flick.
I see lights. Dead means lights out, right?
Flick.
Wait, are those fluorescent lights?
Flick.
Heaven would have better lighting, right?
Flick.
Unless this isn't heaven.

Before Dee could open her eyes, another wave of pain rocked her body. She tried to catch her breath in between the swells. With every inhale, the smells of disinfectant and urine burned her delicate lungs.

She heard weary footsteps shuffling across the floor, and before she could open her eyes, a man with a warm milk-and-cookies voice asked, "What do we have here?"

He gently placed his hands on her forehead and the pain instantly dissipated. Now her body was pulsating with mellow, peaceful energy.

"Another victim of the Triple Moon, perhaps?" he inquired.

She glided on a smooth current until he pushed open her eyelid and shined a bright light into her shocking violet eye, causing him to recoil and fumble the light.

Dee's pain returned with a rush causing her body to shoot up like a rocket. "Is this Hell?" she asked, blinking away the blazing fluorescent lights.

"Also referred to as Chicago City General," he chuckled as he recovered his composure and took a step toward her bed. He was wearing the standard-issue, green scrubs with copper stains, remnants from his other patients. His trainers looked like they had run several marathons.

"Now, I need you to lie back down. Can you do that for me?" he asked.

"Yes," she whispered.

"Is it okay if I help you?"

Dee nodded. He gently placed his hand on her back and slowly guided her down. Gazing up at him, she noticed his sad, red-lined, hazel eyes, framed in dark circles. Salt-and-pepper stubble covered his square jaw. Collapsing his towering frame over hospital beds night after night left his shoulders permanently hunched over. This broken man held her life in his hands.

His eyes read hers, acknowledging without words, her fear, and her pain. He gave her a caring, fatherly smile. "I am the best ER doctor here. My job is to make you better. You got me?" he said, placing a reassuring hand on her shoulder. And for some reason, Dee believed him.

"Now, I am going to get the nurse in here to get you something to help with the pain," he said, winking before turning to leave.

Dee closed her eyes. She heard the floor creak and opened them to find a man standing in her room. He had dark, wild, curly hair and warm Mediterranean skin. He wore a white T-shirt with a harness around his shoulders. Dee frantically pressed the call button. Before the nurse entered her room, he had disappeared.

"There was a man. He had muscles and tight jeans," said Dee pointing at the empty corner.

"Sounds like my kind of man," the nurse teased, smacking her gum as she pulled a syringe out of her pocket.

"You didn't see him?" Dee asked.

"No honey, I didn't," the nurse said, plunging the syringe into Dee's arm. "But if I do, I'll be sure to send him back to your room. Okay, doll face?"

As the drugs infiltrated her veins, Dee found herself in a field surrounded by semi-darkness and an expanse of soaring trees. She glanced up at the sky. There was a round iridescent moon on the rise over the tips of the trees. What did Tabitha Anthea call it? It was the Hay Moon. It was the seventh full moon of the year. She heard the trees sway as a woman in a dark robe emerged from them. Dee couldn't make out her face because it was covered in a hood. The woman walked to the center of the field, lifted her arms to the sky, and a ten-foot-high flaming bonfire appeared. Then, more women filtered out of the shadows in flowing robes circling the pyre. Dee counted twelve in all.

Slowly, in a trance-like state, they circled the fire, chanting, "Aperiesque ostium."

"Aperiesque ostium."

"Aperiesque ostium." they repeated.

Suddenly they stopped and pointed at Dee. She found herself walking toward them. When she looked down, she was wearing the same flowing dark robe.

"Numero tredecim," they chanted softly at first, but as Dee got closer to them, their chanting became thunderous.

Their words, "Numero tredecim," were pounding her eardrums, vibrating in her chest. Dee was now a part of their circle. They pointed at the fire. She knew what they were calling her to do. She lifted her foot but couldn't do it. She could feel the white-hot flame on the sole of her foot. It sent an electrifying jolt through her entire body.

Dee's eyes sprang open. Disorientated, she peered around the room. There was an IV in her arm. The early morning sun was trying to break through the broken, grimy blinds barely hanging onto the window. There was an authoritative knock at her door, and before she could say 'come in,' a man entered her room holding a legal pad and a file.

She knew for sure he wasn't a doctor, dressed in skinny jeans and vintage Doc Martens. He gave Dee an easy smile as he dragged a chair to the side of her bed.

"I'm Jonathan Berwick," he said as he sat down.

He had the presence of a rock star with his auburn hair shaved at the sides and slicked back on top, bright blue eyes, and a sleeve of spiral tattoos up and down his right arm. The molecules in the room danced around him, changing as he moved.

"Are you in a band?" Dee blurted out.

Jonathan's face broke into a large smile, making his eyes twinkle. "Nope, just a social worker who plays a mean air guitar."

Dee pushed the button, trying to move the bed so she could sit up. Instead, she moved her feet up and her back down. Jonathan stood up. When he took the control panel from her, he brushed her hand. His touch sparked a magnetic silver shock between them.

"Get a load of that. Someone has some extra electrons," Jonathan said, grinning.

She watched as he pressed the buttons, studying the two thick leather cuffs with fleur-de-lis etched into them he wore on each wrist.

Once he fixed her bed, he handed over her journal.

"This was recovered by one of the paramedics."

It was covered in dirt and dust. She clutched it to her chest like a little girl holding onto her blanket.

"How are you?" Jonathan asked.

She gave him a weak smile. He sat down and leaned in, closing the space between them. "You are one brave woman," he said.

"Excuse me?"

"You fended off two attackers last night," he stated as he opened her file.

"Honestly, I can't say what happened. I can recall bits and pieces, the rain and thunder, the angel church..." she replied.

"Well, I can tell you something, Delilah, what you went through will be a test."

"I don't understand."

"When something like this happens to a person, it can forever alter their lives. They can't get over it, or they work to get their life back to normal like it was before, or..." Jonathan paused.

"Or what?" Dee asked, unable to push down the rising anxiety building up in her tightening chest.

"Or it changes them, makes them stronger and braver than they ever were before," Jonathan said, leaning back in his chair.

"So, my options are my life is ruined forever, I can go back to the status quo, or I can become a hero?"

"Pretty much," he replied with a casual shrug.

"Do people say you're good at your job?" she asked.

"Normally, I work with addiction patients, but with the crazy moon last night, they have me working double time," Jonathan said, leaning in like he was telling her a secret.

Outside her hospital room, voices were whispering angrily. On the other side of the door, a man's voice said, "Your only job was to protect her."

Dee couldn't hear the response.

"Then how did she end up in my ER?" the man asked.

Jonathan stood up. "Hey, I'm going to grab you some water." Dee watched as he walked across the room. He had a large silver chain running from his belt to his wallet tucked in his back pocket.

When he got to the door, it flew open, almost knocking him over before he jumped back. In the door frame stood all six feet of Tabitha Anthea, Dee's guardian, dressed in her signature burgundy wrap dress and matching lipstick. As always, her black skin was radiant, and not one of her deep brown sculpted finger waves was out of place.

She pushed past Jonathan. "My peanut buttercup," she said as she set her weathered vintage Louis Vuitton doctor's bag on the chair. When she sat down on the bed, she placed her hand on Dee's forehead. "Let me take a look at you."

Dee pulled away from her. "Thea, I wasn't attacked by a fever."

Tabitha Anthea shot a look at Jonathan. "No, you were attacked by something much worse."

Jonathan met her stern gaze. "It's time for Delilah to know what is lurking in the dark, don't ya think?"

"I think it's time you left, son," she replied in a sharp tone, stating their conversation was over.

She wrapped her muscular fingers around Dee's hand. "If anything, I mean anything happened to you."

"Is that pie I smell?" Dee asked.

"Muffins," she answered as she opened her bag and pulled out a container.

"Thea, when did you have the time?"

"You know I can't help myself. Baking relaxes me," Tabitha Anthea replied, handing Dee a mouth-watering, still-warm-from-the-oven cinnamon muffin.

Dee pulled her into a hug. "Thank you."

She pulled away from Dee. Their eyes connected. Dee leaned toward her, and they touched foreheads. "I am always here for you," Tabitha Anthea said.

"No matter what," Dee replied.

July 19 @ 5:55 pm - The Hospital
State of Mind - Lucky to be Alive?

I'm lucky to be alive. That's the refrain I keep hearing from the nurses, the doctors, Thea, and the cute social worker, Jonathan

Berwick. The minute he sat down; I had this feeling like—I know this guy. How do I know this guy? Then I don't even know what happened to me??? I was walking by the church, there was rain, thunder, and that's all I can remember.

Even though I don't remember what happened, I remember what it felt like. It felt like darkness. It felt like being trapped in a bad dream that wouldn't end. It felt like I was trying to scream but nothing would come out of my mouth. I had this pressing sensation on my chest, like my heart was going to explode. I will never forget that feeling. It will haunt me. It was like nothing would or could ever be good again... like I no longer wanted to live.

I would do anything never to feel that way again.

Right now, my head hurts so bad. It won't stop throbbing and my hands feel all tingly. I don't feel at all like myself. It's like I'm outside of myself looking in and watching. I'm all disconnected.

Can they reconnect me?
Is that a thing doctor's can do?

When Jonathan walked into my room, I felt
like this instant calm wash over me. It was
like sitting on a beach on a sunny day
listening to the waves and children laughing.
His voice, the way he said my name, my real
name, not my nickname. It sounded like a
song—Dee-lye-la. It sounded so beautiful.

————————————————————————————————

Five

"I think for the sickness I have;
I am in great danger of death."

Dee, wearing nothing but a thin hospital gown, found herself
walking down the middle of State Street through a dense haze.
The sidewalks were empty. Boarded-up storefronts with
graffiti of the Triple Moon painted on them lined the street.
Underneath the L tracks, she could see a turned over car on
fire.

As she walked down the street, she began to feel
lightheaded. A band of horses galloping rocked the street. The
city melted away from her, turning into an open field filled
with dead bloody soldiers dressed in armor. A woman
appeared in front of Dee. She had short black hair and wore a
chainmail suit with an arrow stuck in her chest. When she fell
to her knees, Dee felt a stabbing pain in her chest in the same
spot.

With a fierce, defiant resolve, the woman stared up at Dee, her face covered in dirt and blood, and said, "Relevez tous les défis avec courage."

Dee repeated, "Meet all challenges with courage."

When she opened her eyes, Dee screamed when she saw a man standing next to her bed.

Jonathan put his hands up in surrender. "It's me. You seemed like you were having a nightmare. I didn't want to wake you up."

Dee pulled the thin hospital sheet and blanket up around her neck. Normally, her body felt strong and lithe, but being in the hospital made her feel weak and frail.

"Get out of my room."

"I need to get you somewhere safe," Jonathan said.

The door swung open. "Not bloody likely," Samuel said, entering the room.

The two men stood on opposite sides of Dee's hospital bed, arms crossed. "Samuel," Jonathan said through gritted teeth.

"Master Jonathan, I was led to believe you had this all in hand?" Samuel asked, shaking his head, his voice dripping in disapproval.

"You were the one who let her wander home under the Triple Moon alone," Jonathan replied.

The two men stood glaring at one another until Samuel broke the silence. "She needs to know the truth post-haste."

"So, you want her to know what you did to her three hundred years ago?" Jonathan asked.

Samuel lifted his right hand with one swift motion; he slowly rotated his palm up toward the ceiling, and Jonathan dropped to the floor. His body was convulsing.

"Is this how it felt the last time you overdosed?" Samuel hissed. "Is this how it felt right after the bliss of the heroin shot through your veins and then sent you into hypoxia?"

"We don't have *time* for this," Jonathan said in between

wheezing, labored breaths.

"What are you doing to him?" Dee yelled. "Stop it!"

Samuel closed his palm. "Just remember who holds the real power," he said, leaving Jonathan gasping for air on all fours.

Dee got out of her bed. By digging her feet into the floor, using the balance she honed doing yoga, she leveraged her medium-sized frame to pull Jonathan up off the floor.

"Enough, both of you. I don't know what you are, but I do know you both are acting like children," Dee scolded.

"You need to come with me," Samuel ordered.

"I can protect you," Jonathan said.

"I want you to both leave my room now," Dee demanded.

Suddenly, Aros appeared in Dee's room. "Aros, our fallen hero, come to save us all," Samuel said.

Dee approached him. She circled him. Dressed in a white T-shirt which outlined each one of his muscles, work boots, thin leather harness that ran under his arms and across his back, and tight dark Levi's he looked like a backup dancer.

She poked him in the chest. "You, you were in my room last night."

He ran his hand through his wild, curly black hair and smiled at her.

Dee's eyes darted between Jonathan, Samuel, and Aros. "Look, I don't know if I'm dreaming or awake right now, but I do know I don't want any of you here."

Jonathan slowly approached Delilah and gently placed his hands on her shoulders. "Delilah, I know this is probably really scary for you, but I'm here to help you."

She slapped his hands away. "You know what's even scarier? Having two strange men," she said, pointing to Aros, "and whatever you are, no offense, in my hospital room watching me sleep."

Aros clapped his hands and pointed at the door. A few

seconds later, the lights went out, and alarms started to wail. The backup generator lights went on, casting an eerie red glow in the hospital room.

"Aros, take her to the fairies," Jonathan ordered.

Moments later, Wolf and Joanna, dressed in lab coats, exploded through the door. Wolf pulled out a gun and fired a polished silver bullet at Delilah. Aros leaped in front of her. They both disappeared before the bullet shot Delilah. Instead, it penetrated the hospital wall leaving a small bullet hole.

Swinging the IV stand like a bat, Samuel hit Joanna in her knees, sending her down. Wolf pushed Jonathan down and jumped on top of him. Jonathan grabbed the cord from the call button and wrapped it around Wolf's neck. Wolf struggled against the cable, trying to insert his fingers between the cord and his neck.

Samuel turned toward the window and kicked it, sending shards of glass sailing through the air. Joanna struggled to get up. Samuel held his hands in front of him, forming a triangle with his index fingers and thumbs, pinning Joanna to the floor.

"Master Jonathan, our train is scheduled to depart. Are you coming?" Samuel said, jumping onto the windowpane.

Jonathan pulled the cord tighter around Wolf's neck, until Wolf finally passed out. Using it as a trampoline, Jonathan jumped onto the bed to propel his body onto Samuel's back. Together, they flew out the window.

Six

"I never saw any fairies under the tree
to my knowledge."

Dee's body felt heavy, like it was filled with stones. One second she was in the hospital room. The next she was—she didn't know.

"Where are we?" she asked Aros.

He didn't reply.

"Can you talk?"

He shook his head and looked down at the floor.

"What happened to you?" she asked as she took his hand. Aros sighed. Then he gave Dee a sad toothy smile revealing a gap between his front teeth which, coupled with his wild wavy hair, made him extremely endearing.

They landed in front of a majestic wooden door, which was framed by a golden arch and engraved with sprite fairies in a field of fiery-red poppies. Dee felt raw and exposed standing there barefoot in nothing but a hospital gown. As Aros raised his hand to knock on the door, it opened before his hand landed on it. Standing in the doorway was a lithe woman with short, platinum blonde hair. When she saw Aros and Dee, she tried to shut the door on them. But Aros wedged his work boot in the door frame.

"Whatever," she said with a shrug, leaving the door open and walking away.

Dee peered inside. It was a dilapidated, abandoned church. The pews were converted to rows of long tables with stools. The floor was a sea of empty Red Bull cans, Amazon boxes, discarded make-up, and designer fanny packs with Gucci, Chanel, and Louis Vuitton logos covering the grimy red carpet. Hanging from the chipped rafters of the vaulted cream ceiling were hammocks filled with gold and silver bedding.

Sitting at the tables intensely focused on their laptops were women, all wearing charcoal gray turtlenecks, leggings, and combat boots. Moments later, Samuel and Jonathan flew through a cracked, stained-glass window. As they landed in the center of the aisle, the women commenced hissing like a hive of angry bees.

Samuel approached the woman who greeted Dee and Aros. "Faye, how have you been, love?"

Faye flashed her teeth, which had turned into razor-sharp fangs. "You know there's an entry price."

Samuel pulled out a thick roll of bills. "Will cash suffice?"

Faye snatched the money from his hands. She raised her hand in the air to show the others the cash. They immediately stopped.

Jonathan ran over to Dee. "Delilah, are you okay?" he asked as he peeled off his faded denim shirt and wrapped it around her shoulders.

The women froze. In silence, they got on their feet, walked

over to Dee and kneeled before her.

Dee glanced down at them. "What's happening?"

"She doesn't know?" Faye asked. "You witches need to get your houses in order."

Samuel leaned into Faye, his nose almost touching hers. "You forget yourself."

Jonathan placed his hands on Samuel's shoulders. "Easy there, boss man. We're all on the same team."

Samuel smacked Jonathan's hand away. "We've never been on the same team. I have urgent business in need of my attention. Do you think you can keep her safe in my absence?"

"You mean to protect her from you? Then yes, I'm perfectly capable of doing that."

Faye placed her body in between Jonathan and Samuel. "You've outstayed your welcome. We don't serve you," she said to Samuel.

"A gentleman always knows when it's time to leave," he replied. He walked over to Dee and took her hand, kissing the top of it. "If you need anything, please call on Mrs. Fairfax."

Dee gave him a quizzical look. "Just say her name three times, and she'll appear wherever and whenever you need her," Samuel explained.

Dee inspected her surroundings. It all seemed like a bad dream, but somehow, she knew it wasn't. "You," she said, pointing to Faye. "What are you?"

"A fairy," Faye replied.

"Like Tinkerbell?" Dee asked as she marched over to inspect her. Once Dee was close to her, she noticed her skin had a pearly iridescent glow, which was mesmerizing.

"If Tinkerbell is a dead soul paying penance for her sins, then yes, like her," Faye said as she pulled a vape pen out of her pocket.

"Is this a dream?" Dee asked.

"More like a living freaking unending nightmare," Faye countered.

Jonathan shot her a dirty look. "Faye, not helpful."

Dee stared at the fairies, who were still kneeling. "You were all there on the night I was attacked?"

"We all saved your ass," Faye replied.

"Delilah, I want to take you home to Tabitha Anthea; she can help us sort this all out," Jonathan said as he put his arm around her.

"Why do you keep calling me Delilah?" she asked Jonathan, shaking his arm from her shoulder.

"Because that's your name, toots," Faye replied, walking back up the aisle. "You're Delilah Johanne D..."

Jonathan quickly placed his hand over Faye's mouth. "Tabitha Anthea will explain it."

"Please stand up," Dee said to the fairies. They glanced at one another, unsure of what to do. Dee waved her arms, motioning for them to stand up. Slowly, they began to rise.

Dee wrapped her arms around her body. She felt cold and exposed standing in the church in her thin hospital gown.

"Faye, you're coming with us," Jonathan said, gathering clothes off of the floor for Dee to wear home. He handed her a pair of leggings and boots.

Faye stuffed her vape pen into her pocket. She walked over to Dee and offered her hand. "Let's motor before those hunters track us down again."

Seven

"The offenses you bring against me,
I have not committed."

When Samuel spotted a small cottage cobbled out of mismatched gray and black stones with a bright red door, he stopped. He put his compass in the pocket of his army green cargo pants. Then, he deliberately made his way around back to the garden, filled with flowers and medicinal herbs.

Perched on a lime green garden mat sat Sage Pentreath, the leader of the Clan. She hadn't changed much since Samuel had last encountered her. She was still a stout woman with a long silver braid snaked down her back, grazing her ankles. He watched her as she pulled out the thorny weeds.

"Don't stand there gaping at my ass; grab a hoe and help," Sage said as she tossed him a small hoe.

Samuel took off his mirrored aviator sunglasses. "I don't do weeds."

Sage gazed up at him with a mischievous smile lighting up her tawny face. "We both know you've never had a problem getting your hands dirty before."

"We have some business to discuss," he said, checking his watch.

She continued to tend to her garden. "Talk and dig. Two birds. One Stone."

Samuel gazed up at the sky. He knew arguing with her was an utter waste of time. He sighed and bent down next to her.

Sage tossed him a gardening mat. "I wouldn't want you to get your pretty knees dirty."

They worked in silence. "How many witches would love to see Samuel Solomon, leader of the OB coven on his knees? And all I had to do was ask," she mused.

"More like order. You stubborn cow."

Sage looked over at Samuel's progress. She took the hoe from him. "That's thornapple."

"They're all bloody weeds to me," he said, standing up and brushing the dirt from his legs. "Your son is causing all sorts of difficulties."

Sage stood up. "I've heard."

"All the way out here?"

"I'm retired, not dead," she said as she made her way toward her cottage. "If you're as tired and as hungry as you appear, come inside."

Sage led him into her kitchen. "Retirement must be treating you well," he said as he admired her French copper stove, Carrara marble countertops, hand-carved cabinets, and stone fireplace.

Sage smiled. "Finally got my dream kitchen and nobody to cook for." She grabbed a wooden spoon and stirred something bubbling in a big iron pot.

Samuel walked over to the stove and peered into the pot. "What do you have there? Eye of newt and roasted toadstool?" he teased.

41

"Beef stew," she said as she pulled out of her cabinet three delicate hand-painted bowls with delicate poppies painted on them.

He leaned in and inhaled the stew. "Smells like the home I once knew, the home the years have long since washed away."

"Good lord, you only get sappy like this when your precious Delilah is around," Sage said as she dished a heaping bowl of stew for him. "Sit down."

He noticed a platter of homemade bread and an assortment of English cheese on a wooden platter on the table. "Stinking bishop, my favorite. I know it was hard to come by in the middle of nowhere."

"Let's say I may have anticipated your visit," she said as she placed a bowl on the floor. "Theodore, lunch is ready." No sooner did the words escape her mouth than a small white dog came tumbling into the kitchen.

Samuel took a bite of her stew. He closed his eyes and savored it as a dull sadness wound its way around his heart. Samuel felt hollow. He took another bite and realized he was homesick.

Sage watched him as he ate. She lit a light-brown clove cigarette. She took a long pull on it and blew the sweet smoke out.

"What do you want from me?" Sage asked as she sat down across the table from him.

Samuel pushed his bowl aside. "I need to call in my chit."

"You've become tedious, Samuel, you and your coven. You conspire to take over the world, while Ascent tries to save it, and the game continues century after century," she said as she stamped out her cigarette into her uneaten bowl of stew.

"The OB coven, we are the descendants of the great King Solomon."

"Please, spare me the lectures about your King and your lineage," she said, putting her hands up in surrender. "We are all descendants of great witches. Some of us know when to walk away and let the humans have at it."

Samuel picked up his napkin and wiped his mouth. "Ah, I see it now. You've got it all figured out. You abandon your coven to hide out in the woods fussing about in your garden and dilly-dallying with your little dog," he said, taking a bite of cheese.

"My coven is safe because of the deal I brokered with the witch hunters. Can you say the same for yours?" she asked, lighting another cigarette.

"You hide out off the grid, making candles and peddling your herbs while your sister, Honey, the Queen of the Impotentem, and her cult thrives. It's disgraceful."

Sage's face twisted in anger. "Mind your tongue, son, or I'll rip it out with my bare hands. This is your war, not ours," she spat as she blew smoke out of her nose like an angry dragon.

"You can't hide away forever."

"Maybe I can wait it out in this life and the next if the humans haven't destroyed the planet. What do you want from me?" she asked as she grabbed his arm.

In one swift motion, he pulled away from her and stood up. "When the time comes, I will collect on my debt."

Sage stared at him. Her face, which usually held a mask of mischief, now held something else, fear. "It's really her, then?"

"Yes. It's Delilah," he said, putting his sunglasses on. "Time for you and yours to get back in the game, my dear."

Eight

"As long as I lived at home,
I worked common tasks."

The night before, Jonathan, Faye, and Dee arrived safely at Tabitha Anthea's home. The next morning, Dee found them sitting on the back porch drinking coffee. The porch was Dee's favorite spot. It was a big old-fashioned wrap-around Thea had decorated with cozy couches, rows of oversized pillows, and candles.

They all seemed so relaxed. Tabitha Anthea was wrapped in one of her cashmere capes with a cookbook resting on her lap and thumbing through recipes. As she watched them, she could see how the house had already affected Jonathan. He seemed at peace with his hands wrapped around a steaming coffee mug, gazing out at the small pond in the yard. Faye even appeared to be content, laying on the couch blowing perfect smoke rings into the sky. Tabitha Anthea's home had always been a haven for Dee. Now she was a stranger, hiding in the shadows.

On the long wooden table, Dee noticed a large book covered in brushed gold leaf. The cover featured an illustration of a sword with a crown resting on the tip and a fleur-de-lis surrounding it. In all her years living with Thea, she had never seen it before. Her stomach flipped and her mouth went dry.

Jonathan set his coffee down and tenderly picked up the book. "This is so old," he said, opening the book. "The magics coming off of it is so powerful, it's making me dizzy."

Tabitha Anthea smiled. "Poor thing hasn't been used in some thirty years. It's like an idling sports car ready to take off."

"You guys, there's a page missing," he said as he showed them the book.

Tabitha Anthea studied the page before it. "I don't recognize the language. It's not Latin." She squinted. "And it's definitely not French or German for that matter."

Jonathan put on his glasses with thick black frames. He looked like a 1960s biology teacher. "I think it's Aramaic."

"Aramaic?" Tabitha Anthea questioned.

"It's the oldest written language," Faye explained, stuffing her vape into her pocket. "Like, Bible old."

They all stared at her, surprised by her knowledge. "What I read a lot," she said shrugging. "When I'm not saving witches."

"There's only one person who can help us," Tabitha Anthea said, glancing at Jonathan.

"Mahai," he replied.

"And your girlfriend, Melia," Faye added in a sing-song voice.

"Ex-girlfriend," he corrected her.

Dee cleared her throat. They were startled to see her lurking in the corner. And she felt guilty for eavesdropping.

"There's our girl," Tabitha Anthea said with too much enthusiasm. The one thing that was comforting was Thea's pajamas. She was always stylish, no matter what. Under her cape, she had on her silk paisley weekend pajamas with a matching headscarf.

"What's that?" Dee asked.

"The D'Arc family grimoire," Jonathan answered.

"But let's do coffee first," Tabitha Anthea said, leading Dee back into the kitchen.

Dee looked around the kitchen. It was the only modern room in the house. Everything else was from another era, but not Tabitha Anthea's kitchen. How could she afford it on a professor's salary? Dee could never work it out. It was probably yet another secret. Now behind the painted lady and the "haint blue" front door, the home she knew growing up held so many. Thea told her the door's color was used in the south to keep out the ghosts and evil spirits. Dee wondered what other malevolent forces were out there in the darkness, waiting for her.

Tabitha Anthea handed her a cup of coffee. Inhaling the warm caramel spicy scent always calmed Dee. This morning, it didn't. Her stomach churned.

Jonathan wandered into the kitchen, clutching the book tightly to his chest.

"Would someone mind explaining to me what a grimoire is?" Dee asked.

"It's a book of spells, family history, ceremonies, definitions of abilities, innovations; stuff your family recorded and handed down through the generations," Jonathan explained.

Dee began laughing. Tabitha Anthea and Jonathan shared a concerned look. She could hear how hysterical she sounded, but she couldn't stop herself.

"I've had not one, but two attempts on my life."

Tabitha Anthea put her hands on Dee's shoulders. "Okay, baby girl, take a deep breath. Don't upset yourself."

"I've been saved by mute fallen angels, fairies, and flying witches."

"Let's have something to eat, and then we can sort this all out," Tabitha Anthea said as she pulled out a loaf of fresh-baked bread and began slicing it.

Dee continued laughing, but it wasn't her normal laugh, it sounded hoarse and a bit hysterical.

"No, really tell me all about the witches." She stared at Jonathan. "And what are you, a warlock or something?"

"We go by witch. We don't buy into all the gender identity politics stuff that humans do. In our world, we're all equal," he replied without one drop of irony.

Tabitha Anthea put the bread knife down. She wiped her hands on the kitchen towel, walked over to Dee, and pulled out a tall kitchen chair.

"Have a seat."

"I am an accountant. I live by the numbers. I live by statistics. The probability that any of this is real is like one half of a half percent."

"And yet, here we are, Delilah," Jonathan said with a broad smile. "Defying all laws of the reality you have known up until this point."

"Stop calling me that," she ordered.

"No," he said as he lifted his coffee cup, took a sip, and placed it back on the table. "It's your given name. It's time you owned it."

Tabitha Anthea went into the pantry and pulled out a bottle of Baileys. "I think we could all use a nip."

As she went to pour some in Jonathan's coffee cup, in a flash, his hand covered it. "None for me, thanks."

"Are you sure?"

He pulled out a coin, shuffling it over the tops of his fingers before presenting it to Tabitha Anthea.

"As sure as the last thirty-five thousand and forty-two hours," he replied, placing it back into his pocket.

Tabitha Anthea signaled them to sit down. She took a deep breath. Dee wouldn't make eye contact with her. She placed her fingers under her chin, lifting her face. Their eyes met. Tabitha Anthea's dark brown eyes always cut right through her.

She casually pushed the grimoire toward Dee. "Place your hands on the book and tell us what you see."

Dee shook out her wrists. She gingerly placed her hands over the book. Her hands tingled, and there was a warm, light glow around the book. She glanced over at Thea and Jonathan. They both nodded. She touched the book. It gave her an electric shock that buzzed through her solar plexus, almost knocking her out of her chair.

Before she could yank her hand away, Tabitha Anthea seized it and forced it back onto the cover. Dee saw the woman in chain mail. This time she was dressed in rags and tied to a pyre.

"Who's the woman? I keep seeing her?" Dee asked.

"Joan of Arc," Tabitha Anthea replied. "You are her heir. Her blood is your blood. Before she was burned at the stake, she had a child while she was awaiting her trial. It's believed that one of her guards raped her. And the reason they waited months to execute her was to allow her to give birth."

Jonathan leaned in. "You are Delilah Johanne D'Arc, daughter of Devlin and Maria D'Arc. Since the 1500s, the D'Arcs have been members of the Ascent coven."

"What's a coven?" Dee asked.

Faye entered the kitchen. "Good grief, we're so screwed."

Jonathan pointed at her. "You, out."

"But I am so hungry," Faye whined.

48

Jonathan grabbed an apple from the bowl in the center of the table and tossed it to Faye. She caught it quickly with one hand and left the kitchen.

Tabitha Anthea encouraged Dee to touch the book again. When she pressed her hand down, she saw an image of a woman with dark curly hair and wild violet eyes.

Dee jerked back. "My mother, Maria."

Tabitha Anthea and Jonathan exchanged a glance.

"She's still alive?" Dee asked, confused.

Thea grabbed the book and pulled it away from Dee. "She cast a strong spell on you when you were a babe."

"What kind of spell?"

"Let's say it's not going to be easy for you to recover your lost memories," Jonathan said, "or figure out what you did to have your soul banished for the last three hundred years."

"And why would my mother take it all away from me?"

"To protect you," Tabitha Anthea replied.

"From the hunters?"

"And the prophecy," Tabitha Anthea said, smoothing Dee's hair back and tucking it behind her ear. "You're the one to lead the witches out of the dark into the light. She was so scared for you. She wanted to give you some type of normal life."

Dee's body shook, and her stomach churned. The cold sweat came next. Tabitha Anthea saw what was happening.

"Are you having one of your attacks?"

Dee nodded and rushed to the bathroom before she started to gag. This panic attack was going to take her down.

"I'll get your meds," Tabitha Anthea called out, rushing to the cupboard to find Dee's medicine.

Jonathan was about to go after Dee, but she stopped him. "It's best to let me handle this."

Dee sat over the toilet, dry heaving. Her body was vibrating. Deep breathing wasn't going to help. She was too far gone. Her thoughts were a turned over jigsaw puzzle. She tried to focus on the black-and-white honeycomb tiles on the floor.

She started counting the black flowers when a gentle tap at the door spooked her. "Can I come in?"

Dee opened the door. Thea was holding a glass of water and one of her pills. "Can you take it?" Thea asked.

Dee shook her head. Her stomach was turning inside out. If she took it, she'd throw it right back up. She needed to give her body and her fear a second to calm down. Thea closed the door and set the glass down on the sink. Dee was shaking so hard that Thea put her arms around her and guided her onto the floor. They both used the massive porcelain claw-foot tub as a backrest. When Dee was little, Thea would hold her so tight, willing the panic to subside.

"I know you're petrified, and none of this makes any kind of logical sense," Thea said, kissing the top of her head. "Courage is not the absence of fear."

"Courage is acting despite your fear," Dee replied before vomiting yellow bile into the toilet.

July 21 @ 1:11 pm - Thea's House,
My Childhood Home
State of Mind - 😱🤯

I'm a witch.
Witches are real???
I'm a witch.

I'm going crazy. This can't be real. Can it?
This is like some weird dream caused by

something I ate. I always have weird dreams when I eat sushi. This is a sushi induced dream. I'm going to wake up and be back to my job hunt and maybe moving back home with Thea.

I'll try pinching myself...okay that hurt. I might have given myself a bruise even. So, this is real then? I mean who even invented the pinch test anyway? Is it even scientific? The thing is that it feels kinda right. That somewhere inside me it feels like ... destiny. My destiny. My birthright. But it can't be me. Can it? I picked accounting because it is the safest profession I could think of. Everyone always needs a good accountant no matter what. An accountant with a panic disorder is not going to save herself let alone anyone else.

And magic and fairies and fallen angels... it is for novels and movies. It's an entire genre that freaks and geeks get all geeked out about.
This is not real.
It can't be.
I'll try pinching myself.
Again.

Nine

"The devil can bring about an effect of magic
without the co-operation of any witch."

Wolf woke up in a damp, grimy cell lined with crumbling
bricks and large iron bars. Everything hurt. He was sure he
had at least one broken rib. Had he been there for a day or a
week? He had no sense of time. On a metal tray sat a stale
piece of bread and a cup of water. He drank the tepid water so
fast it poured down his chin. He stuffed the dry bread into his
mouth, chewing it twice before swallowing it. He took a deep
breath and heaved it all back up.

Images suddenly came back to him like a movie in fast
forward. He was kidnapped from the chapel during his
evening prayers. First, his sect, the witch hunters, shaved him
and dunked him in a vat of holy water. They dressed him in a
thin white linen robe. Then came the torture. Over several

hours, he was bound and gagged. They submerged him in glacial water over and over. And finally, using a flaming hot poker, he was branded on the top of his right hand with an "H" for heretic. It was all torture techniques designed for witches right out of *The Hammer of the Witches* playbook. This tactic was an old standby for his father, Gart, who saw a poetic license punishing hunters with the same tactics used to try witches.

An overhead light clicked on. "How are ya doing, son?" Gart asked as he pulled up a stool next to Wolf's cell.

Wolf turned his head toward him but didn't respond. Gart sat with his arms folded against his expansive chest. His square jaw grinding and snapping a piece of gum like it committed a crime and he was punishing it. He still wore his gray hair high and tight, a holdover from his Marine days.

"We had to do it. That whore bewitched you, son. It can happen to the best of us," Gart explained. "We had to cast the she-devil out of you."

"How's Joanna?" Wolf asked.

"She's a hunter through and through. She did her time in the hole like a champ."

Wolf could hear the pride in his voice. It was a pride he had always reserved for others, but never for Wolf. All Wolf had ever wanted to do was make his father proud. And that's why he had executed the ill-fated hospital attack on the witch. This time, it was all on Wolf. It was his plan, not Gart's, that had gone south.

Gart stared at Wolf as though he was a calculus equation, he couldn't quite crack.

He sighed and said, "Son, I don't think you're ready to come out of the hole yet."

Wolf knew better than to argue or ask for a medic to examine his rib.

"Do you have anything to say for yourself?" Gart asked.

Wolf turned away from his father. The overhead light was beaming down on him like a spotlight.

Gart slammed his hand against the cell. "Stand up, Wolfgart, or so help me, God."

Wolf slowly turned onto his stomach and placed his hands underneath his shoulders. He tried to pull himself up but was too weak.

"Now!" Gart yelled.

Again, Wolf tried to get up, but his arms shook. Gart pulled out keys from his pocket and unlocked the cell. He grabbed Wolf by the arm and yanked him up off the floor of the cell. He threw him against the wall and held him up by pressing his arm into Wolf's chest. The pressure from standing made his limbs shake uncontrollably.

"Do you believe the power of God is stronger than the power of the devil?" he shouted.

"Yes, sir."

"What is the difference between a miracle and witch-craft?"

"The intention, sir."

"Is evil an involuntary act or a voluntary act?" Gart yelled, so worked up into a fever that spittle landed on Wolf's face as he screamed at him.

"Voluntary, sir."

"We are doing God's work, and your soul must be clean. You can't allow the devil into your heart," he said, pounding on Wolf's chest.

"Father, my soul, is pure," Wolf said through unstable labored breaths.

"My son, we are the only soldiers standing between the moral and the nefarious forces threatening our world. Delilah will release an evil the likes of which hunters have never seen or faced before. The civilians no longer have any faith in us. Do you understand me?" he asked as he shook Wolf.

Wolf nodded. Gart released him, letting his body fall to the ground like a sack of flour. Gart threw a copy of *The Hammer of the Witches* at him, slamming the door to the cell shut and locking it behind him.

Ten

"Twice he refused and rejected me."

Perched on two ornate, giant, royal blue velvet, and gold thrones, Dee and Jonathan were waiting for Mahai at his antique store. The Golden Triangle wasn't the usual hodge-podge of other people's junk. It was like a carefully curated museum. Each piece was expertly placed in a collection and lit like fine art.

Dee read the placard out loud. "French Baroque, wedding chairs. Circa early 1800s. $139,000." She quickly hopped off the chair. "I don't think I want to risk breaking something I'll never be able to buy."

Jonathan was distracted by his phone. "So, Melia is your ex?" Dee inquired, trying to get his attention.

His head shot up at the mention of her name. "Yes. We broke up a while ago," Jonathan said, looking around. "When we're together, bad things happen."

"Is Mahai a witch too?"

"No, he's a Gana. They're nomadic mystics, worshiped by the Romani people."

"Like gypsies?"

"They prefer to go by Romani."

"Habibi," a man called out as he walked toward them.

Jonathan jumped off his throne and ran over to him. "Mahai."

The two men wrapped their hands around the inside of their elbows, shook their arms three times, and touched foreheads. "Peace be upon you, my dearest boy," Mahai said.

"Peace be to you, my uncle," Jonathan replied.

Mahai released Jonathan's arm. He then pulled him into an embrace, lifting him off the ground and shaking his body like a rattle. He put him down and took Jonathan's face in his hands. Staring deeply into his eyes, he said, "Clear eyes, bravo, my child."

He pounded his fist against Jonathan's chest. "Your heart is full. No more demons chasing you. I rejoice that you no longer expose yourself to such bad things."

He released Jonathan and turned to Dee. "My lady, Mahai Symeon Nicolae Andri, and your faithful servant."

"The Lyft driver?" Dee asked, suddenly recognizing him.

The man who stood before her appeared the part of a king, as he claimed when they first met, with his black plaid suit, starch white shirt open—just enough to reveal a hint of an outline of a tattoo on his chest, and a bright pink rose pinned in his buttonhole on his lapel. She was struck by his lively, clear eyes, warm olive skin with a hint of stubble, and cropped dark hair.

Gazing into her eyes, Mahai took her hand and kissed it. "I do whatever work is needed, my lady."

He was dashing. Dee found herself grinning and giggling

like a teenager with a crush.

Mahai pointed to the back of the showroom. "Come, my children, tell me how I may serve you."

He led them through the store. Dee's eyes attempted to drink in the furniture and the artwork. She stopped in front of a statue of a woman, her hands together in prayer, wearing gold and royal purple robes with a large gold crown on her head. Her eyes were glistening with tears. Her mahogany skin glowing.

"The Black Madonna, she is our patron saint, the goddess of fate," Mahai said, with reverence in his voice.

They stopped at a wall in the back. Mahai pressed on a painting of a crest, and it opened. They stepped into his sparse office. With bare walls, it was a crimson box with matching walls and carpet. The center of the room was a sizeable black lacquer desk sitting on a circular oriental rug.

Mahai put his hand on Dee's arm. "Please, my child, rest your feet. I see your spirit has not caught up to your body, and it is making you so very weary."

The chair was so plush she sank into it. On Mahai's desk, there was a large leather desk pad with an ink jar and pen. Across the desk were a series of daggers with scorpion-shaped golden handles resting on wooden stands. Dee found Mahai had quickly cast a spell on her. She was in his thrall. If he had told her to jump into the Chicago River, she would've said yes. And Jonathan was right there with her, with a wild, silly smile on his face.

"We have a translation we were hoping you could help us with," Jonathan explained. He nodded at Dee. She pulled out a copy of the D'Arc grimoire page from her purse and handed it to Mahai.

Mahai put on a pair of glasses with clear frames, resting them on the tip of his nose. He reviewed the page, then he removed his glasses and folded his hands on his desk. "It's from the time of King Solomon. He created a language using a mixture of Hebrew and Greek. This language is ancient, as you can imagine."

Jonathan sat on the edge of his seat. "Can you translate it?"

Mahai smiled, taking off his glasses. "I know of only one person who can. She is a professor of ancient languages at the University of Chicago."

Jonathan stood up, snatching the paper from Mahai. "No." He folded the paper and stuffed it into his pocket. "We'll find someone else. Anyone else."

"My son, she is the expert," Mahai said in a soothing voice. "She knows more dead languages than even the dead."

"Who?" Dee asked.

"Melia," Jonathan replied as he charged toward the door.

"Come now, my son. Enough time has passed, no?" Mahai called after him.

Mahai turned to look at Dee. "What can you do? They have a complex relationship. She's the only one I know who can assist you in your journey," Mahai said.

She smiled at him. "Thank you for your help."

Mahai shrugged and nodded at the door, signaling their meeting was over.

When she caught up to Jonathan, he was pacing the sidewalk.

Dee placed her hands on his shoulders. "Look, there's so much I don't understand. Nothing makes any kind of sense to me right now. But whatever is going on here, we can figure it out. Together."

Jonathan pulled away from her. "Four years ago, I was in a bad place." Shaking his head, she could see he was trying to push back the tears.

Dee took his face in her hands. "You don't have to tell me anything or explain anything you don't want to. Okay?"

"Delilah, our powers can do strange things to us.

59

Sometimes, it's easier blocking it all out than trying to deal with it. Do you know what I mean?" he said, wiping his nose with the back of his hand.

"I am not sure I do, but I want to understand."

Jonathan let out the breath he was holding. "I was an addict. I mean, I'm a heroin addict. I'll always be one."

Dee remained silent, giving him the space he needed to finish telling her his story.

"Mahai helped get me clean. He tried to help both of us. For me, it stuck. But Melia kept on using it. She never had any intention of stopping."

Jonathan sat down on the curb, and Dee joined him. The street was quiet. The store was on one of those small hidden streets, lined in bricks. Jonathan took Delilah's hand in his. His hands were capable and warm. As they sat together, she felt like she had known him forever. She leaned her head on his shoulder. Jonathan glanced down and gave her a tender smile.

"Delilah, my job here is to help you find the truth. I can't let my shit get in the way," he said, squeezing her hand.

Dee stood up, offering him her hand. "Before we track down your mysterious ex, can we get a pizza or something? I'm starving."

Jonathan took it, and she pulled him up onto his feet. "I got you. I know the best place."

"Don't we all?" she said, teasing him. "Maybe my place is better than yours."

"You'll have to trust me on this one."

Eleven

"There is no wrath above the wrath of a woman."

Dee hadn't even laid eyes on Melia, but she had already decided she didn't like her. The mercurial Melia chose to meet in a dive bar that reeked of stale beer and cigarettes near the campus. Jonathan was on his fourth Diet Coke and was ready to parkour off the drop tin ceiling. Dee was never much of a drinker and didn't know what to order. She asked about their wine list, and the waitress, without a hint of irony, told her they had two—a red and a white.

Dee checked her watch. "She said eight, right?"

Melia was over an hour late.

Jonathan gave her a withering stare. "If she shows up before ten, we're lucky."

"You don't have to stay," she said, trying to swallow her sip of white wine.

It definitely didn't taste like wine. The taste reminded Dee of something—the time when she tried an apple cider cleanse a few years ago. It was apple cider wine. *Is that even a thing?* she wondered.

He took her hand in his. Her body felt all warm and tingly.

"There's no way I'm leaving you on your own with Melia." He released her hand and grabbed her glass of wine. "I can't watch you try and drink that swill any longer. At least let me get you a beer."

She watched him walk over to the bar. Jonathan had an ease about him, a boyish charm. He made her feel so comfortable even in a seedy bar. He smiled at the surly waitress and immediately disarmed her. They even chatted as she poured her beer.

"He's so very handsome, no?" A deep smoky voice with a Mediterranean lilt whispered in Dee's ear. "See his tight bottom, a succulent peach ready for a bite."

She turned to find a woman standing next to her table. With her long, thick black hair, intense green eyes lined in black, and her full lips, she was striking. Dressed in a tight black sleeveless dress to show off her sleek muscles and hourglass figure, and wrists lined with old bracelets, her beauty was intimidating. In her oversized black tee, jeans, and her beat-up Chuck Taylors, Dee felt like a bug Melia wouldn't think twice about squashing under her spiky Louboutins.

"Delilah," she purred, kissing her right cheek then Delilah's left, leaving the scent of jasmine lingering in the air.

When Jonathan returned to the table and saw her, his face fell. "Melia."

"Yiannis," she said as she greeted him with a kiss, branding his cheek with her vivid red lipstick.

He set Dee's beer down. "You're late," Jonathan growled. His body became rigid like he was bracing for a car crash.

She smiled. "My apologies, my class went over." The

waitress placed a glass of amber liquid in front of Melia. "Thank you, my darling," she said with a wink.

He noticed her drink. "They have Lagavulin, here?"

"They bring it special for me," she said, offering Jonathan her glass. "Would you like a sip?"

He put his hands up. "No, thank you."

"It's your favorite, no?" she asked with an innocent expression, knowing full well, Jonathan was sober.

He took the glass from her hand and set it on the table, splashing the precious whiskey. "Melia, we need your help with a translation."

"Of course, anything for my beloved."

Dee noticed Jonathan flinched at the word "beloved" like she had punched him in the stomach. She pulled out the copy and set it in front of Melia.

"Aramaic," she said, nodding her head. She picked it up and traced her fingers over the words, using her shiny ebony-colored nails to mark her spot.

She smirked as she handed the paper to Dee. "It says 'guardian of the ring.'"

"I don't understand," Jonathan said. "What does that even mean?"

"Where's the rest?" Melia asked, shrugging. "There's more, no?"

"The grimoire, my family's grimoire, it's missing a page," Dee interjected.

Melia took a sip of her drink. "I am certain your mother, Maria, knows where it is."

"My mother is dead."

Melia glanced at Jonathan, shaking her head and pointing her finger at him. "Yiannis, isn't one of your many important steps, honesty?"

"Melia," he hissed.

Dee could feel the panic rising inside her. "Jonathan is my

mom alive?" she asked, her voice cracking. "I don't under-stand." She felt like the time she went over her handlebars on her bike and had the wind knocked out of her.

With a wicked smile, Melia nodded and downed her drink.

"And Tabitha Anthea, she kept her from me?"

"Delilah, we were only trying to protect you."

Dee stumbled off her barstool. "And who will protect me from you?" She started toward the door, and Jonathan caught her arm.

"Let me explain," he pleaded.

Her anger was now bubbling like a rolling pot of boiling water. "Where is she?" He tried to look away, but she wasn't going to let this go. She grabbed his face and shouted, "Tell me!"

The bottles over the bar began to rattle and shake. "Delilah, you need to calm down. You don't have control over your powers yet. You could bring down this entire bar."

"I don't care," she said, seething.

"Lowood Mental Institution," Melia said, leaving the bar.

Dee took a deep breath, trying to control her anger back. "She's where?"

"You're drawing too much attention." With force, Jonathan took her by the arm, threw money on the table, and herded her quickly out the door.

"So, help me, if you tell me Tabitha Anthea will explain it, I'll lose my shit."

Melia was standing on the curb, smoking a cigarette, watching them like they were putting on a play for her amusement.

"This is not for me to tell you," Jonathan pleaded, shaking his head. "This is not how this was all supposed to go down."

"Rigorous honesty," Melia interrupted him. "Isn't it like, step one?"

"Melia, maybe it's time for you to go."

"After four years, you called me, Yiannis. You asked me for my help," Melia said, stamping out the cigarette with her red-soled shoe.

"Tell me the truth, for once," Dee implored him.

"The magics Maria cast was too much for her body and for her mind," Melia explained. "You can't perform a spell like that without consequences. We all know this. And she knew it."

Dee pushed Jonathan, knocking him off balance. "I thought you were the one I could trust."

Out of nowhere, the burly bouncer appeared. "Hey, you guys. I don't know what kind of love triangle bullshit you got going on here," the bouncer said, spitting chewing tobacco into a plastic cup while sizing them up. "And my hats off to you, for punching way above your weight, sir," he said. "But ya gotta move it along before I call Chicago's finest."

Melia pointed at Jonathan, then snapped her fingers, and like a dog answering his master, he scampered over to her. Dee watched as Melia snatched Jonathan's arm and pulled him down the dark street into the foggy night.

Twelve

"I am about to endow thee with many secrets."

Dee was alone, unsure of what to do or where to go next. She remembered Samuel telling her to say Mrs. Fairfax's name if she needed anything. Dee whispered, "Mrs. Fairfax," three times into the night and glanced to the right and to the left—no sign of her.

She shouted, "Mrs. Fairfax," three times up to the sky.

Still nothing. Feeling silly for believing she would appear out of thin air; Dee made her way toward the L station. Her entire life up until this point had been a lie. The thought her mother had been alive all these years. She couldn't begin to understand why Thea would keep it from her. It didn't add up.

A blaring car horn cut through Dee's thoughts. It was idling on the street, a vintage black Mercedes with huge headlights.

"Hurry and get in, my dear, before the po-po gets here," Mrs. Fairfax yelled over the loud rattling engine.

Dee didn't see any sign of the police as she got into the car. Mrs. Fairfax gave her a big smile. "Where shall I take you?" She was dumbfounded. Dee hadn't been back to her apartment since she left for her job interview—which was last week? Was it even safe to go there?

Reading her thoughts, Mrs. Fairfax said, "I'll take you to Thornfield. We'll get some food in you, and it'll all be right as rain soon enough."

"Thornfield?"

"Mr. Solomon's manor."

They drove through the city streets in silence. Dee noticed every stoplight went from red to green the moment they approached it. Samuel's home in the light of day was a sight. But at night, all lit up, it was spectacular. Before her job interview, she was so nervous she didn't notice the two domed turrets looming over the street like a castle.

Mrs. Fairfax led Dee into the house through a narrow hidden side door. They finally landed in the kitchen after snaking around a series of maze-like hallways. It had rows of stark white cabinets and a massive wooden table in the middle filled with bowls of strawberries, raspberries, and blueberries. Silver pastry stands filled with an assortment of macarons, scones, cream puffs, and tarts lined the marble countertops throughout the kitchen.

"Please, sit," she said, tying an apron around her waist. "What can I get you?"

There was a snug breakfast nook under a stained-glass window with a place setting ready for her. "Scrambled eggs?"

Mrs. Fairfax smiled. "And a spot of chamomile tea to help calm your nerves."

"I don't want to be any trouble," Dee said, sitting down.

"Pish posh, it is my pleasure," she replied, setting a tea

kettle on an ancient black cast iron stove that seemed like it needed a lump of coal instead of gas.

"I trust Mrs. Fairfax is taking excellent care of you, Delilah?"

At the sound of his voice, she felt the blood move through her veins like there was an invisible cord between them. Samuel said her name, stretching and pulling on the "D" like gooey taffy. Seeing him standing in the arched doorway, she had to stop herself from running over and throwing her arms around him. Watching as he slowly loosened his tie and took off his blazer, carefully folding it before placing it on the back of a kitchen chair, she was mesmerized by his slow, deliberate movements.

Seeing him standing there, looking at her like he was so relieved she wasn't hurt, she couldn't handle how his response made her feel.

"I should go," Dee said, standing up. "I don't know why I'm here."

Samuel took a few hesitant steps toward her with his hands up like she was a cat he was trying to catch before it ran up a tree.

"Delilah, I told you to call on Mrs. Fairfax," he said, leading her back to the table. "It's good to see you safe and sound."

Their kindness struck something inside her, and before she could stop herself, big wet tears rolled down her face. Samuel sat next to her, pulling her into his muscular chest. Dee melted into his embrace, feeling for the first time in days, the uneasiness that had a vice grip on her entire body gradually release its hold.

"I'm acting like such a child. All I ever wanted was a family. My family. And to know my mother is alive."

He removed a handkerchief from his pocket, and it smelled like lavender and sandalwood. He tenderly wiped away Dee's tears. "After all you've been through, the fact you're still standing shows an indelible inner strength."

Mrs. Fairfax set the eggs and a steamy cup of tea down on the table. She squeezed Dee's shoulder before hanging up her apron and leaving the kitchen.

"I'm sorry. I don't normally gush tears onto strangers' chests," she said, pulling away from him, trying to hide her embarrassment and maintain whatever shred of dignity she may have had left.

"Delilah, we've known one another for many lifetimes," he said with a melancholic smile.

"I have so many questions."

"I can only imagine," he said, his eyes widening.

She blew her nose and looked at him expectantly. "How do we know each other when we just met the other day?"

Samuel sighed and gazed up at the ceiling. "You know when you first began learning math? Everything you learn builds on itself; you can't master complex equations until you have mastered all the basic rules and understand all the variables."

She liked the lilt to his voice and the way he used his hands to underscore his point.

"So, learning about what it means to be a witch is like solving a math equation?"

"In a sense, yes."

She was quiet. There was only one thing that mattered to her.

"I want to see my mother as soon as possible."

"It has already been arranged. Mrs. Fairfax will take you tomorrow." He pointed at her plate. "Now eat, before your eggs get cold."

After she had finished, Samuel insisted Dee spend the night at Thornfield Manor. She was too tired to argue. Twisting and turning through another series of hallways, they stopped at an intricate gold door with roses carved into it.

Holding it open for her, he placed his hand on the small of her back. His hand on her body sent a current up and down her spine.

The room was like nothing she had ever seen before. It had light gray, paneled walls with a huge white and gold four-poster bed. There were two white chairs in front of the fireplace, embroidered with the same image from her family's grimoire—a sword with a crown on the tip of the hilt and two fleurs-de-lis.

Above the fireplace, over the mantel, was a painting of a naked woman, with a sky-blue dress pooled at her feet, a look of defiance on her face, daring the viewer to try and look away.

As Dee moved closer to the painting, she noticed something. "Is this me?" she asked, pointing at the woman's stark violet eyes.

Samuel's eyes lit up. "That painting." He sighed, shaking his head with a grin on his face, lost in a memory. "Come, let me show you where you can find a toothbrush and some fresh towels."

White roses filled every table in the room. She leaned over to smell a vase with white roses.

"They're my favorite."

"I'm well aware."

Even though she protested, he insisted on tucking her into bed. He waited for her to brush her teeth and change into a pair of silky pajamas laid out for her in the bathroom.

"Samuel, may I ask you a question?"

"Of course, Delilah," he replied, helping her into the large bed.

"Were we, I mean you and I... a couple?"

"In another lifetime, yes, we were."

"Were we in love?"

"So much so we risked everything to be together," he whispered. "You see, in our world, witches from different covens do not—"

"Date," she said, finishing his sentence.

"We stay with our kind," he explained, pulling the covers over her and gently tucking them in.

"Aren't we all witches?"

"Yes, but you are an Ascent and I, an OB, and we stay loyal to the coven we are born into. It keeps the bloodlines pure. It's to maintain order in our otherwise chaotic world."

"Are we like Romeo and Juliet then?"

"Our love story may have been the inspiration for Shakespeare," he teased. As he gently kissed her forehead, she wanted nothing more than to pull him into her. She reached up and lightly touched his neck.

Then she slowly traced the angry scar running along his neck and stopped at his chin.

"Who did this to you?" she whispered.

"Delilah," he sighed.

His breath was warm and inviting against her face. Without thinking, she drew him closer and pressed her lips against his. At first, he was reserved; she wondered if she had misread the situation. She was about to pull away from him when his body crashed into hers—his determined lips claiming hers as her body faded into his.

He ripped his body away from hers and stood panting by the bed. He wiped the side of his mouth with his finger.

"Delilah," he growled.

She smiled up at him.

"Samuel," she replied, attempting to mimic his serious tone.

"What am I to do with you?"

She wanted to say *anything you want* but didn't.

"Sweet dreams," he said, turning off the light.

Thirteen

"My mother told me that my father often dreamed
that I would run away with a band of soldiers."

Dee woke up feeling refreshed, with a big, juicy smile on her
face. That kiss. She kept replaying it in her mind. Not sure
what possessed her to make a crazy bold move. It was so
unlike her, she thought, stretching and rolling around in the
luxurious bed, shaking off the remaining embers from her
dreams.

Next to her bed, resting on the night table was her journal.
She picked it up and held it. *How'd it get there?* she wondered.
Must be magic.

Her fingers itched to write down her thoughts, her
feelings, her observations. She had so many thoughts swirling
around in her head.

July 24 @ 8:16 am - Thornfield Manor
State of Mind - Hopeful

Where to begin? My mother isn't dead. I'm still processing that information. It's like a long-lost childish wish that she'd appear one day in my life very much alive. I can't begin to know what it is going to be like to see her, to hug her, to talk to her. I have so many questions.

Will she be proud of me?
Or disappointed that she lost her powers to save me?

I can't begin to know or comprehend what she sacrificed for me. And for what??? For me to live this less than extraordinary life of an unemployed, unloved, unremarkable accountant.

And what type of supernatural possession got into me to kiss Samuel? That's not the way I roll—ever. Where'd I muster that courage??? IDK. I saw that portrait of Delilah, I mean of me, my past-life self. She looked like the kinda girl who just took what she wanted from life and didn't give a F.
Me?
I can't even swear in my journal.

But that kiss, that kiss knocked the breath outta me. I've never been kissed like that. Not in this life anyways. I could feel how much he wanted me in every molecule in my body. I felt every nerve tingle.

———————————————————————————

Leaving no detail at loose ends, Mrs. Fairfax had filled the closet with clothes Dee's exact size. She picked out an oversized, pale blue blazer with a white tee and skinny jeans. It was her style, but a better version.

Once she was dressed, Dee stood in front of the portrait in her room. The woman staring at her was the Delilah Samuel truly loved. Not her. The fact was, Dee was only a phantom playing a trick with his heart. Realizing this truth, the sunny, cheerful feeling she woke up with quickly turned overcast.

Somehow, she managed to find her way back to the kitchen. Mrs. Fairfax was drinking a cup of tea, humming a tune. When she turned around and saw Dee, she jumped and nearly spilled her tea.

"Ah silly me, for a moment, I thought you were a ghost."

Dee smiled. "It must be weird for you. I look like her, but I'm not her."

Mrs. Fairfax set down her cup. She took Dee's hands and inspected her from head to toe.

"The cut of your character is solid gold. Hers was a polished brass at best."

On the long drive to Lowood, she checked her phone. There were long, rambling, apologetic text messages from Jonathan and concerned voice mails from Tabitha Anthea. Jonathan and Thea, she would deal with later. Right now, she had enough on her plate. She was going to see her recently undead mother. Hugging the bouquet she brought for Maria to her chest, she tried to remember the time they had together.

All her memories of her mother were cut up, bits and pieces of pictures pasted into one blurry collage.

Dee had a strong aversion to hospitals. All she knew about mental institutions were from movies. When they arrived at Lowood, she was pleasantly surprised. From the outside, it resembled a sorority house with large, white Corinthian columns, soft pink bricks, and a clay Spanish tiled roof.

As she approached, the large mahogany reception desk was almost cheerful, with an arrangement of sunflowers, a flat-screen TV displaying the weather conditions and the day's activities like a hotel. Then the hospital smell assaulted her; it was two-parts institutional soap and one-part urine. Her heart battered against her chest, echoing in her eardrums. Her mind went blank. For a moment, she forgot where she was. Gathering every ounce of strength she had in her, she willed herself to remain steady.

Dee instantly forgot the nurse's name who escorted her to Maria's room. The nurse was skilled at one-sided friendly banter and didn't stop until they reached their destination. The door was slightly ajar. The sound of classical music drifted into the hallway. Before the nurse left her, she gave her an encouraging smile.

Alone in the hallway, Dee took a gulp of air and tapped on the door.

"Hello?"

A voice sounding like a melody Dee once knew and loved said, "Come in."

Dee crept into the room. Sitting in a large wheelchair was her mother, Maria. She was a skeleton. Her hands were bent like branches, which she held tightly to her chest. She appeared older than her years, with chunky, wiry gray streaks in her black hair and eyes outlined by shadowy, swollen bags.

Tears instantly filled Dee's eyes, and she dropped the flowers, ran over to her, and embraced her.

"Momma," Dee said, hugging her tightly.

Maria patted her shoulder. "There, there mon petit chaton."

"My little kitten," Dee said. Maria unfurled her arms and hands, wiping the tears from Dee's eyes with the back of her hand. "I forgot that's what you used to call me."

The door slammed shut and standing with her hands in fists at her sides, fury in her eyes, and a tight smile on her face was Tabitha Anthea.

"Dee. Outside. Now."

Dee stood up. "No."

Maria took Dee's hand, kissed the inside of her palm, and then wrapped Dee's fingers around it. A light turned on within Maria as she tapped into an inner force.

"You are Delilah Johanne D'Arc. It's your name. It's your birthright. Use it. And bring only dignity and honor to it."

"Delilah, please, we need to talk," Tabitha Anthea said.

Maria put up her hand. "Tabitha Anthea, I'm having a good day. I want to spend the moments of clarity I have with my daughter. You have done your task and have done it well. Now, go. Please."

Delilah saw something she thought she'd never see, Tabitha Anthea backing down. She opened the door. "I'll be right outside."

"Very good," Maria said, smiling.

Delilah picked up the flowers, setting them on a table next to Maria.

"Please, sit down; we have much to discuss."

Delilah pulled up a chair next to her. Her mind was racing. She had so many questions.

"I did what I did because I thought it was the only way to shield you from our world." Maria squeezed her eyes shut. "Delilah, I must ask you one thing."

Delilah took her hand. "Yes, anything."

Maria gave her a rueful smile. "It may not be something you can give."

They sat together, holding hands. "I am asking you to forgive your father, Anthea, our coven. Me. All of us."

Delilah didn't know what to say. She wanted to say yes, of course, I forgive you all for everything. But Delilah didn't think she could. She wasn't able to get over all the time and all the years that had been lost to this lie. It was too much. All this time, her mother was only miles away.

Maria, reading her thoughts, patted her hand.

"Think about it for me. You have a long journey ahead of you. If you can pave the way with mercy, it will be less cruel for all involved."

Delilah didn't understand. She changed the subject, hoping the business would be a distraction for both of them. "I need to ask you about our grimoire."

"The missing page," Maria interrupted, pointing to her bed. "Look under the mattress."

She wondered if Maria was having an episode, but she decided to humor her. She reached under the mattress and pulled it up. There was a gold vellum envelope with Delilah's name written on it. She set the mattress down and opened it. There it was.

Maria waved her over. "You must drink the poppy tea to learn the truth. Only then you'll be safe once you recover your past."

"The poppy tea?"

"Yes, drink the tea. Learn the truth."

Delilah shook her head.

Maria was repeating it and rocking back and forth. "Drink the tea. Learn the truth. Drink the tea. Learn the truth. Drink the tea. Learn the truth. Drink the tea. Learn the truth."

Delilah felt her heart drop. Maria was scaring her. She wasn't making any sense. She tried to hold her hand, but

Maria pressed her sharp fingernails into Delilah's palm. She screamed, and Thea ran into the room. She pulled Delilah's hand away from Maria. Her palms hurt; there was blood oozing out of the little moon-shaped scratches.

"Your visit is done for the day," Tabitha Anthea ordered. "Now go before you upset her more."

Delilah sat in a small garden on the Lowood grounds. She was paralyzed. The events of the last week came tumbling down on top of her.

I didn't ask for any of this. I don't want any of it.

There was a tight ball of pain living behind her heart. She always knew it was there. It held her heart welded together. Seeing her mother, Maria, come apart at the seams, right in front of her, the pain, the anguish she had been holding detonated. It hurt so much. It felt like a heart attack. She couldn't breathe. She put her hand to her mouth, trying to stuff it back inside.

On her knees in the garden, she peered up at the sky. "Please, please help me."

Fourteen

"What I said, I said for fear of the fire."

Delilah felt a hand on her shoulder. She wasn't sure if minutes or hours had passed. The touch anchored her back to the present.

"The nurse gave her something," Tabitha Anthea whispered. Her voice sounded raspy and broken. "She's asking for you."

Delilah couldn't move. "I'll set her off again."

Tabitha Anthea helped her stand up. "Let's clean up your hand and take you back to her."

Delilah shook her head. There wasn't a chance in heaven or hell, she was going back into the room.

Tabitha Anthea grabbed her shoulders. "Kid, you are in it now. There's no going back." Shaking her, she said, "Your mother wants to see you and so help me with all that is holy, in this world and the next, you're going."

After the nurse had bandaged Delilah's hand, she was sitting next to Maria's bed. Maria seized her hand and kept running her fingers over Delilah's knuckles.

"Please stay with me," Maria pleaded. "I know I shouldn't ask this of you. It's unfair."

Seeing her in the hospital bed, she was like a broken doll made out of glass and held together with Scotch tape, one fall away from coming apart. When their eyes connected, Delilah saw an intense globe of light and felt a transfer of energy from Maria to her. It hit Delilah right in the middle of her chest and took her breath away. It was like she was watching a movie about Maria's life and pressed fast forward. Their eyes met again; she saw the moment Maria held her for the first time. Delilah felt it, unconditional love, in every cell of her being. To experience Maria's memory of holding her after she gave birth to Delilah was such a gift.

Delilah climbed into the bed and folded Maria into her arms.

"We are going to get through this. I'll be your light. I will guide you out of this darkness. I promise," Delilah said.

They held onto each other until sleep claimed them. After dawn, Delilah woke up. There was a tiny red velvet pouch in her hand. She pulled it open, and a silver 45-caliber bullet fell out. She held it up, examining it.

She tried to wake up Maria gently. "Momma."

Maria's body was rigid.

"Momma?"

She pressed her fingers to Maria's neck in search of a pulse. There wasn't one.

Delilah kept shaking her.

"Momma, please," she repeated.

Aros appeared. He scooped Delilah into his arms and teleported her to Samuel's kitchen. On landing, Delilah lost control of her limbs. Her body became a jackhammer propelled by adrenaline. The velvet pouch and bullet tumbled from her hand because she couldn't control the shaking.

A man approached her. "May I examine you?" His voice sounded familiar to her.

"Who are you?" she asked, her teeth chattering from shock.

Pulling a blanket over Delilah's shoulders, he replied, "I'm your father."

Moments later, Delilah fainted.

Fifteen

"The stars influence the devils themselves
in the causing of certain spells."

When Delilah regained consciousness, she was in the four-poster bed in the room at Samuel's mansion. Her forehead had turned into a piece of wood that someone was pounding a rusty nail into it.

The door opened, and she heard heavy footsteps. She slowly opened her eyes to find her father, Devlin, holding a glass of water, appearing concerned. He set it down on the nightstand and helped her sit up.

He sat down on the bed. He placed his hand on Delilah's leg.

"Delilah, I'm so sorry."

She crossed her arms. "For what? For letting me think you were both dead? For not telling me I'm a witch. Or that there are witch hunters were trying to kill me? Or my mother is dead?"

"For all of it," he replied, glancing away from her. "For all of it." He rubbed the stubble on his chin. "I can't imagine you'd believe we were—"

"Trying to protect me," she interrupted. "The more everyone tries to protect me, the more people seem to get hurt. All I want is the truth."

"Then the truth you shall receive." He stood up. "Are you hungry? I think the truth will go down better if you have some food in you."

He offered her his hand and gently helped her out of bed.

They walked to the kitchen in silence. Delilah was surprised to find it was empty. No Samuel. No, Mrs. Fairfax. No fallen angels or feisty fairies.

She sat down and watched her father as he carefully made two sandwiches. He didn't ask her what she wanted; he assembled two turkey sandwiches leaving off mayonnaise on one of them. He remembered she hated mayo. Sitting down, he placed a plate in front of her. She watched as he folded his hands, closed his eyes, mouthing a silent prayer.

To her surprise, she was hungry. While they ate, Devlin put his hand on her shoulder and held it there. She was conflicted by this display of intimacy from him. Half of her wanted to pull away from him like a petulant teenager, and the other half wanted to crawl into his lap. In the end, she didn't pull away from him.

A shot of adrenaline hit her. "Why didn't the hunters kill me?" she asked, setting her sandwich down.

Devlin wiped the crumbs off his hands. "The Sect is on another mission now. One that involves more than killing one witch."

"I don't understand."

"They stole the page from our grimoire. The one Maria

gave you. It will eventually lead them to uncover what the D'Arc family has kept hidden since the Hundred Years' War, the power to command good and evil."

"And I led them right to it and handed it over on a silver platter," she said, the realization washing over her like a shower running from warm to ice cold.

He put his hands on her shoulders. "At this point, they don't know what they have. They only know they have something. They can't use the spell without the ring."

"Guardian of the ring?" Delilah said.

Devlin shot her a confused look.

"Melia translated it for us."

"Does Mahai know about the page?" he asked, the concern rising in his voice.

Delilah nodded. She felt like a child getting called out by her teacher for giving the wrong answer.

"Did I mess up?"

Devlin shook his head and said, "You need answers."

He began rooting around the kitchen, searching for the wine fridge. "And I need wine."

After he found a bottle of Sauvignon Blanc, he suggested they sit outside in the garden. Bursting with several varieties of roses, hidden stone paths, it was a proper English garden. The sun was setting over the surrounding high rises. It was a pleasant night with a nice cool breeze off the lake. Waiting for her father to talk, Delilah sipped her wine. It tasted like summer, with hints of citrus, herbs, and a creamy finish. For a fleeting second, life almost seemed normal.

"I can't begin to imagine what you are going through," he said, downing his wine in one gulp. "And I sure as hell know that words aren't going to make it any better."

He poured another glass of wine. "Maria's funeral is set for tomorrow."

"Already?" she asked, her voice cracking.

It was too much to process. Delilah had just found Maria, and now she had to plan her funeral and mourn her, again. It didn't make sense.

"We bury our souls right away to prevent them from getting lost in this world," he explained. "But our coven is refusing to give her a proper burial."

"Can't we find a funeral home?"

"We aren't like humans. Without a proper witch burial, her soul won't transition on to Summerland. Her spirit will be stuck in purgatory," he explained. "She's suffered so much in this life; her soul deserves to rest."

"And Summerland is?"

"It's an eternal summer between heaven and earth. It's the waiting area for our souls before returning to earth."

"Why won't our coven bury her?" she asked, knowing she didn't want to hear the answer.

"The D'Arcs have fallen out of favor with our coven." He got up and began to pace around the patio. "They're demanding you unify; you swear your fealty to Ascent."

"I don't get it. Wasn't I born a D'Arc? Born into Ascent?"

He ran his hands through his hair.

"Yes, yes, you were. This is why we tried in vain to hide you from them," Devlin said, kneeling in front of her and placing his hands on her knees. "Why we sacrificed so much, so you could have your own life." His voice cracked with frustration. "To end up here, it's not what we wanted for you."

"What did you want for me then?

"We wanted you to be free to live a normal life."

Delilah snickered. "And in what world would that have even been remotely possible? Did you guys think you could outmaneuver a prophecy?"

She met his eyes and, with a hard gaze, hissed, "And all I wanted was my mom and my dad."

Devlin sat down and poured more wine. "It was ill-conceived at best, but we thought we were doing the right thing."

She paused. "I'll do it," she said, drinking the rest of her wine. "I'll unify or whatever."

He moved closer to her, and she could smell the sweet wine on his breath. "Before you agree, you must understand what it means. You're making a sacred vow."

"I don't understand."

"You can't turn back. Once you unify, your life belongs to our coven; you'll live in service to Ascent."

Delilah and Devlin sat up talking through the night. Once the sky turned from an inky black to purple, he left her alone after he provided her an out. The D'Arc family owned a home in Domrémy, France, he explained, placing an envelope with a passport, and a stack of euros on the table. He told her it was time for her to decide, as they had all made enough decisions on her behalf.

As she made her way into the house, Devlin's words rang in her ears. "It was time for her to decide," she whispered to herself. The decision in front of her was to run and save herself or stay and sacrifice herself. Delilah was being asked to give up her life for a family, and for a coven had turned away from her. There was much she didn't know about this world. Up till now, she had only experienced death and deceit.

Delilah sat in the chair in her room, opened the envelope, and a piece of parchment paper fell out.

Written in calligraphy were the following words, "Every man gives his life for what he believes. Every woman gives her life for what she believes. Sometimes people believe in little or nothing, and so they give their lives to little or nothing. One life is all we have, and we live it as we believe in living it—and then it's gone. But to surrender who you are and to live without belief is more terrible than dying— even more terrible than dying young."

Underneath the quote, it read "Joan of Arc. The Maid of Orleans. 1431."

July 26 @ 4:44 am - Thornfield Manor
State of Mind - Fucked

I have to sacrifice everything to save my mother's soul from wandering the earth for eternity. This witch stuff is super fucked. Oh, BTW, you need to make the decision now.

Her body was so warm and so alive when we fell asleep. And when I woke up, she was cold and dead and gone. I lost her twice in one lifetime. All those moments stolen from us. There's so much I don't understand about this world. But I'm starting to understand the profound loss. I had Thea growing up. She loved me like an eccentric auntie. But feeling my mother, having a taste of her love, even for a moment was something I don't know how I will recover from, that loss.

They say grief is unexpressed love. I have gallons of it bubbling up inside me—it feels like it is choking me. She gave her life to save me and where did it get us? Alone. What will happen when I hand over my soul to Ascent? Will it lead us out of the dark or deeper inside of it?

I don't think I can do this.

I know I can't.

I don't have the faith or the courage that Joan of Arc had. It would be so easy to take the money and run and keep running.

——

Sixteen

"Go forward bravely. Fear nothing."

Standing alone with her hands on her hips, Delilah studied the angel church. Her church. It all began right here on these steps under the Triple Moon. She had made her decision to hand over her life to Ascent. The building started to sway back and forth, becoming pixelated. She rubbed her eyes, and the front door turned into a bright white arch.

Faye shuffled outside, blinking against the bright sun. "Yo, hurry up. Will ya?"

Delilah took a few tentative steps toward the entrance, unsure if they'd disappear and suck her in like cosmic quicksand. Once she entered, the arch disappeared, and she was left standing in a hallway.

"What's happened to the church?"

Faye waved her hands. "It's called witchcraft."

Delilah was frustrated at every turn; she never knew what was happening.

Faye took pity on her. "There are witches in your coven who can use their minds to alter physical reality. They take matter and bend it to what they see in their mind."

"I'm in someone's imagination?"

Faye began explaining real slow. "Think of it like this... before you have a building what do you really have? Humans with their hands and machines take pieces of wood, steel, plastic and build a home. For us, supernatural's we use our mind and our will to build it instead of our hands. Got me?"

"Is the church still here then?"

"And Schrödinger's cat is still alive in another quantum reality," she said sarcastically, leading her down a hallway lined in white ceramic subway tiles, a marble floor lit by gleaming ornate gold candelabras.

They entered a bathroom covered in small blue glass tiles that formed a wave pattern giving the impression they were standing inside of a swell.

Faye handed her an ivory satin kimono with hand-painted white and black swans on it. "Take off your clothes and put this on."

Delilah sat on a little bench and put her head between her knees, trying to calm herself down. *This is a colossal mistake. I should've taken the one-way ticket to France.*

Faye patted her on her back. "We don't have time for a nervous breakdown, so suck it up and get naked because your Benefactor is waiting on you."

Signaling for Faye to turn around, she said, "Some privacy, please."

"Good grief, we've both got the same parts," Faye sighed, turning away.

"What's a Benefactor?"

"Like your sponsor, your teacher, your sensei, your Yoda."

Delilah removed her jeans and T-shirt, folded them into a tidy pile and put on the robe. "Ready," she announced.

Faye pointed at a white door.

"Get in the tub, take off your robe, and wait," she said, wheeling around and heading to the door.

"You're leaving me?"

"This is my stop." Faye strolled back over and swept Delilah into a bear hug. "You got this."

With trepidation, Delilah opened the door, and to her surprise, it was a blush pink room with a gold leaf, oval-shaped inground bathtub filled with rose petals in the center. Gentle, inviting steam drifted up into the air; she dropped her kimono and lowered her body into the warm water. Every muscle in her body relaxed; her bones felt like jelly as she inhaled the fragrant oils with an aroma of frankincense and oranges.

She was so tranquil. With her eyes closed, she didn't hear the door open, or her Benefactor enter.

"Hey there, Delilah," a friendly voice said.

Her eyes sprang open. Jonathan stood next to her in the water, naked, wearing nothing but a big stupid grin from ear-to-ear on his adorable face. Normal people are supposed to be embarrassed by wanton displays of nudity. Jonathan had no such inhibitions.

"Get outta here now," she yelled, pointing at the door.

In spite of himself, Jonathan glanced down at her breasts and gave her a lingering appreciative glance. Covering her chest with her arms, she yelled. "You can't be here. I'm waiting for my Benefactor."

"I'm right here," he replied with a smile, pointing his thumbs at his head.

The whole right side of his chest was covered with tattoos. Delilah noticed a tattoo of a little boy's face over his heart with dates underneath. Without his leather cuffs and head-to-toe black, he appeared carefree and innocent.

Her mind started racing. *What did she know about witches? Pentagrams? Pointed black hats? Booms? Goats, there were always goats, right?*

Delilah blurted out, "I'm not having sex with a goat."

He erupted with laughter. At that moment, Delilah saw an image of Jonathan, as a little boy, running through the woods laughing.

When he placed his hand on her shoulder, Delilah's breath hitched in her throat. "I don't know where you are getting your intel, but we are not into sex with animals," he teased.

"I'll remember not to Google 'witches' in the future," she said, making a joke and trying to hide her discomfort.

He clapped his hands together. "Let's get on with it. We have a sanctuary full of witches anxious to meet you."

Slowly Delilah removed her arms from her chest. Jonathan's eyes were no longer playful and friendly. They were raw with longing. Their bodies were drawn together like two magnets closing the gap between them. Gently he took his fingers and traced a line down her spine. Her body began to tremble as he put his hand around her neck and pulled her toward him. Standing nose to nose in the water, she took a deep breath. He stroked the side of her arm lightly with his hand, his eyes searching hers. Lost in his cobalt eyes, leaving her body aching for him, her only thought was, *I want him. Now.*

Jonathan, reading her mind, looked away from her.

"Delilah," he croaked between rough breaths, "what we had together was another lifetime."

She didn't retreat. Instead, she held Jonathan's gaze and placed her hand over his tattoo of the little boy.

"Tell me about him."

He stared into her eyes.

"He was my little brother. Joey. I was supposed to take care of him, and I was so messed up on some bad shit. We were in the woods. My safety was off."

She cradled the side of his head in her hand. "Jonathan."

Jonathan placed his hand over hers; as tears streamed down his face, she guided him toward her, into an embrace. He wrapped his arms around her. She could feel him struggling, unsure what to do, wanting to stay in her arms, but knowing he shouldn't.

With a measured, graceful movement, he traced her cheek with the tip of his nose and tenderly placed his soft round lips against hers. Holding onto each other, he gave her one long, deep, perfect kiss. Then he eased away from her with a downcast smile.

He was trying to regain control. "Cross your arms over your chest and turn away from me," he ordered.

As he picked up a small ornate bowl with angels engraved on it, she noticed his hands were trembling. He filled it with water from a bottle with a label that read, "Florida Water Cologne."

Standing behind her, with his warm breath caressing her neck, he said, "Please tilt your head back."

Jonathan poured the water over her forehead.

"Delilah, from this moment on, you will forsake all else. Your mind, your heart, your body, and your spirit now belong to Ascent. And so, it is."

"We must descend in order to ascend," he said, immersing her under the water then slowly guiding her up.

Once she was steady on her feet, Jonathan quickly stepped out of the tub and put on his robe. He picked up her robe; looking away, he held it open for Delilah to step into.

Placing it on her shoulders, he said, "Faye will help you get dressed for the unification ceremony. After it'll be Maria's transitioning ceremony."

She tied the kimono tightly around her waist. She could

feel the sting of tears trying to escape.

"Delilah, what you're doing, here today, it takes courage."

"Someone once told me you either go back to normal after a tragedy, or you never recover, or you become courageous."

"Sounds like a genius," he teased.

"Is it still brave if you didn't have a choice?"

"You could've bolted, and you didn't," he said, punching her in the arm. "I'm proud of you."

Faye opened the door.

"Did you two kids enjoy your seven minutes in heaven?" Faye asked, taking Delilah's hand. "Come on, princess, time to get you ready for the ball."

Faye ushered her into a room covered in fleur-de-lis wallpaper with a large bench and a small vanity. Faye pointed to the clothes hanging on the back of the door and turned around.

After Delilah had dried off, she put on the white wrap dress with a fleur-de-lis embroidered in gold on the back. She noticed a hair tie and lip gloss on the vanity, so she pulled her hair into a low ponytail and applied a swipe of gloss.

Once she was dressed, she said, "I'm all set."

Faye turned around, holding a large white sash. "The D'Arc coat of arms." She placed it around Delilah's waist and tied it on the side of her hip.

Delilah looked down, and it was embellished with the same sword with a crown on the tip of the hilt, two fleurs-de-lis on the side from her family's grimoire, and the D'Arc name underneath. She ran her fingers over the stitching; it didn't appear to be made from thread.

"It's your ancestor's hair," Faye explained.

Her fingers recoiled like she had touched a hot stove. "Really?"

"Come on, it's time to get you unified," she said, pushing Delilah toward the door.

Seventeen

"But I loved my banner forty times better
than my sword."

Faye led Delilah down the hallway. They stopped at a glossy red door with a knocker shaped as two intertwined fish. Faye pulled out a black stain blindfold from her jean jacket. Delilah could feel the bile churning in her stomach creeping up her throat. She inhaled sharply, hoping she could keep it down.

"Turn around," Faye ordered, holding up the blindfold.

Delilah jumped back. She didn't sign up for blindfolds. A dry heave tried to escape; she began to cough and sounded like a rabid barking dog.

Faye reached out and took her hand.

"This is seriously messed up on all levels. You got thrown into this world, and now you have to give this life over to virtual strangers."

Delilah's stomach seized, and she threw up on Faye's high tops. "I'm so sorry," she said, wiping the vomit from her mouth with the back of her hand.

Pulling out a bandana from her back pocket, she wiped Delilah's face. "Nothing bad is going to happen to you there." She looked Delilah in the eye. "I promise you on my car-broiled blackened dead soul."

Delilah's hands were shaking. She reached out for the blindfold and put it over her eyes. Faye tightened it. "Let's do this."

The door knocker reverberated throughout the hallway and rattled inside Delilah's chest. Her mouth was so dry. She squeezed Faye's hand as she was led into the sanctuary. The marble floor was cool against her bare feet.

"We're going up three stairs," Faye whispered, slowly guiding her up the steps. Once they were at the top, Faye took her shoulders and moved her body. "See ya on the other side."

Delilah's knees were trembling.

"Who will stand as her Benefactor?" The voice echoing through the sanctuary belonged to Tabitha Anthea.

A painful silence followed. Delilah willed herself not to pass out. Her heart was drumming in a steady beat against her chest. *Was Jonathan going to leave her hanging?*

She could hear the door grind open.

"I will," Jonathan called out, and Delilah let out the breath she was holding.

"We must descend," a chorus sang out to her left. "In order to ascend," another chorus to her right replied. Their lyrical voices filled the room.

"Hey there," Jonathan whispered in her ear as he removed the blindfold from her eyes.

Delilah blinked back the bright spotlight focused on her face. She scanned the room; it was filled with people from every nationality. Their bright beaming faces were smiling up at her. The women were in the same white dress Delilah wore. The men had on white short-sleeved button-down shirts with pointy military collars buttoned up to their necks, and kilts.

Above their heads floated a massive cathedral ceiling painted light blue, and cotton candy clouds continued to swirl toward infinity as cherubs drifted among them. The beauty of it made her dizzy.

Standing at the altar under a large gold arch covered in white silk, with images of a sword, fleur-de-lis, a rose, two intertwined fish, and a swan hand-painted on it, was Tabitha Anthea.

"Jonathan Augustus Berwick, will you stand as Benefactor for Delilah Johanne D'Arc," Tabitha Anthea said, handing a sharp blade and a goblet to Jonathan.

"It was decided by the sky," Jonathan replied.

"You alone will be responsible for training and guiding her soul from this day forward. What say you?"

"It was decided by the stars."

"In doing so, you agree to live the remainder of your days until your last breath in service to her. What say you?" Tabitha Anthea continued.

"It was decided by the coven."

"The unification now begins," Tabitha Anthea instructed.

Delilah watched the man standing closest to the altar hold out his hand as Jonathan ran the blade over his palm and squeezed blood into the goblet. The entire coven, one by one, pressed their blood into the chalice while chanting, "We must descend in order to ascend."

The sound of their chanting was a lullaby lulling her into a hypnotic state. She barely registered Jonathan handing Tabitha Anthea the blood-filled goblet. In one deft movement, he ran the icy blade over her meaty palm and pressed her blood into it. Quickly Jonathan tied her hand with a linen cloth. He handed Delilah the knife and presented his hand as an offering. She was awakened from her trance, her hands trembling as she attempted to slice open his palm, until finally, he forced his hand into the blade, raking it over the sharp edge drawing his blood.

Tabitha Anthea mixed the blood in the chalice. Then dipped her thumb into it and pressed it onto Delilah's forehead. "May your inner eye always see the truth."

Repeating the movement, this time, Tabitha Anthea imprinted her bloody thumbprint on Delilah's heart. "May your heart know valor and charity."

"The blood of your blood is now mine; the blood of my blood is now yours," Tabitha Anthea said, as she brought the goblet to her mouth and took a sip from it.

She offered the goblet to Jonathan; he took a taste leaving a small trace of blood on his lips. Jonathan handed Delilah the goblet. For a moment, she had a vision of drinking it and spewing witch blood over the entire coven like a possessed demon.

Seeing her hesitation, he said softly, "Take a small sip. It's more for show than anything else."

Delilah knew precisely what she had to do, what was expected of her, as the goblet touched her lips, and the copper penny smell filled her senses. The coven chanted, "Honor, honesty, and mercy." She took a long pull letting the slick oily blood run down the back of her throat.

Jonathan removed the goblet from her hands. "You're a total bad ass. Now stop it before you get sick," Jonathan said, setting the goblet down and wiping the blood from her lips.

Eighteen

"I was the angel and there was no other."

When she focused on the coven, they were all holding large white candles, wrapped in ropes. Gently, Jonathan took Delilah's hand in his. His touch calmed the rolling tide inside her.

"Good job, kid, now here comes the hard part," Jonathan said, tucking a stray hair behind her ear.

The door opened, and Aros, along with three other angels, entered carrying a rustic pine coffin on their shoulders with their arms crossed at their chests, their heads lowered, walking slowly up to the altar. Behind them was her father dressed in black, carrying a bouquet of black and red irises.

Once they reached the altar, they called out in unison, "Un, deux, trois, quatre." Then with military precision, they placed the coffin down in the center.

Tabitha Anthea carried a large gold bowl, a cloth, and set them on the table. Devlin took Delilah's hand and led her to Maria's coffin. It was open. Maria was wrapped in silver linen and silk lined with gold trim. On her head sat a crown of white and pink roses; she seemed so peaceful. She was ethereal.

Devlin took the cloth and dipped it into the water, then handed one to Delilah. His eyes were hollow as he lifted Maria's foot and began tenderly washing it.

Maria was dead. They had just found each other, and now she truly was lost to her forever.

I was supposed to care for her. I was going to save her.

Delilah's chest constricted as she choked out a sob; it made it hard to breathe like she was trapped underwater, drowning in her tears. Tabitha Anthea placed her firm hands on her shoulders, enabling her to do this final act for her mother.

When they had completed their task, Tabitha Anthea approached the podium and sang out, "O God, by whose mercy the faithful departed find rest, look kindly on your departed handmaid. Grant Maria Antonia D'Arc may share in the joy of your heavenly kingdom and rejoice in you with your saints forever."

"And so, it is," the coven replied in unison.

"May your soul know no dismay."

"It is so."

"May there be a beautiful welcome for you in Summerland. May your soul remember your one true home," Tabitha Anthea called out.

"We know it is so."

"May your soul know tranquility. May you rest in peace, old friend."

"Amen," they chanted together.

Each member of the coven, one by one, made their way to the altar in a slow march to place a white rose inside of Maria's coffin. Devlin put the bouquet of irises in last. Once again, the angels lifted the coffin onto their shoulders. As they walked out of the sanctuary, members of the coven touched the coffin, murmuring prayers. Devlin enclosed Delilah in an embrace and led her out.

—·—

IDK what day it is @ half past whatever -
MY Apartment
State of Mind - Hollow

All I do is sleep, eat ice cream and watch the Golden Girls. I have little to no energy— even showering is like too much. It's just me and Faye all day, every day. No one else. No Jonathan, Thea, Samuel, coven. Truth be told, I don't have the energy for anyone, definitely not supernatural types. At least Mom's soul has been saved, count that as a win. I wish I could trade places with her, give her back the years she lost. I would exchange my wasted life for hers in a heartbeat.

I'm useless.
Why am I even here?
I have nothing to give to anyone.
I'm just so tired.

I just need to close my eyes and hope that they don't open. I want to go to sleep and never wake up again.

——————————————————————————————

Nineteen

"I have asked my voice to counsel me whether
I should submit."

Delilah knew anxiety. It was an old friend of hers. Depression
was a new pal who joined the party. Soon, the three of them
became besties. It found her the day after she gave her life over
to her coven and transitioned her mother, Maria. She felt as
though she was living in a dense fog that held her down no
matter how hard she tried to break through it. She couldn't.
Eventually, she stopped trying.

Faye became her self-appointed body man. Her job was to
babysit Delilah, to guard her against the hunters, and to
protect her from herself. Together they camped out in
Delilah's vintage one-bedroom apartment watching classic
black-and-white movies eating chips and Twizzlers. Her
apartment wasn't much, but it was cozy. And it was all hers.

A big comfy security blanket to wrap herself in and pretend the last few weeks didn't happen.

She had invested in an expensive couch from a pricey furniture store. The salesperson called it a "chesterfield." The rich peacock color caught her eye, and the fact it was velvet and had deep-set cushions was also a bonus. To set off the couch, she had painted the walls a dreamy sky blue.

For the last week, Faye had been permanently parked on the floor, on a furry beanbag. She was right at home, scrolling through the channels, lounging in a pair of black joggers, an oversized *Rage Against the Machine* T-shirt, and rainbow-striped socks.

"Hey, you want to order Chinese?" Faye asked.

Delilah shrugged. "Sure." She tossed Faye her phone. "Use the app and order whatever you want."

When she stood up to stretch, she caught wind of a smell, a mix of cat litter and stinky cheese. Showering was for people who had lives they had some control over. Delilah couldn't remember the last time she had changed her depression uniform, pair of yoga pants, and a garbage ready tee with holes in the armpits and sky-blue paint stains.

"Do I smell?" Delilah asked, leaning over Faye.

Faye took a whiff. "Yeah, but I've smelled worse."

"Maybe I should light a candle or something?" Delilah asked as she dug through a drawer in the end table.

It was full of old batteries, a pair of broken sunglasses, and extension cords. Looking inside the drawer made Delilah tired, so she slammed it shut.

"I ordered a ton of food. Check out what's on," Faye said, pointing to the TV.

"*Rebecca*, I love that movie."

Delilah grabbed the blanket, crumbled in a ball on the floor, and fluffed her pillow to settle in, when the buzzer rang.

Faye glanced at her wrist, even though she didn't wear a

watch. "That was fast," she said, popping up to buzz the delivery person.

Delilah slowly got up. "I'll get us plates and pop," she said, walking into the kitchen.

Faye was on Samuel's back with his neck in a chokehold when she returned to the living room.

Samuel implored, "Please, for the love of God and everything holy, call off your bloody fairy."

Setting the plates and the pop down, she nodded at Faye. Before jumping off his back, Faye gave his neck a final squeeze. "It wasn't the delivery person."

"I came to check on you," he said.

"She's doing just peachy," Faye replied, pulling on his arm, leading him to the door.

Samuel gave Delilah a look that sent a wave of heat through her body. For the first time in days, she felt something other than like she was drowning in pain.

"Faye, can you give us a moment?" Delilah asked, not taking her eyes off Samuel.

Shaking her head, she said, "No can do, boss. I'm here to protect you from everything, even bad decisions."

"Faye!" they both yelled in unison.

Their eyes locked in on each other—the air crackling with the energy traveling between them.

Faye put her hands up in the air. "Fine. I don't want to be a third wheel anyway," she said, picking up her messenger bag and her boots. "For the record, I do not condone, nor do I give my consent to whatever may or may not happen here."

The door slammed shut behind her.

Samuel took in her apartment. "What's happened to your flat?"

Delilah glanced around. Her cozy nest had veered into frat-house territory with empty potato chip bags, plates with half-eaten food sitting on the coffee table, crushed Red Bull cans on the floor, and blankets strewn everywhere. If depression had a room, this was it.

"Have you had a bath recently?" Samuel asked.

"If you've come here to insult me and my home, you can fuck off."

Samuel folded his arms across his chest. "I am so sorry for your loss, Delilah."

"Thank you for your kind words. It means so much to me," she said, stomping to her bedroom and slamming the door; hearing it rattle against the hinges gave Delilah so much satisfaction.

Then came a succinct light tap on her bedroom door. "Why do you even give a shit? Covens are not supposed to interbreed. They need to keep the bloodlines pure for loyalty."

He released a deep sigh. "Because Delilah, you stubborn cow, if you haven't realized it by now, I am in love with you."

It was too much for her. She yanked open the door. "Love, me? Seriously? You don't even know me. You love the Delilah in your painting. And I gotta tell you, I'm not her."

His face broke into a smile. Delilah wanted to throw a punch and break each and every one of his perfectly white teeth.

"I think a bath would do you a world of good," he said, rolling up the sleeves on his dark-blue dress shirt.

She watched as he went in search of her bathroom. Moments later, she heard the shower running.

He stood in the middle of her living room, with his hands on his hips like he owned the building.

"Are we doing this the easy way or the hard way?" he asked in a husky voice.

"I have had enough of you for the rest of this lifetime and the next," she said, holding her front door open. "It's been a pleasure. Next time you're in the neighborhood, feel free not to stop by."

Samuel calmly closed the door, picked her up, and marched her to the bathroom. He set her down in the shower, and like an angry alley cat, she tried to escape. Kicking off his Gucci loafers, he jumped in the shower with her.

They stood nose to nose with the water running over their bodies, panting like they were going to devour one another. Staring into Samuel's eyes, for the first time, she saw another version of herself reflected back. In his eyes, she was wild, reckless, self-assured, powerful even.

She reached out and slammed her body into his. Their lips collided. The world fell away from them. Time slowed down. The water fell softly like snowflakes over them. When she unbuttoned his shirt, the lights flicked on and off. From that moment onwards, they were both clawing at their clothes.

Naked and exposed, a light-pink halo surrounded them.

Delilah touched the scar on his neck. "Who did this to you?"

"A vengeful lover." His voice filled with lust.

"Do I need to take someone out?"

"I assure you; they were punished."

He took her face in his hands and kissed her roughly. The energy running between them made her legs tremble. When Samuel pushed her body against the wall, bathroom tiles shot across the room, colliding in mid-air and exploding.

He lifted her off her feet and situated himself deep inside her; the walls around them began to rattle and shake. They moved together, their bodies pushing and pulling away from each other.

Delilah pushed his hair out of his face, gazed deep into his eyes, and ordered, "Don't come."

"There's my girl." he growled, slowly setting her down. On his knees, he took her leg and threw it over his shoulder. He gripped her bottom with his hands; she set his mouth firmly on her sex.

107

"That's better," Delilah purred.

Slow and deliberate, he continued. When Delilah's body was on the brink, so close, about to splinter into pieces and explode, suddenly, he stopped.

He studied her. Then demanded, "Do you want me?"

Delilah bucked against him. The frustration, the desire was boiling over. She looked away from him as pieces of the ceiling crumbled around them.

"Say it," he urged her on, pressing his fingers deep into her flesh.

She peered down at him, and with a yearning, a longing for something she remembered but had never felt before, she whispered, "I want you."

Samuel was grinning. "You want me?" he asked, continuing to tease her.

She barely whispered, "Yes," before Samuel drove his tongue into her, making her body convulse and shake over and over again.

He steadied her by placing his firm hand on her chest. Standing up and sliding himself back deep inside of her, the walls shook as though they were going to collapse around them. Delilah could feel his orgasm, every surge, every tremor as if it were her own. When he was finally spent, the walls gave one last shudder.

Twenty

"A woman either loves or hates;
there is no third grade."

The cawing of black crows woke her up. As Delilah opened her eyes, she tried to shake the feeling of the dream. Intuitively she just knew crows were a sign. What she didn't know was what they represented. She grabbed her phone and googled "black crows."

The Internet confirmed what the pit in her stomach was signaling. "There is no doubt the crow is the omen of death."

She tossed her phone on the floor. The events of the night before were slowly coming back to her. Delilah blushed as she remembered how she ended up in her bed with Samuel. It wasn't that she had any regrets. Because she didn't. None. She couldn't pinpoint how the gears had shifted in their relationship.

Yes, of course, she wanted him. *Who could deny him?* He wasn't only handsome. He was also the right amount of broken. It gave her the impression she had enough glue in her emotional arsenal to put him back together again. For all he was, he wasn't whole without her.

Trying to shake off her nightmare, she watched him sleep. It was as though a sculptor had chiseled him out of marble with his sharp cheekbones, perfect chin with a dimple set in the middle, and his V-shaped widow's peak. She watched his chest rise and fall, studying the scar running up his neck, wondering what happened to him.

Slowly he opened one eye, cocking his eyebrow. "Delilah, love, go back to sleep."

"I had a bad dream."

"Crows or chanting witches?" he asked, pulling her into his warm and muscular chest.

"Crows," she said as she burrowed into him, inhaling him, taking in his vanilla and sandalwood scent.

"Would it help if I told you, it's only a dream?" he asked, kissing the top of her head.

"A death dream. I've had enough dying for two lifetimes."

"Someone's been using the Internet," he teased. "Would you like to hear a bedtime story?"

She remained silent. She had so many questions for Samuel, but there was one person she wanted to know more about.

"You can ask me anything. Anything at all."

"Maria, what do you know about her?"

"Your mother was quite a witch. She was a legend."

"I wish I knew more."

Wrapping his arms tightly around her, she melted into him. "Your mother, Maria, stood up to the Immaculates in front of everyone in our world. It took a profound level of courage."

"The Immaculates?"

"Has your coven taught you nothing of our ways? The Immaculates are our judges and our jury. They have the final rule over our world."

"Like a monarchy?"

"Exactly. There was a case, about thirty years ago, a witch gave birth to a baby sired by a witch hunter. As you can imagine, covens do not mate with covens, and they sure as bloody hell don't mate with the witch hunters."

"Was my mother the witch who gave birth to the baby?"

"No, she stood up for the witch from another coven. She had no personal gain for speaking up. Before the Immuculates handed down their sentence, your mother said, 'Why should a baby be punished? What if this baby was meant to broker peace between the witches and the witch hunters? Love is love. Can't we love who we want and put an end to this gruesome thousand-year holy war we've been fighting?'"

"What happened next?"

"The baby was sent to live with the witch hunters for a life of torture. Your mother was put into the Closet for weeks."

"Do I even want to know what the Closet is?"

"Think of solitary confinement but worse, a vast dark hole of nothing."

"It sounds horrible."

A reflective shudder ran through his body. "I can attest it is."

"You've been in witch jail?"

"Delilah, our love, in another lifetime wrought dire consequences for both of us."

A wicked smile broke across her face as she ripped the duvet cover off him and forced her body against his.

"So, our love is criminal."

"You're not in need of rest?"

"I'll sleep when I am dead," she said, her mouth finding

him in the darkness.

"Did we really cause an earthquake?" she asked, giggling into his chest.

"It was barely a five."

"I think we should try for a ten then?" she said, moving her hips, claiming him with her body.

The next morning the skies rumbled and shook like the gods were at war, covering the city with an onslaught of rain. Delilah wondered if last night was real or a fantasy. Then a very real Samuel, wearing nothing but a black pair of boxer briefs, entered her bedroom holding two steaming mugs.

"Morning," he said, handing her a cup and kissing the top of her head.

She sat up in bed, pulling the covers over her body. "Thanks," she said, taking the coffee from Samuel.

As he sat down, she noticed a mark on his left ankle, a circle with a dot in the middle. She traced it with her finger.

"It's the OB witch's mark, the larger circle symbolizes infinity, the female force; the circle in the middle, the Bindu, is the male force," he explained as he took a sip of coffee and winced. "You need a better coffeemaker."

She offered him her arm. He slowly traced her witch's mark, sending currents rippling through her body.

"Your mark, the spiral, is found in rock formations all over the planet, and means the journey of life."

"And the Clan?"

"The Witch's Knot, the malefic winds that blow the forces of calm and chaos."

She set her cup down on her bedside table. "And what part of the body is their mark located?" she asked, stretching her body, allowing the covers slipping down, revealing her nipple.

Samuel traced a witch's knot on the center of her chest with the tip of his finger, leaving a trail of goosebumps. "Right here," he whispered, his voice hoarse as he took her nipple in his mouth. She could feel his arousal against her leg as she reached down and pulled off his briefs.

The buzzer rang. They ignored it. Samuel's mouth, his firm lips, his tongue, explored her body. She lost herself in him. This time the buzzer interrupted them with a long persistent wail.

"Faye," Delilah shouted, rolling out from underneath Samuel's body. She grabbed her blue robe with white clouds, hanging from the back of her bedroom door.

"I'm going to kill her," she said, tying her robe around her waist and running toward the urgent buzzer.

"Faye, what's your deal?" Delilah asked, opening the door.

It took a moment for her to register it wasn't Faye standing in her doorway.

"Hey, there, Delilah. How've you been?" Jonathan asked, dressed in a gray hoodie, jeans, and high tops, holding two coffees and bagels.

Delilah was frozen. She couldn't move her body or open her mouth to speak.

"Did you tell Faye to bugger off?" Samuel called out from the bedroom.

Jonathan pushed past her, entering her apartment.

"I will if I see her," Jonathan responded, as he set down the coffee and bagels on her small round kitchen table.

Samuel walked into the room, buttoning his shirt. "Master Jonathan."

"Samuel," Jonathan replied, pulling out a kitchen chair. "Do you have any plates?"

Delilah grabbed three plates and set them on the table. Without a word, Samuel sat down; they sat in silence drinking coffee and eating bagels like they weren't in the middle of some unholy love triangle.

"That was some earthquake last night," Jonathan remarked, taking the last bite of his bagel.

Delilah's face flushed red. Her cheeks burning, she pulled her robe tightly around her to conceal how exposed she felt.

Jonathan brushed crumbs off his hands. "I don't want to know what's going down here."

"Watch it," Samuel warned. "Before you cast any tones, check your yard; how's your gypsy queen?"

"Feeling yourself, aren't you, Solomon? Came charging in on your black horse to save the day."

"I waited for your people to do something, but alas, they left her here with Faye to rot."

Jonathan ignored the dig and continued. "Because as your Benefactor, I would have to report you both."

A smile broke across Samuel's face. "You are Delilah's Benefactor."

"Yes," Jonathan answered, crossing his arms over his chest.

"This is fantastic news," Samuel said, taking a large bite out of his bagel.

"I don't understand?" Delilah asked.

Samuel took Delilah's hand and kissed it. "It means that as your Benefactor, Master Jonathan has taken a solemn oath not to shag you."

"This isn't a game. I'm not a trophy you two can pass back and forth," Delilah said, yanking her hand away from Samuel. She could feel the fury rising as she placed her hands on the table and began to dance and jump, spilling coffee, and bagels onto the floor.

"Delilah, you need to take a deep breath and calm down before anyone gets hurt," Jonathan said in his social worker's voice.

Her anger rattled the windows against the weathered windowpanes.

"Don't tell me to calm down," she hissed, creating a wind tunnel around her body, blowing her hair and robe.

"WTF! I'm gone for less than twenty-four hours, and you clowns broke her?" Faye yelled, running into the kitchen.

Faye put her arm around Delilah. "Those fools don't deserve your anger."

Delilah stared at Faye; her eyes were wild; she couldn't focus on her face.

"Let it go," Faye instructed, patting Delilah on the back.

The table stopped dancing, and the window stopped rattling. Delilah started coughing, and it was like she was trying to expel some energetic hairball.

"There you go, boss."

She grabbed Faye's hand. "Thank you."

"I got you, sister," Faye said as Delilah pushed her chair away from the table.

"What do you want?" Faye directed her question at Jonathan.

He glanced at his watch. "It's time for your training to begin."

"Why would I go anywhere with you?" Delilah asked.

"Because your Benefactor gave you an order," Samuel replied.

Delilah looked to Faye for confirmation. "Sorry, dude, that's how it works."

Twenty-One

"Accursed be he who uses this knowledge
unto an evil end."

Jonathan and Delilah made their way through the pouring rain. By the time they had reached Graceland Cemetery, they were both drenched. Jonathan pulled out a map from his backpack and led them around the grounds with a flashlight. It felt like the eyes on the statues on the headstones were following them.

A few years back, Delilah did a Halloween tour there with her former co-workers. She remembered a few details; it was one of the oldest cemeteries in Chicago built back in the eighteen-hundreds, and of course, the grounds were haunted. Wandering through the cemetery, she felt lost in time in a Victorian garden.

As they reached their destination, situated in the middle of the cemetery, the air went from humid and muggy to cold.

"Tell me what we're doing here," Delilah demanded.

"Maria cast a spell on you when you were an infant to lock down any past life memories. We need to access the supernatural electromagnetic energy here to counteract her spell," he explained.

There was a small rowboat sitting in the pond. Delilah pointed at it. "Do I even want to know?"

He pulled out a thermos. "You're going to get in the boat and drink this poppy tea."

"And what if I say hell no?" she asked, crossing her arms.

"What did Maria tell you?"

"Drink the tea and learn the truth," she replied, holding out her hand, reaching for the thermos.

As she settled into the boat, the rain stopped. She looked up at the gray sky; it felt like it was pressing down on her. Her breaths were coming in quick staccato bursts.

"Once you're in the middle of the lake, drink the tea, and close your eyes. It should take hold pretty fast. I'll be right here waiting for you," Jonathan said as he pulled out a pop-up tent from his backpack and started to set it up.

"What if I have like a bad acid poppy trip?"

"It should chill you out and relax you more than anything. I'm right here. Okay?"

She stepped in the boat and began rowing it to the middle of the pond. Once she stopped, she saw apparitions coasting above the water, a little girl with a parasol, a man checking a watch attached to a chain at his waist. Delilah turned back to ask Jonathan if he could see them, but the lake was encompassed in a dense fog. Her hand shook as she unscrewed the thermos.

She drank the bitter licorice tea down and screwed her eyes shut. Her mind slowed down as she chanted, "Reveal the truth."

Just as she was about to drift off into sleep, images played like a movie reel. It was night-time. The darkness was profound, with no streetlights or headlights. The muddy road was lit by candles hanging from wooden posts. Delilah was surrounded by crude buildings made of planks of distressed wood. One building looked as though it was fashioned from a hull of a ship. The smell of dirt, burning wood, and manure overtook her senses.

Delilah wore a tight, white linen cap covered by a black-hooded cloak. Her thick, heavy corset pinched into her stomach. She felt a baby kick inside her. With each step she took, her feet were getting stuck in the viscous mud. Her heart was pummeling against her chest as she walked at a brisk pace, glancing over her shoulder. A sharp contraction almost brought her to her knees as she held onto a wooden stake with a horse tied to it. The horse whined and bucked at her.

Closing in on her was an angry pack shouting, "Kill the witch!"

Her senses were leading her way. All she knew was she needed to get to safety. Delilah about cried with relief as she ran up the church steps. Her body was covered in a cold sweat, and her legs were jelly about to give out on her. It took every ounce of energy to pound on the heavy lancet-shaped wooden door. Her knuckles were raw and bloodied from the sharp inlets carved into the door.

Any moment the crowd would arrive at the steps; they were closing in on her fast. Too fast. Her thoughts were a wild freight train about to go off the rails.

I have to get inside. Inside we'll be safe. Open the door. Please.

The door scraped against the wooden floorboards, and she fell inside. She felt a wave of relief as the sounds of locks falling into place echoed through the sanctuary. Samuel, wearing a long black cloak and a long white clerical collar, pulled her up onto her feet. She fell into his arms, into safety.

Torches danced outside the stained-glass windows, as rocks sailed through them with the inflamed crowd circling the church. Followed by torches, the wooden pews were kindling, spreading rapidly into flames. The door began buckling under pressure from a battering ram thrusting against it. They had moments until they would be burned alive.

Delilah focused on Samuel. His eyes were black and dead as he wrenched her hands behind her back and tied them with a rope.

Was he planning on feeding her to the bloodthirsty mob?

She fell to her knees, tears streaming down her face. "Our child, save our child. I beg of you."

He jerked the rope, pulling her up on her feet while waving his hand, opening the church door.

"The child your carry in your belly is an abomination. You brought this down upon your head."

The crowd parted to let them pass. Delilah could feel the heat from their torches on her back. She was like a wild animal cornered, with adrenaline pumping, her stomach churning, an icy cold sweat streaming down her corset.

"Witch!" an old woman yelled, spitting in Delilah's face.

Delilah could feel the spittle slithering down her face and chin. Samuel towed her through the crowd by the rope. The throng beating like a single heart, pumping hate toward Delilah and her unborn baby, pushing and shoving her.

Delilah's only thought was—*tonight, I will die.*

Suddenly stopping, Delilah crashed into Samuel's back and fell to her knees. He kicked her back, knocking the wind out of her.

"This woman knows Satan. This woman holds Satan in her heart," Samuel hollered.

"I am carrying his child," Delilah screamed into the night

119

winds, pointing at Samuel.

Pulling Delilah up to her feet by her hair, he said, "Blasphemy! This witch attempted to seduce me to dance with the devil, but as a man of hearty faith, I persevered against temptation."

"Kill the witch!" the crowd chanted as Samuel pointed to a fresh grave with an open coffin surrounded by lanterns.

Samuel held up his arms, silencing the crowd.

"Delilah D'Arc, you have been accused of witchcraft and are hereby sentenced to die by the power instilled in me by our Lord God and the good people of Salem."

Delilah strained against the ropes in an attempt to break free, only to tighten them. She focused her attention on the torches and summoned the wind. As she took a deep breath, tiny funnels circled up from the ground, pulling the torches out of the dirt and hurling them into the crowd. The mob scattered like roaches. A torch landed on Samuel's neck, setting his long clerical collar on fire, burning his neck and face.

The sky opened up, dropping heavy wet rain from the clouds, pelting them as lightning bolts shot out of the heavens. Delilah broke free of the binds and ran from the open grave. Samuel caught her and tackled her. She dug her fingers into the ground, into the dirt, scraping large rivets, as Samuel pulled her back to the coffin.

"Dust to dust, dirt to dirt, now I command this earth," she chanted, as the ground began to quake and split open.

She gazed up at him; the skin on his neck and chin was charred black; he tossed her into the coffin. Slamming a piece of wood over her, she cried out as the nails, one by one bore into it, sealing her in her living tomb.

The moment Delilah was fading into unconsciousness, the wood was peeled back, and standing over the grave, her black cloak whipping in the wind and rain, was Tabitha Anthea.

Reaching into the coffin, she yanked Delilah out; placing her hand on Delilah's head, Tabitha Anthea mumbled a spell. Delilah was convulsing, trying to catch her breath. The graveyard had descended into chaos. The horde had turned on one another. They were now using their shovels, sticks, and axes to fight each other. Tabitha Anthea carried Delilah to a carriage, and they fled into the shadows of the night.

"Delilah, wake up," Jonathan said, shaking her.

When she opened her eyes, he said, "Thank God. Can you sit up?" He packed up his backpack.

She slowly sat up in the rowboat. Her mouth felt like it was stuffed with cotton.

"Look, um, we unleashed something, and we need to get outta here like now," he said, helping her out of the boat.

In the distance, she heard a crowd yelling, "Kill the witch!"

"Where am I?"

"You're in Graceland Cemetery. You uncovered a memory and, in the process, might have unleashed a seventeenth-century pissed off mob of Salem townsfolk," he explained.

The sounds of chanting were getting closer.

"You brought with you, from your memory, an angry mob who wants to kill us."

"And the good times, keep going. Can we unleash them?"

"We can stay here and try, or we can run like the wind and lock 'em in the cemetery," he said as he put on his backpack.

He took her hand. "Let's go."

As they started running, Delilah's legs were wobbly like she got off the gym's stationary bike. The cemetery was surrounded by a screen of misty fog and darkness; they couldn't see where they were going.

Running in circles, Jonathan and Delilah stopped at a mighty oak tree; looking up, they saw two nooses hanging from a thick branch. There was no way out; the mob had them surrounded and was going to hang them.

Delilah remembered the spell from her memory. She laid on the ground. "Dust to dust, dirt to dirt, now I command this earth," she chanted.

Nothing happened.

"What the hell are you doing?" Jonathan screamed. "Get up! Now."

She ignored Jonathan and continued to chant; gradually, the earth around the tree began to pull apart forming a circle, leaving Delilah and Jonathan on an island under the tree. A moat formed, protecting them from the throng. Moments later, the ground swallowed the Salem townsfolk sending them back in time.

Twenty-Two

"For there are three things in a person:
spirit, soul, and body."

Waking up at Tabitha Anthea's home was disorienting for Delilah. After drinking poppy tea, recovering a memory, and fending off an angry ghost mob, she was spent. Then there was the fact that Samuel had tried to feed her and their unborn child to an angry mob. There were two things she desperately needed: coffee and answers.

Delilah wasn't at all surprised to find Jonathan in the kitchen wearing an apron with large juicy roses on it, making strawberry crepes and homemade whipped cream. Faye was in the yard smoking and swinging on a rope swing.

"Where's Thea?" Delilah asked as she poured herself a cup of coffee.

"She was gone when I woke up," he said, placing a plate of

crepes in front of her and sitting down.

"I have so many questions."

"I can only imagine."

"In that life, I gave birth to a baby?"

"Babies. You had twins," he corrected her.

"What would bring Samuel to try and kill us? It doesn't make sense. What happened to them?"

"You have more memories to recover."

Tabitha Anthea's perfume entered the kitchen before she did.

"You're all up, I see, finally," she teased, unwrapping her cashmere scarf and placing a velvet jewelry box in front of Delilah. "Maria wanted you to have this."

At the mention of Maria's name, Delilah felt a hitch in her chest. The grief always surprised her like someone was piece-by-piece digging out her heart with a melon baller. She opened the box and inside it was a dark gold round pendant with her family's crest on it. Gently she picked up the necklace; it had tiny indentations all over it. On the back, there were the words "anneau gardien" engraved on it.

"Garden of the ring," Delilah said out loud.

Tabitha Anthea took the necklace and placed it on Delilah's neck.

"Jonathan, can you give us some space?" Tabitha Anthea asked.

"Sure," he said as he stood up and placed his cup in the sink. "I'll grab Faye, and we'll head into town to pick up supplies."

Tabitha Anthea examined Delilah.

"How are you holding up?"

"Super. Couldn't be better."

"You're always welcome here. No matter what. You know that, right?" Tabitha Anthea said, sitting down.

Delilah nodded. "I know after the funeral, I don't know, I

wanted to be alone." She took a sip of coffee. "Do you really want Samuel Solomon at your door?"

Tabitha Anthea snorted. "I can handle that boy. Don't you worry about me."

"Of course, there's nothing that can bring you down."

She took Delilah's hand in hers. "There's first love, there's bad love, and there's—"

"True love," Delilah said, completing her sentence. She knew this speech all too well.

"First love, it never leaves you fully, becomes part of you—bad love. Bad love gets into your blood," she said as she set Delilah's hand on the table and patted it. "It isn't easy to shake. It can take lifetimes."

"It feels like I have lost my mind, Thea."

"What do they say? It wouldn't make for sanity living with the devil. He's caused you enough trouble and heartache for ten lifetimes. But I know one thing for sure, when the time comes, you'll do the right thing."

Delilah suddenly felt hungry and couldn't resist Jonathan's crepes. Tabitha Anthea placed her hand on Delilah's shoulder. It felt good to be with her in her childhood home again. She felt cared for, and she felt safe for the first time in weeks.

"Thea, you were there in my memory. You saved me."

"The Salem Witch Trials were a dark time for our people," Tabitha Anthea said as she got up and poured a cup of coffee.

"Need a topper?"

Delilah nodded. "Because twenty witches were killed?"

"Those poor women who were hanged weren't witches. They were innocent humans caught in cross hares sacrificed by the OB's greed."

"The Salem Trials were a bunch of hysterical young girls."

Tabitha Anthea sighed. "They were under a spell to create chaos. It was one of the most diabolical uses of witchcraft. By the late sixteen-hundreds, the trials were dying down in

Europe; humans were starting to lose their appetite for torture. OB wanted to secure their foothold in the New World, so they used the trials as a distraction."

"They created the trials as a way to gain what?"

"Land, in those days, power was in land ownership. You have a town completely upside down; people lost their lands, their farms, it allowed OB to take it all over."

Tabitha Anthea shook her head. "Humans, distract them with chaos; wars, stock market crashes, disease and they turn on one another, and OB, in turn, continues to amass more wealth and more power."

"Why don't we stop them?"

"Honey, that's what we've been attempting to do for centuries."

―――――――――――――――――――

October 30 @ 10:10 am - My Old Bedroom
State of Mind - Pissed Off

Anger, it's not an emotion that I personally have had a lot of experience with. I've never allowed myself to lose control and to be angry. But now, now, I need a thesaurus to describe what I'm feeling... enraged, infuriated, wrathful. I don't know what to do with this rage.

It feels nuclear.

Samuel fucking Solomon, that man, or that witch, the father of my children?!?!

I'm a mother.

I was a mother.

The deeper I go into this world the less I understand. I no longer know who I am anymore. I don't know who I can trust. Before my life was less than exciting, but at least I knew, or I thought I knew who I was. The world had order. The world made sense. This world is utter chaos. I don't understand any of it or my place in it. The answers are out there, and I will find out what happened to my children.

Whatever it takes.

Twenty-Three

"All witchcraft comes from carnal lust."

It was All Hallows' Eve. Delilah had never paid much attention to it. And as an adult, she avoided Halloween like New Year's Eve; in her mind, it was only worse because people were in costume and drunk. Faye had insisted Delilah go to their annual party. Apparently, it was the one night a year the witch world called a truce, drawing up the white flag for one evening. Delilah wanted to go to see if she could find answers to the long list of questions she now had.

Faye even went so far as to say, "It's our Christmas Day. Everything is right and tight for one night only: peace, love, and liquor."

"What could possibly go wrong?" Delilah muttered to herself.

"After everything you've been through, don't you need to

get drunk and get stupid?" Faye chided.

Delilah was never much of a drinker, but Faye had a point. Even though she had her reservations, too many to count, she found herself standing on a deserted street in front of an imposing limestone castle. The door was framed by two massive stone turrets that ran the building's length from the sidewalk to the roof. Over the years, the building has changed hands and has been reincarnated as "The Chicago Hotspot." Tonight, the humans had found other places to haunt.

The streetlights flickered on and off like they were transmitting morse code as the two stone gargoyles pulled their claws up from their gravel perches, tugging at the masonry like it was chewing gum. They zipped up toward the night sky, then buzzed past Delilah's ear, leaving her feeling winded and exhilarated.

The bricks around the door moved in a wave motion, and the door flew off its hinges and splintered into pieces, leaving a dark cavity in the center of the castle, with fog pouring out of it as a staircase dropped down, followed by a rolling red carpet.

Delilah took a few cautious steps toward the entrance. Then two large stone fire pits appeared on either side of the staircase. Dressed like a punk rocker, with a platinum blonde pointy mohawk, a safety pin through her nose, stood Faye at the top of the stairs.

"Whatcha waiting for? An embossed invite?" Faye shouted.

The fog formed the words, "Happy All Saints' Eve," as Delilah climbed the steps.

Faye punched her in the arm. "Wasn't sure you'd show."

She stopped and looked Delilah up and down. Delilah was wearing a silver tunic with a hood made to resemble chain mail, a bodice made of lightweight armor with her family crest in the middle flanked by two crosses, black leggings, and knee boots with brass buckles up the sides. And to finish off her costume, she was carrying a sword in a holster around her waist.

"Nice. You went full-on, JOA. Huh?"

"JOA?"

"Joan of Arc. Come on, let's get you an adult beverage," she said, putting her arm around Delilah and leading her into the party.

Delilah followed Faye inside. They walked down a long narrow hallway, the fog and smoke pooled at their knees. She couldn't see past her thighs. It was so thick she wanted to slice through it with her fake sword.

When she glanced up, a specter appeared. A bride, her throat slashed open, bloodied, her wedding dress torn. She ran through Delilah's body, leaving her feeling like she had bees covering her skin. Then her knife-wielding groom, missing an ear, the side of his face a gaping wound, his tuxedo shredded.

Faye put her hands up in surrender. "Begone, you obnoxious poltergeist."

And the ghost groom disappeared in a puff of smoke.

She reached out and took Delilah's hand.

"This place is hella haunted. So much crazy shit went down here, makes for some interesting party crashers."

At the end of the hallway was a hexagon-shaped room lined with backlit mirrors, with mirrored balls hanging from the ceiling. It was an infinity room filled with multiple Delilahs and Fayes. Delilah stood in the center and slowly turned around. They were standing inside a three-dimensional kaleidoscope.

The room went dark, and a demon voice hissed. "Spirits are no longer at rest as they roam across the land. Tonight, you will rise to meet them."

The room fell away. Delilah and Faye were standing in the middle of the illuminated LED dance floor surrounded by wasted supernatural beings dressed in costumes. All of them, witches, angels, fairies, Romani, and hunters, dancing their faces off to the body thumping EDM. They were all lost in a trance under flashing laser lights and smoke machines. Two dueling deejays were pumping out the music on thirty-foot high platforms under circular spaceship lights. Every so often, cannons would explode, launching sparklers and confetti into the crowd.

Delilah took a deep breath; the smoke smelled funny.

"What's up with the smoke?"

"It's like the highest-grade weed, primo shit," Faye answered. "Breathe it in and feel the beat, sister."

Faye left Delilah for the epicenter of the dance floor. Delilah made her way to the bar. It was a band of neon lights with black-and-white veined marble countertops. All the liquor bottles were lined up on glass shelves and lit underneath like pieces of art.

The bartenders all wore white collared shirts, sleeves rolled up, and thin leather suspenders. As Delilah opened her mouth to order, the bartender, a slender woman with close-cropped dark hair and tattoos dancing up and down her lithe arms, said, "Vodka, tonic with a twist of lemon."

Delilah nodded; she had read her mind; that was her go-to drink order. She set the drink down in front of her; as she lifted it to her lips, a booming animated voice said, "Cheers."

She turned to find a hulking man, dressed as Thor, standing next to her, holding a foamy beer.

"Cheers," Delilah replied, clinking glasses.

She took a sip. It was hands down the best cocktail she had ever tasted.

Thor smiled. "Yeah, I know, right?"

She looked into his eyes. One was brown the other blue. He reminded her of someone, but she couldn't place him. She wondered why his eyes were two different colors.

"Heterochromia of the eye," he said.

"Excuse me?"

"You asked why my eyes are two different colors. It's a genetic thing, something to do with the uneven distribution of pigmentation in the iris."

"I don't think I asked you about your eye color, not out loud at least. What are you, some mind-reading witch or something?" Delilah replied.

"Mind-reading witch hunter," he said, holding out his hand. "Wolfgart Zandt. Friends call me Wolf."

Delilah stood there with her mouth open, gaping. He had this easy-going boy-next-door way about him, but she knew he was a cold-blooded killer. She shook her head and started to walk away.

He gently placed a hand on her arm. "Delilah, tonight I'm a regular guy talking to a regular girl at a party."

She pulled her arm away from him.

"Wait, you know me?"

"Everybody, and I mean everybody, knows who you are," he said, taking a long drink from his beer.

"Is that supposed to be comforting? I don't understand how this all works. So, for three hundred and sixty-four days a year, we're in a holy war, for all intents and purposes we hate each other, but on one night, we push it all aside, and party like it's 1999."

"I don't know if we do hate each other, in so much as we've been at war for so long, we don't know another way," he said, draining his beer. "Maybe you'll be the one to show us there's a better way. We can live in peace for three hundred and sixty-five days a year."

She set down her drink and crossed her arms over her chest. "Are you messing with me?"

"I would never mess with you. Think about Joan of Arc; look at what a teenage girl was able to accomplish. You could do even more with this life, so much more."

"Where the freak have you been?" Faye yelled into her ear. "Been searching for you for hours."

Faye stopped short in front of Wolf. "Wolfgart."

With an exaggerated bow, he asked, "Faye, Queen of the Asphalt Sprites, may I get you a beer?"

Faye clapped her hands. "I'm all good, hoss," she replied, pulling Delilah away from the bar.

Delilah glanced back at Wolf, and he saluted her.

Once they were out of earshot, she said, "I like, leave you alone for two seconds, and you're having a tete-a-tete with Wolf Zandt; his dad is the leader of the Sect. You know the hunters who killed your mother and tried to kill you. WTF, Dee."

Delilah stopped suddenly. "It's Delilah."

"What?"

"My name is Delilah."

"Whatever," she said, leading her to another part of the club with a velvet rope and a bouncer, dressed in a black suit, sunglasses, with an earpiece, guarding the entrance. He put up his hand to stop them.

"She's with me," Faye said as he unhooked the rope and let them in.

The room was draped in red velvet curtains with small little gold tables throughout it. On the stage was a voluptuous woman performing a burlesque number for a room full of captivated fairies. Faye pointed to an empty table, and they sat down. An androgynous man, with legs that went on forever, dressed as a cigarette girl with a short pink skirt and a pillbox hat, came by with a tray with straps around his neck. The tray was filled with cigarettes, joints, and opium pipes. Faye signaled him to move on.

The club host was a petite woman with her lips painted blood red, her hair slicked back, dressed in a tuxedo. She came over to their table with a bottle of champagne, a gold bucket filled with ice, and two glasses. As she poured the champagne, she winked at Delilah and blew her a kiss.

Delilah leaned over to Faye. "Tell me about the Sect."

Faye took a long drink of champagne, her eyes focused on the dancer on stage who was performing a number with large fans made of long pink and white feathers.

"No way, sister. Not tonight."

Delilah grabbed her arm. "Please."

"Listen, this is my one night off from all that shit, and if you think I'm gonna spend it giving you a history lesson, you are bananas."

"Faye. Pretty please, with sugar on top."

"B-A-N-A-N-A-S," she replied, clinking Delilah's glass. "Go and ask Jonathan, your big daddy Benefactor. I'm sure he'd love to educate you on the Sect's thousand-year master plan to rid the world of evil."

Delilah took a sip of champagne.

Faye clapped her hands. "There you go. Drink up. Have some fun," she said, pouring more champagne into Delilah's glass.

The bubbles went straight to Delilah's head, leaving her feeling fizzy. The dancer gave her final twirl and exited stage left. The fairies let out a collective groan.

Faye turned to Delilah. "So, what's up with you and Solomon?"

"Are we gonna have some girl-talk now?" Delilah could make out a slight slur in her voice.

The dance floor began to fill up as a sad tune played. Faye stood up and offered Delilah her hand. "May I have this dance, my lady?"

Delilah drained her drink and followed Faye to the dance floor. Faye pulled her close. She hadn't realized how well-built and taut Faye was under all her oversized T-shirts and leggings.

"You deserve better than him," Faye whispered in her ear.

Her breath was fiery against Delilah's skin. The eerie music filled Delilah with a sense of yearning. She rested her head on Faye's shoulder as they swayed in time to the song. When the music ended, Faye pulled away from Delilah. Faye turned away and wiped her eyes with the back of her hand, trying to hide her tears.

"You should go. This room is for fairies only."

"Thank you." Delilah leaned in and kissed Faye on the cheek.

"For what?"

"For taking care of me after Maria died."

Faye shrugged her shoulders. "It was no biggie."

Delilah squeezed her shoulders and met Faye's stony gaze. "It was a huge biggie."

Faye put her hand over her heart. "On my honor, I will continue to serve you."

Delilah stumbled out of the burlesque show and found herself in a room titled "Hydration Station." The room was lined with distressed bricks and lit with small round fire pits lining the walls. The large square pool in the middle was deep turquoise and was under an ancient stone arch. A man and a woman with mermaid tails lounged by the side of the pool.

Steam rose from the water, inviting Delilah into the pool. Slowly she peeled off her costume and entered the water. The mermaid rolled into the pool and swam over to her. She opened Delilah's mouth and blew into it. Giving Delilah a burst of oxygen set all her brain cells at attention. She felt so alert, like she had downed a double espresso. Feeling so alive, so refreshed, all Delilah wanted to do was to go dance. She jumped out of the water, and to her surprise, she was completely dry. Back in her costume, she headed to the dance floor.

A night's sky filled with a big, luscious Harvest Moon

surrounded by stars hung over the dance floor. Delilah felt a hand on her shoulder. It was Aros. He pulled her into an embrace, and together they danced. The sky exploded with fireworks. Bursting with thunder and light, the crowd clapped and hollered after each new blast. She never had in her life felt so wild, so free. The crowd was one giant organism, one big body moving in sync to the music. And she was a part of it. All of it. There was no past, no future, the moment. Aros was in rapture. It lit up his entire body. He placed his hand on Delilah's heart and transferred the energy to her. Together on the dance floor, they had a mystical experience.

Then an unrelenting thirst set in.

"Water," Delilah screamed over the music.

Aros shook his head. Alone, Delilah swam through the crowd in search of something to drink.

Once she was off the dancefloor, it was a labyrinth of hallways leading to another fantastical party. She heard a man singing, "Witchcraft."

The voice sounded like home to her. She followed it into a nightclub. It was all Las Vegas circa Rat Pack era with men in custom tuxedos and women in gorgeous gowns dripping in diamonds and furs. The room was filled with tables covered in satin tablecloths with candles in the middle. Clouds of smoke drifted over the tables as bright spotlights lit up the stage.

Delilah almost fainted when she recognized the man standing in front of a big band singing. It was her father, Devlin. And the most surprising part wasn't the caliber of his voice; he could give Ol' Blue Eyes Frank Sinatra a serious run for his money. It was the woman dressed in a cherry red brocade sleeveless ballgown with white opera gloves sitting front row eyeballing her dad like he was fresh from the grill Porterhouse. Devlin grabbed her hand and pulled her onto the stage.

Never missing the beat, he sang, "Witchcraft, crazy

witchcraft, I know it's taboo."

Swaying to the beat, gazing into Devlin's eyes like a teenager with a crush was Tabitha Anthea. It was so wrong to watch them. Delilah felt as though she dove into the ocean and couldn't tell the surface from the floor. They appeared to be happy. And in love. She couldn't figure out if it was Halloween or reality. Through the crowd, she made eye contact with Tabitha Anthea and did what every grown woman did when confronted with the fact that her guardian and long-lost father were lovers. She ran.

Running through the corridors, Delilah realized she still needed water. From the corner of her eye, she saw a fountain. It was majestic. In the middle of four tiers was the goddess, Venus, holding a pitcher with water flowing out of it. So thirsty, Delilah stuck her mouth under the water and drank from it. The water tasted like the freshest spring water. She was eating the water, letting it run down her face and chin.

"Delilah, what are you doing?" Tabitha Anthea asked.

She pulled her mouth away and wiped it with the back of her hand.

"The question is, what are you doing with my dad?"

Devlin entered the alcove and put his arm protectively around Tabitha Anthea's shoulder.

"Delilah, Thea and I are in love, and we have been for some time now."

"Wow," Delilah said, pushing past them both.

She was speechless. *How was she supposed to react to this news? Happy? Angry? Confused?*

Tabitha Anthea tried to reach out to Delilah, but she shook off her hand. Walking away from them, she heard Devlin say, "Leave her be for now. She'll come around."

This night was turning into a rollercoaster ride with sharp turns and loop de loops. Turning another corner, Delilah saw Jonathan, dressed like a Greaser with a pompadour and black motorcycle jacket, standing underneath a waterfall of silver confetti. His eyes were closed. The smile on his face was serenity itself. She stood frozen, watching him until he opened his eyes.

"Hey, De-lye-la," he said, drawing out her name.

Something about him was off, way off. "You okay?" Delilah asked.

He put his sunglasses on and stuck his thumbs out. "For sure, baby girl."

Delilah walked over to him and removed his sunglasses.

"You don't look good." His pupils were tiny little pins.

"I feel fine," he said, holding onto her shoulders and opening his eyes wide to prove he was totally normal.

"How about we find a twenty-four-hour diner? We can get some coffee and food in you," Delilah suggested.

"He doesn't need any coffee," a voice with a thick Mediterranean accent informed her.

Delilah turned around to find Melia dressed as a Flamenco dancer. "He looks higher than a fucking kite," Delilah replied.

Melia took a step into Delilah's personal space. They were nose to nose. "I think you should run along and let this go."

"Excuse me?" Delilah spat back.

"My advice would be to walk away now before you get hurt," Melia countered.

Jonathan put his arms around them both and set sloppy kisses on both their cheeks. "Ladies, can't we all just get along?"

"Jonathan!" they both yelled in unison.

Melia pulled away. She placed her fingertip under Delilah's chin. "You don't want to tussle with my uncle or with me. It won't end well for you."

Delilah stood staring Melia down, every muscle in her body taut and tense.

Melia ran her fingers over Delilah's costume. "Adorable."

Swatting Melia's hand away, and catching her wrist, Delilah gave it a hard twist.

"You don't want to mess with my family or me," Delilah warned.

Pulling her arm away, Melia laughed like it was all in good fun.

"Come now, Delilah, we can be friends, no?" Melia leaned in, kissing Delilah on each cheek.

She pushed Melia away. "Jonathan, I'm so disappointed in you."

Melia wrapped her arm around Jonathan. "Come, my love, there's still so many more pleasures to be enjoyed."

She watched as Melia, again, pulled Jonathan away into the dark. He turned around and mouthed, "Sorry."

Delilah was feeling exhausted. Trying to find her way out was like trying to find the exit in a casino, nearly impossible. She found a door with a flashing red light about the threshold. In her mind, red meant exit. Opening the door, she discovered it was another room. This one featured hand-woven oriental rugs, lush floor pillows, and an ornate gold hookah.

Smoking like a king on his throne was Mahai, lounging on a gold pillow. His crisp white shirt, still neatly tucked into his suit trousers, was open with his sleeves rolled up to reveal his tattoos, which were works of art. His chest provided a canvas for a sun with a face in the center surrounded by rays. Two identical daggers featuring eyes at the top of the hilt graced his forearms. As the emperor of the night, dark kohl outlined his eyes, and black polish on his graceful feet.

"Delilah, come join me," he said, patting a furry pillow next to him.

In a trance, she walked over to Mahai and sat down. The moment she sat down, Aros entered and found a spot on the other side of Mahai.

"Ah, my children, come for a visit; let your Theo, your

uncle Mahai tell you a story."

He inhaled from the pipe; the smell was dirt, tobacco, and coffee. He signaled for them to place their heads on his lap.

Delilah shot back up onto her feet. "My sword. I've lost it."

"It's of no matter, come and sit, my darling girl," Mahai said, trying to reassure her.

Like a child, she snuggled into Mahai; he began petting her hair.

"Do you know of the story of the Grigori, of the angels, of Aros's people?"

He didn't wait for an answer. "Jacob dreamed of a ladder which would connect the earth to the heavens so the angels could travel between the two realms. Jacob then built an altar and his ladder. The Grigori used it; with the ease of light, they'd journey back and forth. It was only when the angels shared a bed with the humans and procreated, they were then cast out, forced to roam the planet without their tongues no less," he said, inhaling the smoke and blowing out.

"What happened to their children?" she asked.

Smiling, Mahai tilted his head back and closed his eyes.

"Mahai, the half-human, and half-angel children?"

He opened his eyes, placed his hand on her face. "Can't you see? My darling girl, you and your kind are their children."

And like that, Delilah, after a slow crawl up to the apex of the roller coaster, was now careening down the other side.

"I don't understand."

"What's to understand? You're made from the heavens, the moon, and the stars. You are magic. This is beautiful. No?"

Mahai held out his arms.

"Come give your Theo a hug and wish me pleasant dreams."

She leaned into him as he wrapped her in his embrace. Tears streamed down her face.

"Listen, my child, meet all challenges with courage," Mahai said.

She pulled away from him. Aros was splayed out, like a starfish, dead asleep. He looked adorable. Despite herself, she giggled.

Mahai clapped his hands.

"Bravo! Darling girl, you can see both the pain and the absurdity that is this life; you'll then know some happiness," he said, dismissing her with a wave of her hand.

Delilah left Mahai feeling soothed. She found she was no longer as anxious to leave the party. A loud cackle drew her attention to a woman holding a champagne bottle in a room to her left titled "Champagne Room." From behind, the woman wore a tight black velvet dress made to accentuate her waist and hug her round bottom. The mystery woman had on a pair of stockings with a black seam up the back.

Delilah realized it was Mrs. Fairfax. She was having the time of her life climbing up a rope ladder to jump into a life-sized champagne glass filled with squishy round gold and white balls. Once inside, she was floating in a bubbly glass of champagne. A man wearing a tuxedo and tails with spats covering his shiny shoes handed her a glass and poured her a drink from a magnum bottle.

Mrs. Fairfax drained the glass. "Hit me again, Governor."

The man nodded and poured her another.

"Delilah! My dear, I've missed you so," Mrs. Fairfax hollered through the streamers and confetti. She snapped at the tuxedo man. "Get Ms. D'Arc a glass."

Mrs. Fairfax signaled for Delilah to join her. She knew arguing with her would be a fruitless exercise, so, as they say, when in Rome or in the Champagne Room at a paranormal Halloween party, do as you're told. Delilah jumped right on in. It made her feel giddy, like a child swinging too high.

"There's my girl," she said, pouring Delilah a drink. "How's your evening been? I want to know everything, and you mustn't leave out a single detail."

With a magnum of champagne between them, Delilah told Mrs. Fairfax about everything that had happened, from her conversation with Wolf to her story time with Mahai.

"My, my, someone has had a night to remember," Mrs. Fairfax said, clicking her tongue. "I'm proud of you."

"For what?"

"The woman who sits before me now is not the same woman I met when I answered the door last summer."

Delilah couldn't argue with that assessment, but it still didn't explain why Mrs. Fairfax was proud of her.

"You were faced with insurmountable circumstances, one after the other, and here you sit with me enjoying a glass of the finest champagne. You made it, my dear," she said, patting Delilah's hand.

"It feels as though I'm only halfway through my journey."

"Quite right, but you made it this far and it's not for nothing." Mrs. Fairfax leaned in. "And Mr. Solomon? Has he figured into your grand adventures?"

She sighed. "Samuel."

"Spill the tea. Inquiring minds want to know," Mrs. Fairfax teased.

Delilah couldn't reconcile the Samuel she knew in this life with the Samuel she met in her memory. He tried to feed her and their unborn children to a bloodthirsty mob. Although Delilah hadn't had much experience with relationships, she was certain she couldn't forgive and forget it.

"It's complicated. I'm not in a good place right now for a relationship. I need some me-time to focus on my priorities."

"Bollocks!" Mrs. Fairfax yelled, leaning into Delilah's face.

"He was going to murder our children and me."

Mrs. Fairfax waved her hand. "Did you ask Mr. Solomon his side of the story?"

"I saw it with my own two eyes. I felt the heat of the angry mob's torches on my back."

Mrs. Fairfax gripped Delilah's hands. "Go find him and hear him out."

She withdrew her hands and climbed out of the champagne glass.

"Keep an open mind, dearie." Mrs. Fairfax pointed her finger, shaking it up and down like an angry schoolteacher.

Delilah had no concept of time. She wondered if, like in *Cinderella*, the clock strikes midnight, and they all turn back into warring pumpkins. This thought made her laugh out loud. To say her night had been surreal was an understatement. There were no words to describe it.

The party had become quiet. Delilah thought the main dance floor was the middle of the wheel, and the rooms were the spokes extending from it. Disorientated, she glanced behind her, and it was a wall of mist. Ahead of her was a forest accentuated by a murky greenish-blue sky. She walked toward it and was at the foot of a gothic stone balcony with an arch framing the apricot Harvest Moon. It was pulling her up the grainy stone steps, calling her closer.

Once under the moon, she howled; she knew it was silly, but it felt so good. Turning her face to the moon, feeling the rays reflecting on her skin, she arched her back and howled again, as though her life depended on it. Wailing into the night, her voice felt hoarse, feeling the strain. Then a howl answered her, bouncing on the treetops. She laughed. It comforted her, knowing someone was out there howling at the moon with her.

"It's magnificent, isn't it?"

Her cheeks flushed red. She didn't need to turn around. She felt him standing behind her.

"I found this," Samuel said, holding her sword. "I wanted to return it to you. Who's Joan of Arc without it?"

Delilah took it from him and placed it back in the scabbard. "She never used it. Of course, she could, and by all

143

accounts, was an accomplished swordfighter. Couldn't bring herself to harm another living soul."

He smiled at her. He seemed tired. Of course, he wasn't in costume; instead, he wore a light-gray cashmere V-neck sweater, jeans, and a pair of light-brown vintage lace-up leather work boots. Being so close to him, she could feel her willpower waning. The air between them crackled and popped. Images of their night together mixed in with pictures from her recovered memory was causing havoc on her brain. And she was starving.

"Now my duty is done, and Jehanne d'Arc has her sword. I may rest easy," he said, giving her a slight bow.

"What about Mrs. Fairfax?"

"I have learned long ago to leave her to her own devices. Goodnight, Delilah."

She watched as he walked away from her. Before she knew what she was doing, she called out, "Samuel."

"Yes?" he asked, turning around with a big smug grin on his face.

"I'm starving, and I can't figure out how to get out of here."

Twenty-Four

"You take great pains to seduce me."

Delilah sat patiently in Samuel's kitchen, watching him cook her an omelet. The kitchen seemed empty without Mrs. Fairfax. The counters were bare. To her surprise, he knew his way around the kitchen.

He placed the omelet in front of her. "Bon appétit," Samuel said, wiping his hands on a white and blue kitchen towel.

She took a bite and moaned. It was so rich and buttery. Samuel added a dab of caviar, sour cream and dusted fresh chives over it. She ate it slowly with her eyes closed, savoring each bite.

When she opened her eyes, Samuel was staring at her.

"Bloody hell, if that wasn't erotic."

Delilah blushed. "I was so hungry, and it was so good."

"No need to apologize. I'd watch you eat an omelet anytime."

She pulled at her costume; the fake chain mail was scratching her neck. "Would you like to slip into something more comfortable," Samuel said, cocking an eyebrow.

Waving her hand back and forth, she said, "I'm not in a place right now where I can do this. Whatever this is. It's too much. Too confusing."

"Eat an omelet with an old friend?"

"Samuel, you tried to kill our babies and me," she said, pushing her plate away from her.

"It was three hundred years ago, under a very different set of circumstances."

"Three hundred and twenty-seven years ago," she corrected him. "There's so much I don't know about our world, about us. How did we meet?"

He smiled at her. His smile told her they shared a fable worthy story. Despite her anger and confusion, she wanted to know their history.

"I can show you how we met."

She shrugged. "Show me?"

"We can access my memory, a bit of time travel. If you're up for it."

"Why not?"

He led her to the library. She hadn't been back in the room since her ill-fated job interview. In the twilight, it seemed so peaceful, like the books were asleep. He kneeled in front of the fireplace. She watched as he carefully placed the logs in the center and lit the kindling. The words "We Alone Open the Door to Perception" were engraved over the marble fireplace mantle, underneath it on the apron the phases of the moon. The legs featured a crow with a flame on the left side and a lantern with a sparrow on the right. And the hearth had a bronze engraving of a compass, with a pentacle replacing the north direction.

"You'll want to get a bit more comfortable," he said,

pointing to her costume.

She watched as he removed his sweater, shoes, and socks until he was in a white T-shirt and jeans. Delilah, in turn, removed her costume and boots, leaving on her black leggings and tank top. He reached for an ornate, ancient wooden box with a crown and a serpent engraved on it. Samuel waved his hand. The box opened, and he pulled out an emerald.

Suddenly, it all became too real, and an uneasiness overwhelmed her.

"Is this a good idea? I mean, should you time travel on a full stomach?"

He placed his hands on her shoulders. His gray eyes were looking through her.

"It's perfectly normal to feel a bit nervous. I promise you; you'll be safe."

"And I should trust you because?"

"Delilah, I have never lied to you. But, if you don't feel comfortable, I understand it's been a long evening," he said, placing the emerald back in the box.

"No, no, let's do this," she said, trying to psyche herself up.

"Are you absolutely sure? I want to make certain I have your consent."

"You have my consent. Let's get this show on the road."

He removed a small dagger from the wall and pressed it into his palm; drawing drops of blood, he squeezed it onto the compass. Then he tossed the emerald into the fireplace; a hologram of flames shot out of it. The fireplace legs expanded upwards toward the ceiling, making it large enough for them to step inside.

"Where are we going?"

"Home," he said, reaching out his hand.

Delilah held on tight to his strong hand and closed her eyes as he pulled her into the flames. Once inside, she had the sensation of diving into the water, the moment when your body enters, and it seems like up is down and down is up.

When she opened her eyes, they were standing in a long hallway with glistening chandeliers filled with thousands of candles, polished parquet floors, arched Palladian windows all lined with mirrors.

"The Hall of Mirrors," Delilah whispered, peering over at Samuel.

When she realized they were both holograms, she began giggling, touching her arm, watching her fingers go through it.

He smiled down at her, his face beaming. "Versailles, late seventeenth century, I was invited by the Sun King Louis XIV to discuss recent scientific discoveries. I had been following the Great Comet. The King was fascinated with anything new."

"This is where we'd all come to try and catch the King on his way from his private chambers to the chapel to ask favors," Delilah said, pointing to the hall.

Moments later, Delilah saw her seventeenth-century self floating down the hall holding a hand-painted fan with images of cherubs in a lush field. Her luscious light-blue silk shantung off-the-shoulder gown embroidered with gold fleur-de-lis and trimmed in white lace was stunning. A regal-looking dark-haired woman wearing an opulent royal blue dress with bell sleeves and a ruby medallion the size of a baseball hanging from her bodice leaned in and said something in Delilah's ear. And she nodded as though she had been given an important assignment.

Delilah then gracefully opened her fan, her eyes set on a fixed prize, making direct eye contact over the top of it with a man a few feet away. It was Samuel. He was dashing with his hair flowing over his shoulders, wearing a long dark, somber slate waistcoat and breeches made from a silk brocade with oversized white lace cuffs and matching cravat.

She lowered her fan and gave Samuel a mischievous wink. He lifted an eyebrow, his signature move, and glanced away from her.

"Who's the woman I am with?"

"Françoise d'Aubigné marquise de Maintenon, she was the King's second wife and the most powerful woman in France. You began life in court as a courtesan, but deftly and quickly maneuvered your way to become her lady-in-waiting."

Glancing around, Delilah sighed. "It feels like home here."

Samuel nodded in sympathy.

"Come, there's more to our story," he said, leading her into a small private antechamber leading into an apartment.

They found Samuel wearing a linen shirt and breeches hunched over a writing desk working in front of a roaring fire. He was lost in his work and didn't notice when Delilah entered his room. With her chin set high, her shoulders back, holding her hands delicately, she waited for him to look up.

"The King gave you a daunting task," Samuel explained.

He glanced up at her, set down his quill, and folded his arms. Delilah clapped her hands. Three stunning women with their hair down around their shoulders, dressed only in salmon-colored silk togas tied at the waist with gold ropes, danced into the room and posed in front of Samuel.

He gave the women a once over shook his head and picked up his quill.

"To find me a courtesan, and I didn't make the job easy for you."

Delilah walked with a clip to the door. No sooner was Samuel on his feet, barring her exit.

"When the King gives you a task, you by divine law must complete it. Otherwise, you fall out of favor and are exiled from the inner circle," he explained.

Delilah spinning on her heels, turned around. He pinned her against the door. Her eyes locked into his, and with one defiant look, she dared him to kiss her, to take her right there. He took a step back, opened the door, bowed, and stepped aside for her to leave.

Delilah nodded at him and said, "Monsieur."

As she went to leave, he seized her arm and kissed her neck passionately.

Present-day Delilah felt the heat of his kiss on her neck. Her past and her present life were merging into one.

With force, Samuel slammed the door shut and led her to the bed by her hand. She pushed him down onto the bed which was furnished in gold leaf and silks. Seductively, Delilah's ghost sauntered over to the desk. Placing both hands on the back of the chair, she leisurely dragged it over to the bed.

As she stood in front of him, his hands landed on her bottom. She slapped them away and scolded him like a naughty child. From her wrist, she untied a blue silk ribbon. Delilah wrapped it around Samuel's neck, using it to pull him toward her. She leaned down and kissed him, pressing her lips against his. His greedy hands landed on her breasts, and she slapped him across his face.

Without breaking eye contact, she started a seductive striptease. Just down to her corset, she presented him her laces, urging him to unwrap her like a present. At first, he pulled at them violently. He was met with another slap until, gently one by one, he removed each tie. The corset fell to the ground, and she kicked it aside playfully with her toe.

Lunging at her, he planted urgent kisses on her bare shoulders. She pushed him down and pulled off his linen shirt. Slowly she slid out of her silk undergarment, leaving it to pool at her feet. He was panting, ready to devour her. Taking her ribbon, she tied his hands together tightly.

Naked, she sat in the chair, placing her feet on either side of him, allowing him the full view of her innermost world. He was transfixed. He sat motionless, mesmerized by her. He leaned into her sex, inhaling her, dropping to his knees before her.

She pulled his head back. "You are my beloved."

"One love, one life, one blood," he said, then sunk his tongue inside her. She placed her hands on the back of his head, forcing him in deeper.

Standing by the fireplace, the twenty-first century Samuel shouted, "Delilah!"

Unable to make out what he was saying to her, she closed her eyes, blissful, and content. Delilah didn't want to leave this perfect memory. Sharp teeth cutting into her thigh shook her out of her reverie. Samuel took her hand, pulled her up, and pushed her inside the fireplace.

Back in the present day, they were both on all fours gasping for breath. Delilah's head felt hollow, and her lips dry. As panic set in, she couldn't catch her breath. She found herself forgetting how to breathe.

Samuel grabbed her face. "Look at me."

Her eyes were rolling upward. "Come on."

Those were the last words she heard until she regained consciousness, with Samuel pinching her nose and breathing into her mouth. He turned her onto her side, patting her back, as she coughed up gritty ashes. Once she could breathe again, he handed her a glass of water.

"What happened?" she asked.

"The only way to preserve the space-time continuum is to be a detached observer. Your past soul and your present soul were converging into one. If they had joined completely, then you would no longer exist, you would've been permanently stuck in the past."

"Maybe the next time you tell me all that before launching me there?" She felt a chill run through her body. "I felt like I belonged there. It was—"

"Home." He finished her sentence, placing a blanket

around her shoulders.

"How did we end up in Salem?" she asked, yawning.

Sitting down next to her on the couch, pulling her into his chest and kissing the top of her head, he said, "That is a story for another day."

Twenty-Five

"And when they left me, I wept, and I wished that
they would've taken me with them."

Delilah sat in front of an unmarked grave covered with white
roses and candles. She had set out a picnic blanket with wine,
fruit, creamy cheese, and crusty fresh bread. Delilah checked
her watch; it was almost midnight, and All Souls' Day would
soon commence. Anxious, she poured herself a glass of red
wine and rolled it around in her mouth, allowing the notes of
blackberry, vanilla, and pepper to play on her tongue.

"Mon petit chaton, you found me."

Delilah jumped up. Maria appeared whole again. She was
glowing with her dark hair set in wavy curls. Her violet eyes
clear and bright. In a pair of black wide-leg pants and a
stretchy asymmetrical tunic, Maria was the epitome of a
French woman. The afterlife was agreeing with her.

"Maman," Delilah said, giving her a tight hug.

Maria took her hand. "Let's sit. We don't have much time."

Delilah poured her a glass of wine. They touched glasses. "Sante," they said in unison.

"Delilah, what you did for me. I'm so proud of you," Maria said, squeezing her hand.

Tears started to form. Delilah looked away from Maria.

"Come, child, you don't have to hide your tears from me."

"I fell apart after your funeral. I lost it."

"Grief, it's not easy to bear. When you were called, you did what you needed to do. To hold yourself to a standard in which you don't ever fall to pieces isn't realistic. No one should ever expect it of you, least of all yourself. True courage is found in putting yourself back together."

"I'm so lost. I don't know who I am anymore."

She took Delilah's face in her hands. "You are Delilah Johanne D'Arc, daughter of Devlin and Maria."

"I feel like a fraud."

"Here's what I do know. You are braver than you believe, stronger than you seem, and smarter than you think," Maria said, holding her hand.

"Are you quoting *Winnie the Pooh* to me?" Delilah asked with a playful shove.

Maria giggled. "I suppose I am. And know, mon petit chaton, I'll always be here for you."

"Aren't you dead?"

"When you need me, just summon a redbird and whisper my name."

"I don't have a lot of experience summoning birds."

"My daughter, you're a witch. Animals are our hirelings," she said, eyeing the cheese plate. "Is that brie?"

Delilah picked up a plate and handed it to Maria. She watched as she tore the bread into pieces and prepared two plates.

"The Sect has the page," Delilah blurted out, taking a plate from Maria.

"Well, it seems as though you have a quest in your future," she replied, taking a bite of bread dripping in brie. "I recommend you drink the poppy tea and recover the rest of your memory."

"You make it sound so easy."

"I have faith in you. Now eat something. All Souls isn't complete until we break and eat bread together. It's tradition."

She reached over and hugged Maria. "I don't want this to end."

Maria set down her dish. "Delilah, you are surrounded by love. I love you; Devlin loves you, and Tabitha Anthea loves you."

She pulled away and inspected her hands. "Maman, there's something I should tell you."

"I know."

Delilah looked at her, shocked. "About Thea and Devlin?"

Maria patted her hand. "You'll find there are no secrets in our world. I know, and I gave them my blessing. Life is too short to stand in the way of happiness. Love is love in all its forms."

"But she's your best friend, and he's your husband."

"What transpires between a husband and wife isn't for others, even their daughter, to understand. Your father was a good husband. I love him, and I want him to be loved. And I ask you to find it in your heart to accept them."

Delilah wrapped Maria in a hug. "I hope one day, I'm half the woman, half the witch you are."

November 2 @ 1:11 am - My Old Bedroom
State of Mind - Bewildered

They say it's a thin line between love and hate. I now understand that saying completely. Can you love and hate someone? Yes, I def can. My emotions are a jumble. But the sex with Samuel, it causes earthquakes, it's that freaking good. I'm now a sex crazed witch!?!? My logical brain is telling me to stay far far away from Samuel for a host of reasons:

1. Tried to kill me and our unborn babies
2. When that's your #1 you really don't need a #2
3. I don't know what his motives really are
4. It's against the natural order of our world
5. And there's Jonathan too

What I do know.

Is that I need more answers. I can't rest until I know the truth. All of it. No matter what it brings. I need to find those answers for myself. It's like when I had to solve the infinite series in calculus. I became obsessed and I couldn't stop until I figured it out. It took me two semesters to solve it. I know I can solve this problem—depose the sums, simplify, isolate, evaluate, and pull it all together.

Twenty-Six

"And I answered the voice, even though I was a poor girl who knew nothing of riding and warfare."

Devlin slammed his hand on the kitchen table, rattling their empty dinner dishes. "Absolutely not. It's too dangerous."

Tabitha Anthea placed her hand on Devlin's. Delilah looked away, and Tabitha Anthea quickly removed it.

"Maman told me I have to recover the rest of my memory."

Devlin pulled his chair toward Delilah, taking her hands in his, nearly knocking over his wine glass. "How many more visits to the ER? And let's not forget, a ghost mob nearly killed you."

She hadn't told them about the time traveling with Samuel. Since their return, her head hadn't stopped pounding, and she was still coughing up ashes.

"Thea, what do you think?" Delilah asked.

She shook her head and started clearing their empty dinner plates. After placing them in the sink, she leaned against the counter and wiped her hands.

"Dee, Delilah, this is your crusade and yours alone."

Delilah stood up too fast and held onto the chair to steady herself, another side effect of the time travel: she was also lightheaded. "You'll help me then?"

"First, I want to examine you," Devlin said as he took her wrist and felt her pulse.

"Fine. Whatever it takes for you two to get on board and help me figure this all out," Delilah replied, easing back into her chair.

"First, you need to tell me what's going on," he said. "Ever since All Hallows' Eve, you haven't been yourself."

"I time traveled with Samuel," she blurted out.

"Do you know how dangerous that is?" Devlin said, admonishing her and her life choices.

Delilah watched as Devlin went in search of his medical bag. He returned with his stethoscope around his neck. Devlin sat in the chair, listened to her heart, and took her blood pressure. Then he placed his hands on either side of her head and closed his eyes.

"I need to do spirit work on you. Your pulse rate is all over the place, and your energetic field is shattered from top to bottom."

"Spirit work?"

Thea put her hand on Delilah's shoulder. "Your dad is a healer. He can read your energy field and make adjustments."

Devlin pulled out a prescription pad and a pen and drew a picture of a body with egg-shaped halos around it.

"We have five energy fields surrounding our physical bodies connected to our internal functions like, for instance, your heart. If these energy systems are out of alignment, it can cause both mental and physical ailments."

Devlin set up a massage table in the living room. He had Delilah lay down on her back while he sat down at her head, with his index fingers on her temples. When he stood, he held his hands over her body and slowly moved them over her. She began moving like a puppet on an invisible string, her back arching, her arms moving, along with her legs. Then Delilah began coughing like she was trying to release an energetic hairball stuck in her throat. She was coughing so hard; Tabitha Anthea placed a bucket under her chin. She vomited sickly yellowish pea-soup-colored phlegm into the bucket.

"How do you feel?" he asked.

"Honestly, I feel better, lighter even."

He took her hand and helped her off the table.

"Let's get you a cup of tea and then an Epsom salt bath. I'm glad you're feeling better, but you're still healing and will need rest."

Delilah could smell Thea's homemade banana bread. She wrapped her arms around Devlin's neck and hugged him. "Thank you."

He was surprised at first, but then hugged her back. "Look, kiddo, I want you to know I'm always here for you, but right now, no more memory recovery or time travel until your spirit and body has had a chance to heal."

She patted him on the back. "Okay, pops."

Later that night, Delilah couldn't sleep. Her thoughts were a jumble. She worried about Jonathan and wondered why he hadn't returned her texts. Lying in bed healing felt like such a waste of time; she had memories to recover and a grimoire page to find before anyone else got hurt.

Delilah sat up in bed and whispered, "Mrs. Fairfax," three times.

This time Mrs. Fairfax appeared right away wearing an apple-green gingham apron holding a bowl and a spoon on her hip.

"Yes, Ms. D'Arc, how may I be of service?" she asked, stirring the batter in the bowl she was holding.

"Do you know how to recover lost memories?"

She looked at Delilah like she was insane. "My dear, I have been recovering lost memories since, well, before you were firstborn over three hundred years ago."

Mrs. Fairfax glanced around her childhood bedroom. She felt self-conscious about her adolescent taste. She wanted to cringe at her choices, including the light pink and mint green striped wallpaper, corkboard filled with her diplomas and graduation tassels, and boy band posters on the walls.

"That Justin Timberlake is a nice-looking young man," Mrs. Fairfax said, whistling through her teeth.

Delilah smiled. "Where do we start?'

"Let's get back to the mansion and get you a spot of poppy tea," she said, offering Delilah her hand.

With a twitch of Mrs. Fairfax's nose and a blink of an eye, they were back in her kitchen. She set down her bowl and found a tarnished metal tea tin with a picture of a poppy on it.

As she put the kettle on, she gave Delilah instructions.

"This time, recovering your memories is going to be different. You will have to overcome a common fear, like spiders or flying, before you can access it."

"Heights. When I was a kid, Tabitha Anthea took me to the Sears Tower; when we got to the observation deck, I passed out cold."

Mrs. Fairfax set a teacup and saucer in front of Delilah. "And you will have a limited amount of time in your memory. You will see three poppies, and once you see the third, you have to leave; otherwise, you will be stuck there."

She took Delilah's shoulders and gave her a wild look. "And your coven, nor Samuel's, have the magics to get you out. Do you understand?"

The kettle screeched, punctuating Mrs. Fairfax's point.

Delilah's stomach churned. The fear was rising within her. She didn't have a choice. She was going to have to push through the panic and drink the tea.

As the tea was brewing, Mrs. Fairfax led Delilah to the domed cupola perched on top of the mansion's roof. It was a room made to practice magic. The cold marble floor featured the OB's coven mark, a black onyx circle with a Bindi in the middle. An artist had painted a mural of ravens in flight set against a purple sky with an orange sunset on a wall.

When Delilah glanced down at her hands, she saw fuzzy waves of energy around her fingers.

Mrs. Fairfax handed Delilah the poppy tea and then placed a red mat in the middle of the circle. "Drink your tea and lay down when you're ready."

Mrs. Fairfax moved a chair near the circle. "I will be right here. And remember, you must get out when you see the third poppy."

Delilah brought the teacup to her lips. "Do I need to do something to leave the memory? Chant? Jump up and down?"

"To get back here, you'll need to hold a poppy in your hand."

Delilah's hands were shaking as she drank the tea. The tea was so much more robust. It was so bitter she started coughing and forced herself to swallow it. It hit her immediately. Her heart turned into a mallet, and her chest, the bass drum booming and marching inside her body. She watched her thoughts fly past her at lightning speed. It was a ferocious panic attack to end all panic attacks. She wanted out now. Trying to stand up was impossible; her body became disassociated from her mind.

Her only thought was, *I don't want to do this.*

When she opened her eyes, she was riding an elevator. It was traveling at high speed as the wind whistled between the elevator and the shaft.

"At 110 stories tall, the Sears Tower is the eighth tallest building in the world," a voice with a thick Mediterranean accent said over the intercom. "The highest point of the twin antenna towers is 1,730 feet."

"That's like six football fields," Delilah said out loud.

"At the top of the building on a clear day, the wind speed can clock in at sixteen miles an hour."

"Can't imagine how fast it is on a cold, windy day."

Delilah looked at her hands, and she saw double. Peering around the elevator, she saw climbing equipment, a helmet, shoes, ropes, and a harness.

The elevator reached its destination, and the doors slid open. Delilah was on the roof of the Sears Tower. As she stepped out of the elevator, a sharp wind slapped her in the face.

"Delilah, don't forget your gear."

She turned around to find Melia dressed in climbing gear with a harness strapped around her waist and thighs and winding a rope around her elbow and hand.

She took the equipment out of the elevator, and the door slammed shut. There was no way out. Melia took the harness and held it open for Delilah to step into it.

"We're climbing to the top of the antenna," Melia said.

Delilah gazed up at it. It was reaching toward the heavens. The antenna had a series of climbing holds attached to it.

"Come," Melia ordered.

They stood at the bottom of the antenna. Melia clicked the carabiners in place and started to climb. Delilah's hands were shaking as she watched her. The wind was picking up and felt like thirty miles an hour.

"Stop wasting time," she yelled down at her, pulling on the rope. "Climb."

Delilah reached up and began scaling the ladder. Her arms and legs felt like jelly with each movement up toward the top.

She made a mistake and looked down. The mini cars and the mini people below seemed like they belonged in a dollhouse. Then she lost her footing and was holding on for her life, as her arms started convulsing.

Melia glanced down at her. "I will have to cut you loose."

Delilah heard the click and held onto the hold. She gripped the foothold and continued to climb. A dense fog surrounded her. She couldn't see how far she had come or how far she would have to go.

"Just keep climbing," she sang out loud until she saw a platform above her head with a ladder leading up to it.

She pulled herself up and sat down. A raven landed next to her and let out a series of staccato caws.

Twenty-Seven

"If I believed that the thing I have dreamed about her
would come to pass, I would want you to drown her;
and if you would not, I would drown her myself."

The world around her melted away. Delilah was standing on
the deck of a ship. The rain, the wind, the weather punished
the vessel for attempting to sail in the middle of a gale. It was
pitching and rocking. It reminded her of a carnival ride.

In her memory, she watched as Tabitha Anthea put a cloak
around Delilah and held her as she expelled the contents of her
stomach into the ocean.

"The baby is coming," Delilah shouted over the rain.

"It's too dangerous to teleport."

Delilah grabbed Tabitha Anthea, and like that, they were
standing in front of a rustic farmhouse.

The town sign read, "East Lothian, Scotland."

A contraction hit Delilah, and she fell to her knees. Her belly was bursting through her dress with congealed sick stuck to the front. Tabitha Anthea pounded on the door. It opened slowly.

A man was standing in the doorway. It was Jonathan.

"What's your business?" he asked, pulling his leather suspenders over his broad shoulders.

"We were told a wise woman lives here."

Gazing past Tabitha Anthea, his eyes landed on Delilah; she was barely holding onto consciousness.

"She's gone to Summerland," he said, attempting to shut the door on them.

Tabitha Anthea wedged her foot in between the door and the jam. "Please, we've come a long way."

"I don't need the misfortune you and them children are placing at my doorstep."

"She can't hold on much longer."

Delilah screamed out in agony. Jonathan ran over to her and carried her into the house. He set her on a small sofa near the fire and placed an ear to her stomach.

Then he placed his hands on her. "Her waters have broken. The weans is ready to come out and meet ye."

"Weans?" Tabitha Anthea repeated.

"Ay, twins." He placed a large pot of water on top of the grate over the fire.

"The babe's crowning and crowning fast," he said as he ran to the pot in the fireplace, poured the water into a basin, and washed his hands, motioning for Tabitha Anthea to do the same. No sooner had they finished, than Delilah was bearing down on a leather strap pushing.

Jonathan placed a screaming, red-faced baby boy on her chest and said, "Healthy set of lungs, babe has."

An hour later, he placed the twin girl on her chest and said, "Yer bonnie lassie."

Delilah's entire body trembled and shook as Tabitha Anthea pressed on her stomach to expel the afterbirth after she gave birth. Jonathan returned with a tea made of calendula and lavender. He held it to her mouth as she drank it.

Tabitha Anthea washed the babies in the basin and wrapped them both in a white cloth. She held the boy in front of Delilah.

"Aaron," she said and kissed the top of his head.

Then she brought the girl over to Delilah.

"Evie," she said, kissing the top of her head.

Present-day Delilah stood watching in the corner with tears running down her face. The love she felt for them, she was overcome by it. They were both so tiny and precious. Her heart felt heavy and light at the same time. *Am I a mother?*

The room began to spin. Delilah sat down and pulled her knees up to her chest. It felt like a tilt-a-whirl going around and around at seventy miles an hour. She squeezed her eyes shut and prayed it would end, but the spiraling sensation kept hurling her through space and time.

Until, at last, it stopped. Delilah was sitting in the middle of a bucolic field. The bright blue sky went on for miles. She breathed a sigh of relief when she heard children laughing and playing. When she inhaled deeply, the smell of grass filled her lungs.

Aaron and Evie ran through her. They were both so happy and healthy, little cherubs, about three years old with their father's caramel hair and her violet eyes. Delilah watched as her spirit and Jonathan's chased after them, leaving them squealing in delight. He took Delilah in his arms, twirled her around, and kissed her. Putting her fingers to her mouth, she felt the sweet tenderness of his kiss.

Evie picked a poppy and pretended to hand it to Delilah's specter and then ran away from her. It was her first poppy. It was almost time for her to return.

At that moment, present-day Delilah heard a carriage on the lane pulling up at a clipped pace in front of the farm. Samuel's ghost, dressed in a dark navy coat trimmed in gold, jumped out of the carriage.

Evie ran into his legs. He reached down and scooped her into his arms. Samuel kissed her cheek. Then he whispered something in her ear, and Evie, utterly enthralled, cackled.

Delilah's ghost came around the bend and stopped. Jonathan, unaware of what was happening, opened the door holding Aaron in his arms. Aaron had a poppy in his hand and kept hitting Jonathan in the face with it and laughing.

That was Delilah's second poppy, but she couldn't leave, not yet. She had to see this through to the end. Time moved at lightning speed. The day abruptly turned dark and stormy as Samuel placed Evie into the carriage. Delilah's spirit held on to Aaron with all her might, as Samuel tried to wrench him out of her arms.

Aaron cried out, screaming, "Momma!" at the top of his lungs.

Samuel leaned in and hissed, "So help me, Delilah, you release this child into my charge, or I'll burn this farm down to the ground."

Delilah released Aaron and fell to her knees.

Jonathan came charging around the corner with a loaded rifle pointed at Samuel's head.

Samuel lifted his hands and said, "Oh, love, I see you've gone and bewitched another suitor and your kind. Is he willing to die for you?"

Jonathan responded by cocking the gun.

"This does not concern you. This is between me and my beloved. We have an affair to settle. I recommend you put the rifle away," Samuel said.

Jonathan fired the gun. Samuel flexed his arm out in front of him and splayed his fingers. In slow motion, the bullet changed its course and went flying back toward Jonathan.

Delilah screamed, "Jonathan!"

Jonathan barely dodged the bullet by falling to the ground onto his stomach.

Samuel stood triumphant with his hands on his hips. "Are you quite finished with your gallantry? The Immaculates have handed down their sentencing. The children are to come back to London with me."

"What is to happen to them?" Delilah asked.

"Once they are of a certain age, they will be made immortal. And I, as their father, will endure the same sentencing," he said.

Delilah's ghost looked up at him with tears streaming down her face.

Samuel continued. "And Delilah, love, your coven has decreed you are to be stripped of all knowledge of your powers living in darkness to the truth of your being for the next three hundred years."

He pulled out a knife from his pocket with a curved blade and a dragon's tail for a handle.

"The Immaculates commanded that I am the one who has been sentenced to condemn you to your life of darkness."

Samuel pulled Delilah's head back. His hands were shaking as tears streamed down his face. "If we do not abide by this ruling, they will send the children to angel hell." He pressed his knife against her throat, dragging it slowly across her neck as blood poured out and down her dress.

And there was the third and last poppy lying on the ground. Delilah tried to reach for it. But suddenly, two girls, with pale, gaunt faces wearing tattered witch hats and sailor outfits, grabbed it. They ran into the woods surrounding the house.

Delilah ran after them. The deeper she ran into the forest, the darker it became. Their sing-song voices called out, leading Delilah further into the darkness.

"Over here. Try to catch us if you can."

Delilah was alone in a dark forest after witnessing Samuel ripping her children from her arms and then killing her. And now, her third poppy was stolen. If she didn't find that poppy, there was no way back from this seventh circle of hell memory. She followed their voices deeper into the forest through the bush and the brambles. Delilah tripped over a branch, falling on her face. The only sound she heard was laughter echoing through the trees, taunting her.

Delilah was on the ground deep in the forest when the little girls appeared by her side. When they laughed, they revealed their rotten and black teeth. In unison, they tilted their heads to one side and chanted, "Dust to dust, we must, take you and break you until you become us."

Twenty-Eight

"I would rather be beheaded seven times
than suffer burning."

Delilah's spirit was standing in her bedroom at Samuel's mansion, gaping at her pale, lifeless body lying on the bed. Surrounding her body was Devlin, Tabitha Anthea, Faye, and Mrs. Fairfax. They were holding what appeared to be her last rights vigil.

Samuel entered, stuffing his cell phone into his pocket. "Sage will be here shortly."

Devlin stood up and walked over to Samuel. "I still don't understand how, after all these years, you convinced the leader of the Clan to get involved in witch matters."

"She owes me a favor."

"And you're willing to use it to help my daughter?"

"Devlin, let me make one thing clear to you, I love Delilah, and there isn't anything I won't do for her."

"Yes, and we see time and time again the price she pays for your love," Devlin said, pointing to the bed.

Phantom Delilah touched her neck. She could feel the cold blade against her warm skin, the sensation of the knife cutting into it. When she pulled her hand away, it was covered in her blood. At that moment, she was back on her knees in front of the farmhouse, replaying the moment Samuel murdered her. Delilah screamed for help, but no one could hear her. Caught in a netherworld between life and between death, as each moment slipped by, she was inching closer to death.

A woman with a long silver braid marched into the room carrying a large bag, a teal and white carpet bag with a worn-out leather handle. Wearing a cashmere camel-colored cape, a stark white cotton button-up, and cropped black pants, she looked more like a granny than a witch. "Move it," she said, pushing aside Tabitha Anthea.

"Sage," Tabitha Anthea said. "Always a pleasure."

Sage stopped. "Thea, by the appearance of things here, your charge doesn't have much time. We can sit down for tea and do a catch-up, or I can save her life. Which do you prefer?"

"Save her life, please," Devlin replied.

Sage leaned over the bed and placed her head on Delilah's chest. Then she opened her eyelids. Her eyes were two blank, bloodshot white orbs.

"Jesus Mary and Joseph, no one said anything about an exorcism," Sage said, removing her cape and placing her hands on her meaty hips.

"Oh, this is gonna be good," Faye said, pulling out her vape pen.

"Not only is she trapped in a memory. The twins are in her," Sage said, digging through her bag.

Looking around the room, Sage pointed at Devlin and Samuel. "I'm going to need you knuckleheads to help me."

"I'm going to assist, too," Tabitha Anthea said, pushing up the sleeves on her burgundy sweater.

"Sorry, toots, I need to harness the male energy for this one. First, we need to fish her out of the memory, and then we need to get the twins out."

"What will you need?" Mrs. Fairfax asked.

"Four strings of barbed wire, a black-and-white television, leather straps, a water board, and a tub filled with Florida Water. We're going to need to get her up to your cupola to perform the ceremony."

As everyone was about to mobilize, Sage said, "I want to make one thing clear; there are no guarantees. There's a good chance if I get her back, she won't be the same."

Once they had assembled all the necessary equipment needed to save Delilah, Sage, Samuel, and Devlin were standing over her body lying on the cupola's ground.

Sage took off her Birkenstocks, pulled out three leather aprons from her bag, and handed them out. She gave Samuel the side-eye while she rolled up her sleeves. Then she pulled out a canister of sea salt and drew a circle around Delilah's body with it. Reaching into her bag, she pulled out a small traveling witch kit.

"I need to sage you first before we get started," she said, lighting the Palo Santo stick.

"Do we have time for this nonsense?" Samuel asked.

"I come from a long line of hedge witches. Let me do my magics, or should I leave your girlfriend in the netherworld?"

"Do yours," Devlin replied.

"You need to take off your shoes. We all need to be barefoot," she said, pulling out a small bottle with a dropper.

"Open wide," she ordered Samuel.

"Do I even want to know?" he asked.

"We are all going to open our third eyes with some cornflower, don't be such a baby."

Sage clapped her hands. "Now, let's begin. Put on your leather gloves. You'll find them in the pocket of your apron."

Sage began to wrap Delilah's ankles and wrists with a bracelet of barbed wire.

"What are you doing to my daughter?"

"I'm trying to save her. The only way to pull her out of the memory is by using pain at the four meridians. We're going to pull and push the wire into her skin."

"No, you're not," Devlin said, unwrapping the wire from her ankle.

"We're wasting time. Time we don't have," Samuel yelled, holding Delilah's arms pulled above her head, ready to tug on the wire.

"I will count down to three; on three, we'll all pull and push on the wire. Got me?"

They were silent.

"Got me?"

"Yes," they both yelled back at her.

"One, two, three," Sage said while pulling Delilah's ankle. "Unite the body, unite the spirit," she repeated.

Blood was dripping from Delilah's ankles and wrists onto the white marble floor. Her body was motionless and limp. Until finally, a guttural scream came from her mouth. It sounded like an animal dying.

"You fucking bitch, stop this right now," Delilah seethed.

"Who's speaking?" Sage asked.

"You know us, you cowardly witch," she replied, her eyes opening wide. Instead of violet, they were blank and bloodshot. When she smiled, her teeth were black.

Sage motioned to the board; they moved her body over to it and strapped her down. Delilah's body was twitching and spasming.

"You can't get rid of us," the Twins bellowed.

Sage pulled on the leather straps hard.

173

"Daddy, these hurts," Delilah whined. "Why are you hurting me? Make her stop. Please."

Samuel moved the bucket of Florida Water by Delilah's head.

"Samuel, don't you love me?" Her body bucked and twisted. "Stop it, and I'll suck your big juicy cock. I promise."

Sage nodded to Devlin. "Now!"

They dunked Delilah's head in the water. She thrashed around. Once her head was out, she coughed up dead flies.

"Who am I speaking to?" Sage asked.

"You know who."

"Delilah?" Devlin asked.

Delilah smiled, revealing a set of sharp rotten teeth. "Oh, daddy poo, it's not her. We're not letting go of her so easy."

Again, they dunked her head. As Sage pushed the television closer to the board, she waved her hand over it, and an image appeared of the forest where the Twins had trapped Delilah.

Once again, they pulled her out of the water. "Pops, it's me. Please help me."

Sage nodded. "One more time."

One last time, they dunked her head into the water. When she came up for air, she coughed out two toads. Samuel picked them up and pointed at the television. The screen went static at his command, then cracked in half, as a high-pitched off-air tone filled the room, and the rainbow test-pattern color bars shot out of it.

"By and by, there's a toad in your eye. No longer shall ye roam, now go to your proper home," Sage chanted.

As Samuel tossed the toads into the television, it flickered then went dark. The television clicked back on, and the Twins were standing in the forest.

Delilah was moaning. Her eyes were closed. She had foam and water dribbling down her mouth. Her wrists and ankles were bloody.

Sage took off her gloves. "Devlin, I got her back. Now you need to put her back together again."

Samuel stood over her and raised his arms above her.

Devlin seized his arm. "I got it."

"I can have this sorted in no time," Samuel said.

"She's my daughter."

Sage took Samuel's arm. "Where can a girl get a cup of tea around here?"

Samuel wouldn't move, his chest heaving, his feet covered in water, and Delilah's blood.

"I am not leaving until Delilah is healed."

Devlin put his hand on Samuel's shoulder. "Son, your work here is done."

Sage led Samuel out of the cupola. He turned around and flexed his hand at the television. The Twins fell to the ground, holding their throats; they began throwing up maggots. Then, he snapped his fingers, turning the television off in a flash.

Twenty-Nine

"But there is no bodily infirmity, not even leprosy or epilepsy, which cannot be caused by witches."

Sage did save Delilah. She was told she was lucky to be alive. With a severe palsy on the left side of her body, leaving her eye squeezed shut and her mouth drooping with saliva dripping down her chin, Delilah didn't feel particularly lucky. Her hands had an involuntary tremor, making it difficult for her to do simple things like brush her teeth. Her body had staged a revolt, and she was no longer in charge.

All she could do was stew in her thoughts and relive her recovered past life memories. This left her with more questions than answers. There was one person who could answer them, but Tabitha Anthea and Devlin wouldn't allow it. She was trapped in her childhood bedroom with her immobile body with her mind running a sprint.

176

Even though she disagreed with Delilah's decision, Tabitha Anthea took care of her, force-feeding her homemade soup. She held a bowl of chicken and rice soup hovering under Delilah's chin.

With Delilah's right hand, she grabbed Tabitha Anthea's arm. "Samm-u-el," Delilah said.

Tabitha Anthea set the bowl down on the bedside table.

"You need to get better, and the only way is to rest."

There was a gentle tap at the door.

"It's open," Thea called out.

Devlin entered with his medical bag. "How's it going, kiddo?"

Pulling her light blue robe with white clouds around her, she muttered no.

"It'll be a quick exam. I promise."

Tabitha Anthea wiped the soup off her chin. "We're asking for Samuel again."

"Not a child," Delilah replied.

Devlin nodded at Tabitha Anthea, and she left the room. He sat down on the bed and held Delilah's hand. "Our only concern is for you and your safety."

She pulled her hand away and huffed like a petulant teenager. "I need answers."

Devlin bowed his head. "Fine. I'll call him."

An hour later, Samuel appeared in her bedroom, unbuttoning the top button on his dark-blue suit. It always surprised her how each time she saw Samuel, he still took her breath away.

Rushing to her side, he placed a kiss on her forehead.

"Delilah, love, I would've been here sooner. There was a ward around the house," he said, pulling a chair over to her bed.

She met his gaze head-on. She challenged him to look away from her disfigured face and body. To his credit, he kept

177

his eyes trained on her.

"You should know I don't care about your face. I am so thankful you're alive."

She snickered. "This isn't living."

"You must have questions."

It was so hard for her to talk. Her throat was always dry, and the paralysis made it difficult for her to form words.

"Children. How are they?"

"Evie is a medic with Doctors Without Borders. She's on the border, helping the refugees." The pride was echoing in his voice. "Aaron is a gadabout wandering around the globe in search of the next socialite and the next party."

Delilah turned away; she could feel the drool inching down her chin. Without missing a beat, Samuel took his pocket square and gently wiped her face.

"And they think their mother hasn't returned from Summerland."

She touched her neck, her fingers tracing the spot where he sliced open her neck. "Why?" she asked, not hiding the betrayal she felt.

"By getting pregnant, you signed death certificates for us all. We had a good life in court, but you wanted more. You always wanted more."

"Bull," she croaked, "shit."

Samuel stood up and paced around her room. Seeing him in her bedroom, dressed in his suit, trying to explain to her what happened lifetimes ago made her grin. Her new life was so at odds with her old life.

"Can you handle the truth?" he asked, sitting down next to her on the bed, placing his hands on either side of her legs.

She nodded.

"Okay, fine, take my hand, and I'll show you why you wanted to get pregnant and blow up our lives at court."

She held onto his firm hand. Feeling the warmth of his

skin set off a hunger deep inside her. She was cursing herself for still wanting him even after knowing the truth.

"Close your eyes," he said in a husky voice. "I will focus on the memory, and you can squeeze my hand when you see us back in Versailles."

She closed her eyes. A movie began to play in her head. It was a film of Delilah laughing and running down a long hallway in Versailles, which was lined with thick, gold brocade curtains. Her hair was loose around her face. She was wearing a sheer, silk, ivory dressing gown with a large pink bow tied under her chest.

A handsome man with long dark hair chased after her wearing only white breeches that landed on his muscular hips. They were playing hide and seek. Tiring of the game, she hid behind a thick gold curtain. He ran past her disappearing down the long hallway.

Delilah peeked out from the curtain. Seeing the coast was clear, she ran in the opposite direction of her suitor. Finally, she reached a series of French doors covered in gold leaf. She opened a door and entered into the antechamber surrounded by candelabras.

Delilah could hear the murmur of voices coming from the interior room. Recognizing Samuel's voice, she made her way into his private chambers. The door was ajar, and she was at the ready to surprise him. Peering through the door crack, she stopped suddenly before opening the door.

Samuel was naked in his bed with his head resting on a man's bare chest. He was petting Samuel's hair. He leaned down and gave Samuel a languid passionate kiss. Delilah slammed the door shut.

Pulling her hand away from Samuel, her eyes popped open.

"The King?"

"You know as well as anyone; you can't deny him."

She slapped her hand against the bedspread.

"Stop lying. You loved the King," she said, placing her hand on Samuel's heart. "I felt it."

"It didn't mean I loved you any less. Everyone had affairs, even you. It was the bloody French court."

"Got pregnant to keep you," she said, slowly enunciating every word.

"You wouldn't have lost me," he said, placing his hands on her shoulders. "You have to believe me."

Tracing the scar on his neck. "Salem?"

"I thought if we went to America, we could disappear in the Witch Trials and would reunite in Summerland," he said, placing his hand over hers. "A fresh start, just the two of us."

She pulled away from his hand. "Go." She felt exhausted like a chain was hitched to her body, dragging her underwater.

"Delilah, how can I make you understand?" he asked, his voice cracking as a tear started down his cheek. She reached over, and with her index finger, brushed it away.

"You can't."

The air around her felt thick. Her eyes were heavy. She had reached her limit for what she could comprehend about her past or her present.

"Our children, don't you want to meet them?"

"Sleep," she said, gathering the comforter and blankets around her, making a nest. "Go. Now."

Devlin opened the door.

"Samuel, it's time for you to let her rest."

"Can I heal her before I go? At least let me do that."

"It's up to her," Devlin said, crossing his arms over his chest.

"Lights off," Delilah demanded, sinking into her bed.

November 13 @ 2:22 pm - My Old Bedroom
State of Mind - Broken

It hurts to hold a pen. My thoughts...are like scattered puzzle pieces that I can't put back together. Faye is always by my side. When I wake up and when I go to sleep. She won't leave me. I had to tell her she couldn't come into the bathroom with me. I don't like people or fairies watching me pee. It's just too weird even for witch world.

I'm Humpy Dumpty—I drank the tea, recovered my memories and now I'm shattered. I got my answers, but I didn't solve the equations.
I'm more, what is the word?
I can't remember words, even simple ones.
Confused!
I'm more confused than I was before.

—————————————————————————————————

Thirty

"I have not clearly understood whether that is
forbidden to me or not."

It was a crisp, late autumn day. The leaves had reached their
full fall color potential. Faye and Delilah were on their daily
hike. It was a convalescent walk through a nearby forest
preserve. Faye had found a short path Delilah could manage.

She was holding onto Faye while Faye puffed on her vape
pen.

"What's this one? It smells different," Delilah asked.

Faye inspected the pen. "Watermelon Wave. Want a puff?"

Delilah shook her head.

"That sounds gross."

The two of them had reached a place of understanding
where they could walk in silence. Even though Delilah was
healing, it was still hard for her to talk. Her body was gradually

unfurling, like a flower bud blooming one petal at a time. Most days, at her best, she felt weary.

"Jonathan?" Delilah asked.

"Nope. I'm pretty sure he's back on the smack."

Delilah stopped and let go of Faye's arm. "Really?"

"He didn't seem right on All Hallows' Eve and the fact he hasn't been around to check in on you," she said, shaking her head. "He's your Benefactor. He took the job seriously. And the stolen grimoire page, there's no way he wouldn't help us search for it."

"We need to go find him."

"Shut up," Faye said, walking away from her.

Delilah followed her.

"We have to find him, find the page, and finish the translation."

Faye took Delilah by the shoulders. "Sister, just because you have stopped drooling and can feed yourself, you're still a hot mess."

Delilah considered Faye and realized what a pair the two of them made. With her head-to-toe layers of black, Faye, including a flannel shirt and fingerless gloves, punctuated like a reverse exclamation point with her outgrown platinum blonde pixie cut. And Delilah, hobbling along wearing leggings and an old puffer coat, her hair wild and curly looking like she combed it with static electricity instead of a brush.

"Can't sit here and do nothing."

"What did you have in mind? Like searching condemned houses, abandoned warehouses, and hourly motels?" Faye asked, stuffing her vape pen into her leather motorcycle jacket.

"Like crack houses?" Delilah asked.

Faye took hold of Delilah's arm. "No, if Jonathan's hanging out with Melia, it would be like a high-end situation."

"A high-end crack house?"

"No stupid, a high-end opium den. And there's no way Tabitha Anthea or Devlin is going to let you go hunt him down."

"We'll tell them you're taking me into the city to get haircuts," Delilah said, walking at a faster clip now that she had a mission.

"Lie to Tabitha Anthea? You got a death wish?" she replied, catching up to her. "No, thank you."

Delilah stopped walking. Her eyes met Faye's. She saw something in them she had never seen before—fear.

"You're scared of Thea?"

Faye peered down at her beat-up knee-high Doc Martens and shook her head.

"What then?" Delilah asked, placing her finger under Faye's chin gently, guiding her face up so Delilah could look Faye in the eye. "Tell me."

"Like you were almost dead. You gotta get better, or next time you'll be dead dead," Faye said, wiping her nose with the back of her hand. "You can't play around with magics, especially if you don't know what the hell you're doing."

"I promise, I won't drink any more tea or go back in time." She crossed her heart. "Scouts' honor."

"This isn't a joke. We need you," Faye said, pushing Delilah away. "I need you."

Faye brought Delilah to an expensive salon to get a Brazilian blow-out, a hair straightening treatment that took forever. It gave them the perfect cover to spend the night in the city. To Delilah's surprise, Devlin was so supportive he gave her the money to pay for it. Faye selected a silver, almost gray color for her hair. Delilah was happy to have her wild curly hair smooth as silk for once.

After the salon, Faye insisted they go shopping. She didn't

want to be seen around town with an accounting nerd. Faye selected a "stakeout chic" outfit for Delilah—a motorcycle jacket with a mandarin collar, a pair of skinny black jeans, and soft leather ankle boots with large buckles on the side.

Together dressed in leather and black, Faye and Delilah resembled bounty hunters standing in a dead-end alley paved in rust-colored bricks slick from the light rain. The door was black with a fire breathing dragon painted in gold, and the fire painted in hues of red and orange.

There wasn't a door handle. Faye lifted her fist to knock on the door, and the dragon moved, lifting his snout, blowing fire toward her. She ducked before it singed her.

"WTF!" Faye shrieked. "A ward?"

"Do we need a password?" Delilah asked.

"Aros, we need your help." The words had just left Faye's mouth, still echoing off the buildings when Aros appeared.

"Can you get us in?" she asked.

Aros nodded. He lifted his arms over his head, and the door creaked open. He turned to leave, and Faye caught his arm. "Hold up, cowboy; you're staying with us. We might need backup."

Aros shrugged and nodded toward the open door. Faye led the way inside, and Delilah followed close behind. The door slammed shut, leaving them alone in an entryway lit by a single red light bulb dangling from the ceiling. Faye walked into it, causing it to sway back and forth like a pendulum, hypnotizing Delilah as she watched it. Music filled the air. It was a woman's voice singing, her voice full of yearning, chanting over the slow pounding drums and sitar.

They continued down a claustrophobic hallway covered in intricate fields of poppy flowers needlepoint tapestries. The sickly, sweet smell of poppy and patchouli overtook Delilah. The hallway flipped. Her stomach dropped. Then her skin turned clammy. She glanced at her feet and realized she was hanging upside down from the ceiling.

Faye slapped Delilah. "You're having a poppy flashback. Get your mind right because we're on a mission."

Delilah rubbed her eyes and tried to shake it off. Aros took her by the hand. The trio halted in front of a thick magenta velvet curtain. Faye pointed at it, motioning for Delilah to open it. Aros ripped the curtain open.

Jonathan, shirtless, with his jeans unbuttoned, was lying in the middle of the room, which was decorated like a circus tent. Bands of thick red and white striped silk fabric met in the ceiling's center, pinned together by a massive crystal chandelier. The floor was covered in all shapes and sizes of cushions in varying shades of reds to pinks.

Delilah's eyes landed on Jonathan's feet. Her heart cracked open when she saw them covered in cuts and dirt. Melia, dressed in a white peasant blouse and leather pants, took a long pull from the hookah, blowing the smoke into Jonathan's face. He turned on his side away from her. They were so far gone they didn't realize they weren't alone.

Delilah kneeled next to Jonathan and placed her hand on his shoulder.

"Hey there."

He looked up at her. His eyes were vacant.

"It's me, Delilah." She pointed to Faye and Aros. "Look who I've got with me. We're all here because we want to help you."

Melia slapped Delilah's hand away. "He doesn't need you. He has me."

Delilah glanced over at Faye. "Keep it steady there, boss," Faye said.

"Jonathan, hey buddy, maybe we can get you out of here. What do you think?" Delilah said.

Melia pulled back Delilah's hair and traced Delilah's chin with her nose as she whispered into her ear. "He doesn't have to choose. He can have us both. We'd be so happy all together. You will see."

Delilah shoved Melia away. "Fuck off."

Melia lunged at Delilah. Before she could make contact, Faye grabbed her arm and pulled her away.

"What do I do?" Delilah asked Aros and Faye.

"Interventions are not in my wheelhouse," Faye replied. "If he doesn't want to leave, I mean, are we going to force him?"

Aros cracked his knuckles.

"I get it; we could try to remove him with force, but if he doesn't want help, is it going to make a difference?" Faye asked.

"Can you guys get her out of here?" Delilah said, pointing to Melia. "I just need a minute to think."

Aros placed his hands on Faye and Melia, and they disappeared.

Looking down at Jonathan, Delilah realized the situation was dire and probably hopeless. She placed her hands on his chest, and she could feel his suffering radiating on a loop between them.

"I don't know what led you here. But I do know this isn't the end of the line for you. You can put this behind you," Delilah said, shaking Jonathan, trying to get a response. "Things are so screwed up right now. I know we can help each other get through it."

Their eyes connected. Delilah felt like she was getting through to him. "I need you. Please."

He shook his head and whispered. "Just go."

"There was a time, in another lifetime, when you saved my life and my babies."

Delilah took hold of his limp hand. She took a deep breath. She cleared her mind of all thoughts and focused on a singular memory she had recovered. It was of Jonathan. He was holding onto her legs, yelling at her to push. Delilah was fighting him. She would rest when he told her to push and push when he told her to rest. Finally, Jonathan released her legs and took hold of her hands. "I delivered my own. I can deliver yours, but you have to put your faith in me, and you'll come out of this. I promise ye."

She held onto his hand, but Jonathan didn't respond.

Faye appeared. "Hey, Aros is going to have to return Melia. He can only keep her for so long before she rips us a new one."

Delilah whipped a tear from her cheek. "No, you're right; he has to come on his own. Bring her back."

Aros and Melia appeared. Melia was kicking and screaming. She tackled Delilah and had her hands around Delilah's neck.

"He's my beloved," screamed Melia.

Faye punched Melia in the face sending her flying across the room.

"It's time for us to move it along. Yeah?" Faye said.

Aros took Delilah's hand, and like that, they were standing in the alley. The night had grown cold. Puffs of warm air escaped from their lungs, filling the air around them like a cloud. In a daze, they stared at the door, each one of them willing, hoping Jonathan would walk out the door.

"Hey, it's time to get you home," Faye said, placing her arm around Delilah's shoulder.

"I can't get any of this right. Can I? I wanted to do this one thing. I wanted to help one person. Every time I turn around, someone I care about is getting hurt."

"Hey now, this one is on Jonathan; this is his deal. It's got nothing to do with you. You're like barely healed, and you are trying to help him. I won't let you play the blame game. K?"

Aros had his hand on their shoulders, ready to transport them back to Tabitha Anthea's house when the door flew open; it was Jonathan holding his leather jacket in his arms.

He careened over and fell into Delilah's arms.

"Please help me," he croaked.

Thirty-One

"I have fared as well as I could."

After rescuing Jonathan from the opium den, they weren't sure where to go. Collectively, they agreed taking a stoned Jonathan to Tabitha Anthea's would bring them a heap of unwanted hassle. Finally, Aros transported them all to Sage's cabin. It took less convincing than Delilah had anticipated getting Sage on board. Sage had a soft spot for Jonathan and seeing him strung out in need of healing did most of the convincing.

Delilah wondered what kind of favor she would owe the leader of the Clan in return. She had the impression with Sage no good deed would go without a favor in return. After watching the hedge witch in action administering herbs to Jonathan, she was more than happy to pay whatever price Sage would eventually demand.

Jonathan was like a newborn baby who needed constant care. He spent most of the night in the fetal position on the bathroom floor, unable to keep even a few sips of water down. The cramping in his legs was so painful. Delilah tried to rub them, but her touch sent him into convulsions. His body ran hot and cold. One minute, his teeth were chattering; the next, he was drenched in sweat.

He would sleep twenty minutes at a time. It seemed the moment Delilah would doze off, he'd wake up like the devil was chasing him through his dreams back toward consciousness.

At dawn, she was holding Jonathan in her arms, watching him sleep as his eyes quickly scanned the back of his eyelids. She was counting the seconds, waiting for him to wake up again. It didn't take long until his eyes shot open.

"You're okay. I got you," Delilah said, with a calm, soft voice.

He held onto her arms.

"Every thought I have is like a hot poker to my brain. I keep thinking about all the ways I let everyone down. Especially you."

Delilah grabbed his face. "All you need to do right now is get better. Put all the other crap out of your mind."

Slapping his forehead with the palm of his hand, he said, "I fucked up so bad."

She grabbed Jonathan's hand. "No more or no less than the rest of us."

"After Maria died, I wasn't there for you."

Her eyes met his. "No, you weren't, but believe it or not, I survived."

"I drove you to Samuel."

"Excuse me? I'm a grown woman making my own choices."

"Delilah, he's a powerful witch."

"And your point is?"

"He can compel you to do things."

Delilah untangled her body from Jonathan's and stood up. "I'm going to get some coffee and something to eat."

She reached down and offered him her hand. "Let's get you to bed."

"You're pissed off."

"I don't want to discuss Samuel with you."

He took her hand, and she pulled him up. He was still weak. She placed her arm around his waist. Together they navigated the hallway in silence.

"I'm not trying to hurt you," Jonathan said.

"I didn't think you were."

"He's not who you think he is."

Delilah didn't respond as they entered a spare room covered in pink and red roses. Sage's dog was sleeping in the middle of the bed. Delilah helped him into it and tucked him under the covers. The dog moved over and curled up next to Jonathan.

"I'm right downstairs," she said.

Jonathan grabbed her hand and kissed it. "Thank you."

She smiled down at him. "Get some rest."

Once outside the door, Delilah wanted to cry. She was exhausted, trying to manage a rolling current of emotions, from grief to fear to anger. She had to admit it. Part of her was angry at Jonathan for getting involved with Melia and using again.

Delilah stumbled down the stairs and into the kitchen. Sage was sitting at the table, smoking a clove cigarette.

"Why don't you take a shower?"

"I'm starving," replied Delilah.

"You have puke in your hair."

Delilah glanced down and saw it.

"I need a piece of toast or something."

Sage pointed at the counter. "Knock yourself out. The bread is right next to the toaster."

"Do you have a problem with me?"

Sage crossed her arms over her chest. Staring down at Delilah, she embodied the crone, in all her unapologetic glory.

"To have a problem with you, I'd have to give a fig about you," she said, stomping out her cigarette into the overflowing ashtray.

Delilah popped a piece of bread into the toaster. She leaned against the counter, trying to muster enough strength to stay upright. Now she was awash in guilt, wondering if she somehow pushed Jonathan off the wagon.

"Look, Jonathan has struggled with addiction for a long time. No one or one thing can push him over the edge. He lives there. He decided to jump."

Delilah turned around. She couldn't quite figure Sage out. Delilah watched Sage remove butter and jam from the refrigerator. She set it down next to the toaster for Delilah.

"Jonathan lost the connection," Sage said.

"Connection?"

Sage set her hand on Delilah's shoulder. "Addicts live in a world of isolation. Their minds are so up their butts they don't know fact from fiction. Sobriety means connection. You being here for him, like really being here, no judgment, support. It's the one thing he needs more than anything."

Sage paused. "Can you do that for him?"

Delilah nodded.

"There's a good girl. I have to run an errand. I'll be gone overnight," Sage said, patting Delilah's shoulder.

"You're leaving?"

"He'll be fine. He has you," Sage said, pausing before leaving. "I made a potion. If he's in a bad way, you can give it to him. For it to work, you'll both need to drink it."

Later that night, Delilah was in the kitchen, loading the

dishwasher, when she heard Jonathan screaming. She ran through the house and up the stairs. When Delilah entered the room, he was still asleep in the throes of a nightmare. She placed her hands on his chest as a rush of adrenaline surged from Jonathan's body into hers.

Delilah was experiencing one of his memories, it was right after Samuel slashed her throat. Jonathan was left alone, holding Delilah's blood-soaked body in his arms.

He rocked her limp body. "I am so sorry I couldn't protect you."

He sat in the lane, holding her, willing her to come back to life for hours until the day turned into night. By the light of the moon, he dug a grave for her in the meadow. He covered her body in a white linen sheet.

Jonathan woke with a violent start. His hands flew to Delilah's neck, and he pressed his fingers into her throat.

"Jon-a-than," she choked out. "It's me, De—" she said, peeling his fingers off her throat.

"Delilah?"

She took his hand. She noticed the vial filled with the potion on the nightstand. They were both shaking. She picked it up and opened it. It smelled like Pine-Sol. It burned her throat on the way down.

"Drink this," she said.

He drank it down fast. Then gagged and coughed. "What the hell was that? Detergent?" he asked, taking her hand. "Please, stay with me until I fall asleep."

Jonathan pulled her into his embrace. In his arms, she felt warm and safe. She could hear his heart beating, and she knew he would get through this. They would get through it together. Then the profound exhaustion set in, and she didn't fight it.

When she woke up, her arms and legs were pinned to the bed. She opened her eyes. It was an impenetrable darkness with a sharp moonbeam cutting through it. On her right was a little boy curled up, and on her left was a little girl sprawled like a starfish. Jonathan was asleep on the floor with a shotgun resting by his side.

Suddenly, she realized she was in bed with her children, Aaron and Evie. She covered their angelic apple cheeks in kisses. *Was she in another memory?*

The moon was summoning her. Before she even realized what she was doing, she was in the meadow running toward the moonlight. Reaching a small hill, she pulled off her nightshirt, extended her arms to the moon, and danced. She felt so free.

"Delilah?"

Jonathan was standing in the clearing, wearing only his breaches with his leather suspenders hanging at his knees, smiling at her. Instead of broken, he looked whole and happy. Without thinking, she ran into his arms. He caught her and twirled her around. They were both caught in the moment like two carefree teenagers laughing at nothing and at everything.

Jonathan set her down. He took her fingers and pressed them to his lips. "You are my peace. You are my light. You are my heart's eternal spark."

"What is happening?"

He placed his hand on her heart. "Let's not break it."

"Break what?"

"The spell."

His eyes locked on hers; with a wide grin, he stepped out of his breeches. Then he reached out and put his hand around the back of Delilah's neck. Without hesitation, he pulled her toward his body. His eyes told her he was going to devour her. Urgently, he pressed his body into hers, and she could feel him straining against her. His lips finally crashed into hers.

He pulled away. "Not here. Under the Hay Moon," he said, leading her up the hill.

Standing face to face, the moonlight reflecting in his eyes, he placed his hand on Delilah's heart, then took her hand and put it on his heart.

"Know this, no matter where you go or who you are with, I will always carry you here."

Jonathan pulled her into his arms, her spirit melting into his; they kissed.

"I will now, and three hundred years from now, always love you," he said.

When their bodies finally came together, a bright light shot through his heart into hers. Together their pleasure began to crest, forcing their bodies to rise off the grass, hovering between the earth and the moon.

Thirty-Two

"I wish you to come back to me with this spell to tighten up our connection forever."

The next morning, Delilah woke up in bed alone. Her mouth tasted like a pine-scented holiday candle. She felt hungover. Bits and pieces started coming back to her, and it seemed like a delicious dream. Her stomach rumbled. A warm breakfast and a cup of coffee would set her straight. Walking down the stairs to the kitchen, she was certain it was a dream.

Jonathan was sitting with his back to the door, eating a bowl of cereal. A memory from her dream, his lips on hers, came flooding back. Delilah felt flush. She steadied herself before walking into the kitchen.

"Good morning," she trilled.

He glanced up and nodded. He didn't give Delilah any indication of whether or not last night had happened. Delilah took a cup from the cupboard and poured herself a cup of coffee.

"How are you feeling?"

Their eyes locked. A hunger rose inside of her. She could feel Jonathan's hands on her body. *Something did happen last night.*

"Good," he replied, shaking his head.

The backdoor flew open, and Sage entered, pulling off her cape, carrying a bag filled with herbs. Her face was bright red from the brisk wind.

"My darlings, how did it go last night without me? I am most certain you found a way to keep yourselves occupied," she said with a wicked smile on her face.

"Sage, you had no right," Jonathan said.

The anger in Jonathan's voice shocked Delilah. She didn't know he had it in him.

Sage placed her hand on his cheek. "If you need to blame it on me, doll face, go right ahead."

Delilah slammed her coffee cup on the counter.

"Can someone tell me what the hell is going on?"

"The potion we drank," Jonathan said, setting the spoon into the bowl. "It was a love spell."

"Hold the damn phone," Sage said, with her hands in the air. "It only works if both parties want it to work. I don't have the kind of power to compel anyone to do anything they don't want to do, let alone two extremely powerful witches."

Jonathan stood up and tossed his cereal bowl into the sink. He pushed by Sage on his way out the door.

"We trusted you," Delilah said, shaking her head in disbelief.

Sage stuck a cigarette into her mouth. "Well, toots," she said, lighting it, "that was your first mistake."

Delilah grabbed two coats hanging by the back door and ran after Jonathan. He was standing in the middle of tall grass, hugging his arms around his chest. She handed him a coat. They stood face to face, staring at one another.

"Please say something," Delilah said.

"I'm sorry."

"What if I'm not. What happened last night, for me, it was—"

"Amazing," he said, finishing her sentence.

Delilah placed her hands on his face. "Jonathan, I lov—"

He removed her hands from his face. "Please don't say it."

"But what about last night?"

"It was wrong. I shouldn't have said it. I'm your Benefactor. I have a job to do," he said, releasing her hands.

"So, we're supposed to pretend it didn't happen and go about our business like normal?"

He placed his hands on her shoulders. "Don't you understand what's at stake? We need to get back on mission."

"You're the one who left me," she spat back, the anger rising in her chest.

Jonathan put his hand on the back of his head and looked up at the cloudless dark gray winter sky. Delilah felt like she couldn't breathe. She squatted on the ground, her head in her hands.

"I don't know how much more of this I can handle. If I can't even trust myself and my feelings."

He got down on the ground and pulled her into an embrace. It felt so good to be in his arms. After a lifetime of being alone in the world, he was her home.

"And it's my job to help you, not make it worse." He wrapped his arms even tighter around her. "In our world, we only get moments. And I'm thankful for what we shared last night."

They sat in the tall grass with the wind whipping around them.

"Jonathan?"

"Yes, Delilah."

"I love you."

"You own a major piece of real estate in my heart."

"Which part?"

He put his hand on her heart. "Left ventricle."

"What about your aorta?"

"That too."

Jonathan released her and stood up. He held out his hand and pulled her to her feet. Together, they walked back to the cabin holding hands.

They found Sage sitting on her sofa in front of a fire, reading a trash magazine. On the coffee table, she had set out tea and cookies.

"So did my love birds kiss and make up?" Sage asked.

Picking up a cookie, Jonathan sat down next to Sage.

"Lady, you are so not off the hook," he said to Sage, biting into the cookie. "You're going to need to call in your son."

"No can," she said, turning the magazine pages, "do."

Jonathan ripped the magazine from her hands.

"Speaking of sons, here's yours," he said, showing Delilah a picture of a man standing next to a starlet at a movie premiere.

Her hands trembled, holding the magazine, studying her son's face. He had Samuel's strong chin with a deep-set dimple right in the middle. His smile was also Samuel's, his eyes laughing, telling a secret to the camera. Aaron's eyes were violet; that was the only trace of Delilah in him. His eyes.

"I need to see my children," Delilah said, throwing the magazine into the fire.

Thirty-Three

"Thou shouldest take great heed and care that this
Key of Secrets fall not into the hands of the foolish,
the stupid, or the ignorant."

Once again, Jonathan and Delilah were waiting in Mahai's office. He had phoned Jonathan to tell him he had something of value for the Ascent coven. This time when Mahai entered his office, there were no hugs. He unbuttoned his dark navy suit and sat down.

"My son—"

Jonathan's hand flew up. "Please don't."

Mahai sat back in his chair with his hands intertwined on his stomach and gave Jonathan a long hard stare.

"I see how it is." He pulled out a piece of paper from the inside of his suit jacket and pushed it across the desk.

"Before Melia left, she translated the page from the D'Arc grimoire for you."

"Where is she?"

Mahai threw his hand up in the air. "Only the wind knows."

"How did Melia get the page?" Delilah asked.

"The witch hunters," he said. His face was smiling, but his tone was malevolent.

"The hunters have the page and the translation?" Jonathan yelled.

Mahai waved him off. "My son, they are impotent without the power to cast a spell. They would require a witch, and of course, the ring. Neither of which they possess."

Jonathan stuffed the page into his pocket and stood up.

"Of course, they are not the only persons searching for this spell," he said, drumming his fingers on the desk.

Jonathan sighed and sat down.

"Mahai, anything you can tell us would be appreciated," Delilah said.

A smile broke across Mahai's face. "Of course, Delilah, I would be more than pleased to be of service to you."

Jonathan moaned, placing his head into his hands. "No, she doesn't want your service."

"Are you asking me for a gift of information?"

"Delilah, no!" Jonathan interjected.

"Yes, please," Delilah said, feeling a wave of relief wash over her.

"And so, it has been agreed," Mahai said, clapping his hands.

"Thank you."

"You just made an agreement to make Mahai an offering that he will determine," Jonathan scolded her, "and whatever he asks of you, you can't say no to him."

Mahai shrugged. "Would you care for some refreshments?"

Before they could answer him, he walked to a white

lacquer and gold cocktail cart. He poured two glasses of bourbon and a glass of sparkling water.

Mahai handed Jonathan the water and Delilah the dark amber liquid. "Saluti," he said, looking Delilah in the eye.

"You two are on a quest, and you don't even know why you are searching for what you seek."

"Mahai, for the love of Pete, you made your agreement; tell us what we need to know," Jonathan growled.

"The ring was a gift from the Archangel Michael to King Solomon as a reward for his humility," Mahai explained as he took a pull from his drink. "It has the power—"

"To control good and evil," Jonathan said.

"This is only half true."

Delilah sat at attention, moving closer to Mahai. "Half true?"

"The ring has the power to control angels and demons," Mahai said, draining his drink.

"That's a lot of power for a coven," Delilah said.

"Or one man," Jonathan said, shaking his head.

"How'd my family get it?"

"Ah, well, the OB started the Hundred Years' War, like they have started wars before and the wars since, as a grab for world dominance. God was not pleased, so he sent the Maid of Orleans in to prove the purity of her faith by believing she was the chosen one to end the war," Mahai explained.

Delilah took a sip of bourbon, and it burned her throat. "Joan of Arc proved herself, so now the D'Arc family guards the ring. Why not take the ring back?"

"He can't," Jonathan answered.

"I don't understand."

"Once an archangel gives a gift to a conjuror, it cannot be reclaimed by the heavens; it has been made unclean by magics," Mahai explained.

"Why not at least disable it or something?"

"Delilah, gifts from the heavens are not like modems you turn off and reboot. The ring now has a power of its own, a power only witches can control," Jonathan said, standing up.

"The heavens give the gifts; it's up to us, their mystical children created from the marriage of the heavens and the humans, to use them to either create or destroy," Mahai said, nodding his head.

Jonathan held out his hand to Mahai. "I hope she finds her way home to you."

"As you well know, not all who wander are lost," he replied, grasping Jonathan's hand, placing his other hand over it. "Be well, my son."

When Jonathan and Delilah stepped out into the cold, they both shivered in unison.

"Now what?" she asked.

"I could use a burger. How about you?"

"We just found out my family has been guarding a ring which can control angels and demons, and there's a spell out there to cast it; a missing ring, and you're hungry?"

"Yeah, but they don't have the ring or a witch, now do they?"

Delilah crossed her arms over her chest. "Fine, lead the way."

Jonathan sunk his face into a double cheeseburger with bacon. She enjoyed watching him eat. He took pleasure in every single bite, moaning with delight each time.

"Samuel is using me to get to the ring," Delilah said, dipping a fry into ketchup.

Using his burger to point at her, "Maybe," he shrugged," Maybe not."

"He wants to take over the world, not save it. He told me as much."

"Well, you know the saying, hold your friends close and your enemies closer," he said, popping the last bite into his mouth and whipping the grease off his face with a paper napkin.

She pushed her burger away from her. "I'm not sure I have the stomach for all this intrigue."

He pointed at her burger. "Can I?"

"Knock yourself out. You seem almost happy about this turn of events."

"We know what Samuel wants, but Samuel doesn't know we know." He took a bite of her burger. "And we're in the power position, and you have the perfect excuse to go see him."

"My long-lost immortal children are not an excuse."

"My bad, it's a reason, the perfect reason," Jonathan said, finishing the last of Delilah's burger.

December 3 @ 11:11 am - The Coffee House
State of Mind - Edgy

When I told Jonathan I didn't have the
stomach for this, I wasn't lying. I have a
shot at the one thing I've always wanted—a
family. Yes, it's completely crazy and upside
down and far from simple. I remember when
Samuel asked me at my job interview what I
wanted. I blurted out a family before I could
stop myself. I remember the loneliness and
yearning I felt. I still feel it. I have this
space, this hole in my heart.

205

Gawd, I sound so cheesy.

But it's true.

Even though Thea tried her best. It was always just the two of us. This abandoned left behind feeling haunted my childhood. There were times, even as I got older, I would pretend my parents were there and I'd talk to them. This went on for a long time. IDK, maybe they could hear me? Who knows?

My children are like an echo in my heart. I can feel what I felt when I went back into the memory—the pain of having them taken away and the joy of waking up with them cuddled up next to me. I remember smelling the tops of their heads... that smell, it's mommy catnip. And their round rosy cheeks, eyes closed, lost in their dreams, like little cherubs. I missed so much. And now, they're grown adults who have lived hundreds of years without a mother. The thought of being a real family, the four of us—of having the one thing I have always wanted.

And then there's Jonathan. I feel in many ways responsible for him. Like, it's down to me to save him from Melia, from drugs, and from himself. Maybe we could just run away from all of this—take the money, and the passports, and go where they can't find us. But he'd never do that. He's too loyal. He'd never leave the coven without fulfilling his duty.

And that's what I love and admire about him.

I wish my mom was here. I have so many questions. I need her guidance, her advice, now more than ever. Honestly, I just need a hug and reassurance that everything will be okay. And if it's not, that no matter what, I can handle whatever comes my way. I just need someone in my corner that has my back no matter what. That loves me no matter what. Right now, it feels like everyone around me wants something from me and their affection comes with a big price tag and lots of expectations that I can't possibly live up to.

I'm not Joan of Arc.
I'll never be her.
Ever.
She was so strong. She had her faith. She was in service of one thing and one thing only. I feel like I'm expected to be in service of everything and everyone.

When the time comes will I be able to put my coven first? The coven that took everything from me. My parents. My childhood. And now, the rest of this life and maybe all the lifetimes from here on out?

—————————————————————————

Thirty-Four

"It is of great power since it compels the Spirits of Venus
to obey and to force on the instant any person
thou wish to come onto thee."

Delilah was left waiting alone in the formal living room. It was a set from a black-and-white movie with walls lined in wood, the sofas all dark velvets set around the fireplace. The last time she saw Samuel, she was still recovering. He showed her why she had risked everything to get pregnant. Her heart and her head were at odds. Even knowing the truth, he had murdered her. He was using her. It still didn't matter. She had feelings for him. More than feelings, she was bound to him in a way she didn't quite understand.

Lost in her thoughts, she didn't notice when Samuel entered the room, until he was standing in front of her; unsure what to do, she stood up and offered him her hand. He ignored it, and instead, leaned in and gave her a prim kiss. His light touch caused her cheeks to flush crimson. There was something about Samuel in a suit. He was sexy in a suit. But seeing him dressed in a cashmere V-neck, jeans, and penny loafers with two shiny pennies, made her heart hammer against her chest.

Delilah gazed past Samuel.

"Evie got in late last evening, and she'll be down in a moment. And Aaron, I reached out and left word, but the only thing reliable about him is that he is—unreliable."

Samuel poured two glasses of champagne and handed her one. "Cheers," he said, motioning for her to sit.

She picked a spot next to the fireplace. "Tell me again, exactly what you told them."

"After many long decades of searching for their mother, I found her."

"And their mortality?"

"I re-framed it as a gift. Not a punishment for their mother's misdeeds," he said, taking a sip of champagne.

"And they know I'm an Ascent witch?"

He reached over to her and took her hand. His fingers wrapped around hers. The flesh of his palm against hers was enough to send a burning hunger throughout her body. She hated that he still had that kind of power over her. She wished she could control her reaction to him and his touch.

"I have not explained your lineage or much else to them. It was easier than telling half-truths and lies. After about a hundred years, they stopped asking so many questions."

The doorbell rang. It echoed through the mansion like a trill alarm. It rang again, in three sharp staccato bursts.

Delilah jumped up and spilled champagne over the front of her sweater.

"I'll answer the door," Samuel said, handing Delilah a napkin. "Take a moment to compose yourself."

"I'm a mess," she said, showing Samuel her shaking hands.

"They will come to know and love you, trust me."

"Daddy dearest," Aaron called out.

Delilah found them in the foyer. Aaron picked Samuel up off the ground and into a bear hug. Aaron wore a long, navy-blue military-inspired coat with a cashmere scarf wrapped around his neck, skinny dark denim jeans, and ankle boots. His hair was longish and combed back from his forehead with a pair of aviator sunglasses resting on top. He reeked of old money and oozed the easy charm of a British monarch. Not surprisingly, actresses and socialites found him irresistible.

"Aaron put me down," Samuel said, laughing, "or I'll send you to bed without any supper."

He set Samuel on the ground. Aaron removed his coat with the same precise movements he inherited from his father. Delilah noticed he was wearing an off-white and navy striped sweater and an antique Bulova watch.

Samuel immediately saw it and grabbed his arm. "You bugger. I've been looking for that watch. I bought it from the Sinatra estate at auction."

Aaron shrugged him off. Like a laser, he set his attention on Delilah. He had the same unnerving way Samuel had of not looking someone over but taking them apart bit by bit with their gaze.

"So lovely to meet you, Mummy," Aaron said, taking her hand and kissing the top of it.

"Stop being such a wanker," a woman's voice teased.

It was Evie. She appeared small in an oversized fisherman's sweater and baggy cargo pants. Her long hair was pulled into a low ponytail. Like Aaron, she also had Delilah's violet eyes. The rest of her was entirely Samuel.

Aaron picked Evie up and swung her around. He set her down and began tickling her like they were children.

"Please stop, you'll make me wee," Evie called out, and he stopped.

Samuel took Evie's hand and introduced her to Delilah.

"Evie, meet Delilah. She has gone through a personal hell to find her way back to us."

Evie smiled at her. "Hallo Mum."

Delilah stepped in and pulled her into a fierce embrace. Finally holding her daughter in her arms, realizing all the moments they had lost, she remembered how it felt when she had found Maria, only to lose her again. Tears filled Delilah's eyes; there wasn't any magic that could fill the void left when you grow up without a mother.

"I have a million questions, and I don't even know where to begin," Evie said, her voice cracking, trying to hold back her tears.

Samuel patted Evie on the back. "Steady on. She won't vanish. I promise."

"Daddy, I'm famished. Please tell me Mrs. F made her famous Sunday roast," Aaron said, sniffing the air.

Samuel led them into the dining room. It was eerie and majestic, anchored by a stone fireplace. The table could seat twenty but was set for the four of them. It was a gothic dinner party with black and gold china under a candle-filled chandelier and a table filled with more candles and deep red, almost black, roses.

"Please let me get your chair for you," Aaron said to Delilah, pulling out her chair like a maître d' at a restaurant.

Samuel set a bottle of champagne into the stand.

Aaron pulled it out. "What kind of swill are you trying to fob off on us this evening?" Aaron asked as he inspected the label. "Ah, a Krug? Really Daddy-o?"

"Pour the champagne and keep your comments to yourself. Mrs. Fairfax has the night off, so I will be serving tonight," Samuel said.

"I'll help," Evie volunteered, following Samuel into the kitchen.

Aaron poured the champagne.

"So here we are. Mummy, tell me, where have you been for"—he checked his watch—"the last three hundred years?"

His question caught her mid-sip, and the champagne bubbles shot up her nose. Instead of answering the question, she choked on her champagne.

"Easy goes it there, Mother."

Samuel and Evie returned with plates overflowing with food.

"What you have here is what's considered an English Sunday dinner," Aaron explained, pointing at the plate. "We have roast beef, potatoes, some veg, Yorkshire pudding, and—"

"Gravy, I forgot the gravy," Samuel said, leaving once again.

"The old man's going soft in the head in his old age," Aaron said. "Delilah, we must know, where have you been all these decades?"

"Aaron, stop winding her up," Evie said, coming to Delilah's aid.

Samuel entered carrying a gravy boat. He set it on the table and sat down.

"Shall we say grace?"

"Grace," Aaron and Evie said in unison.

"I opened the door for that one, didn't I?" Samuel said, giving Delilah a warm smile.

"You'll never learn. We are pagan heathens who refuse to pray to your merciless God," Aaron teased.

"Shut your gob and pass the gravy," Evie said with a wink.

"It's our tradition to have a proper Sunday roast dinner when we're all in the same time zone," Samuel said.

Watching how they fell so effortlessly into being a family

made her heart swell and ache at the same time. *This is it, what I've always wanted. A family to call mine*, she thought as she emptied her champagne glass.

"Where did you fly in from?" Evie asked.

"Paris," Aaron answered, his mouth full of Yorkshire pudding.

"Aaron do not speak with your mouth full," Samuel scolded. "Still dating the blonde actress who was up for the Oscar last year?"

"You'll have to be a wee bit more specific."

"You're truly horrible," Evie said.

"Don't worry, love will catch you one of these days, Aaron, and when it does," Samuel said.

"Like it caught you, Father?" Aaron shot back, turning the fun, easy banter upside down.

Aaron wiped his mouth with his napkin and set it on the table.

"You'll have to forgive me, Delilah. Our father has been rather tight-lipped about the whereabouts of our mummy all these years. So please excuse me if I am gobsmacked by the prospect of sharing a Sunday roast with you."

"Aaron," Samuel said in a warning tone.

"I have spent many lifetimes searching for her. I have traveled to the far ends of this bloody planet. Now I'm supposed to sit here and play happy family with some woman who shares nothing with us other than the same peculiar eye color?"

"You are supposed to keep an open mind and give her a fair chance," Evie said.

"Who are your people? From whence do they hail? What do you do for a living?"

Samuel threw his napkin on the table.

Delilah put her hand up. "No, Samuel, it's fine," she said, folding her napkin and placing it on the table. "Up until a few months ago, I was an accountant from a small town. I have recovered my past life memories, and since then, I have recently learned I'm a descendant of Joan of Arc."

"You're an Ascent?" Evie asked. "We're semi-bloods? Like the unicorns in the witch world?"

"Delilah was cast out of her coven and out of her powers when it was discovered she sired children from two covens. Now, she's come back," Samuel said, filling in the rest.

"How'd you reclaim your memories?" Aaron asked.

"I drank poppy tea."

"Not once but twice, and she almost died," Samuel said with pride.

"Okay, so you're a total baller," Aaron said, shifting in his chair and leaning toward Delilah. "This man, our father, has kept his shit together for centuries. He's been a good father to us and deserves better."

"Aaron, that's quite enough," Samuel said, signaling them to return to their dinner.

In silence, they pushed their food around their plates. Samuel got up and poured more champagne. He stopped at Delilah's seat, placed his hand on her shoulder, and gave her a reassuring squeeze.

"If you love each other, then it's all worth the pain it caused?" Evie said, looking at them both. "You do love each other?"

The question hung in the air between Samuel and Delilah.

Samuel's eyes locked on Delilah's. "Delilah is my beloved now and always."

"You're ruining my appetite," Aaron said, turning back to his plate.

Once they finished dinner, Aaron took Evie out to a private club. Delilah and Samuel worked side by side cleaning the kitchen.

"You didn't answer Evie's question," Samuel said, drying

a platter with a dishtowel.

"Which question?"

Samuel set the platter down. He placed his hands on Delilah's hips.

"You know which question," he said, pulling her closer, his lips grazing hers. "Am I your beloved?"

He was pulling her into his thorny web. His words, his breath, his lips were spinning silk around her heart, making it impossible for her to wiggle free.

"Delilah, I want to marry you," he whispered in her ear. "Will you marry me?"

She pulled away from him and reached for the counter to steady her wobbly knees.

"Marry you?"

"I can give you the one thing you have always wanted—a family."

"Can we get married? Won't our covens come after us? The Immaculates?"

"After three hundred years, we will be together," he said, pulling her into his arms. "All you have to say is yes."

She couldn't look at him.

"Ah, I see. Not quite convinced." Samuel let Delilah go. He grabbed the tea kettle and filled it with water.

"Is there someone else?" he asked, placing the tea kettle on the stove, his back to her. "Master Jonathan has his foot in the door, once again."

Part of her wanted to reassure him; there wasn't anyone else. She wanted to go to him to wrap her arms around him and comfort him.

Her heart screamed, *Yes, I want to marry you.*

Her brain screamed, *Run for your life.*

Thirty-Five

"Thou art taught in what manner the Magical Arts
may be reduced to the proposed object and end."

It was an unseasonably warm night for December in Chicago.
Delilah had decided it was time to summon Maria and find out
once and for all where she had hidden Solomon's ring.
Jonathan and Devlin were in the yard building the bonfire.
Tabitha Anthea was gathering the items for the altar. She
watched as Thea gathered the Palo Santo smudge stick, a
bottle of red wine, white roses, and several white quartz
crystals.

Delilah was on edge, still suffering from PTSD from the
last time she practiced magic. Even though Devlin assured her
this was completely safe, Delilah still had her reservations.

Jonathan entered the kitchen, smelling like wood and ash
from the fire.

"We're ready when you are," he said, squeezing Delilah's arm.

"Help me with the altar," Tabitha Anthea instructed. "Dee, your dad is here, I'm here, it's going to be alright, I promise."

"I'm totally fine," Delilah replied, giving her a reassuring smile.

"I call BS," Faye said, entering the kitchen. "You're freaking out."

"Faye, not helpful," Jonathan scolded her.

"Whatevs, you weren't around the last time. I was," Faye said, opening the refrigerator and pulling out leftovers. "She was a hot mess."

"We are losing the night sky," Devlin called out from the yard.

One by one, they filed out into the yard. It was so quiet out in the country. Delilah gazed up, and the sky was full of stars. She forgot living in the city; she rarely, if ever, saw the stars. Their beauty always held a special kind of magic for her. Even before she knew magic was real. The big sky and the bright stars reminded her how small she was compared to the universe.

Tabitha Anthea set the items around the bonfire. She lit the smudge stick and began enveloping each of them in the smoke. Devlin handed Delilah the bottle of wine.

"Maria's favorite. You'll need to take a sip and pour some into the fire," Devlin explained.

Tabitha Anthea tossed the stick into the fire, and flames shot up. "We're ready when you are," she said to Delilah.

Delilah took a sip of the wine. "The Spirits which are created of Fire reside in the east, those created of Wind in the south. And between the east and the south lives Maria D'Arc. I call on the Spirit. I call on the Wind. I call on this Fire. Return our celestial spirit Maria to this physical plane. I call on you now, Maman," she chanted as the wind swirled around her.

Then she poured wine into the fire. Not sure what to expect, Delilah was puzzled when nothing happened. She glanced around the circle they formed around the fire. They stood with their eyes closed, asleep, standing up.

Delilah was again alone in a spell. Panic set in. She felt dizzy.

"Delilah, my love, you are perfectly fine."

She turned around, and Maria was standing behind her. She wasn't flesh and bone; she was a ghost.

"We don't have much time, dear one. Take off the necklace," Maria said.

Delilah fumbled with the clasp until she was able to remove it.

"Good girl, now hold it over the fire."

Delilah placed the necklace over the fire.

"Say after me, show me the band that controls the doors to good and to evil."

"Show me the band that controls the doors to good and to evil," Delilah repeated, and lightning lit up the sky.

"Repeat it," Maria said.

"Show me the band that controls the doors—" As the words left Delilah's mouth, lightning struck the necklace, and it burst into flames landing in the fire.

"Finish the spell," Maria yelled over the lightning display.

"To good and to evil." Delilah completed the spell, and the bonfire went out.

Delilah looked around the circle, and Maria was gone. Then Devlin, Tabitha Anthea, and Jonathan opened their eyes.

Devlin ran over to Delilah. "Are you okay, kiddo?"

Delilah nodded.

"I don't think the spell worked," she said.

"It did," Jonathan said, pointing to the pyre.

There it was—a gold ring with a six-pointed star. It appeared so harmless. She couldn't believe a humble ring held so much power.

"I was wearing it this entire time?" Delilah said, fishing it out of the ashes.

The magics coming off the ring made everything around her go blurry. She dropped it on the ground, unable to handle the energy.

Devlin picked it up. "Let's get inside."

Tabitha Anthea went to work making a pot of tea in the house and pulling out cookies from the pantry. Devlin set the ring down in the middle of the kitchen table. They stood around it, waiting for something to happen.

Faye walked into the kitchen. "Why's Delilah's necklace on the table," she asked, pointing at the ring.

"You see the necklace?" Jonathan asked her.

"Yeah, the necklace is sitting on the table. Did you guys find the ring or what?"

They all exchanged a knowing look.

"It's a glamour," Jonathan said, picking up the ring. "We can see it because we assisted with the spell."

"You guys are freaking me out," Faye said. "I'm going outside for a smoke."

They sat in silence, drinking tea, staring at the ring in the center of the table.

"Will it go back?" Delilah asked.

Devlin shook his head. "What did Maria say exactly?"

"Show me the band that controls the doors to good and to evil."

Once the words left Delilah's mouth, the ring burst into ashes and returned to the necklace.

"Well, then, I guess we now know how it works," Tabitha Anthea said, clearing the table.

Delilah picked up the necklace, expecting it to be hot, but it was cool to the touch. She put it back on. She held the round medallion in her hand. No magics were coming off it now.

"Did you know?" she asked Devlin.

He shook his head. "She kept it all a secret from me. It was safer that way."

"Can we talk? Alone?" Delilah asked Devlin.

Tabitha Anthea nodded, and Jonathan got up, and they left the room.

"Samuel asked me to marry him."

Devlin reached over and took her hand in his. For the first time in her life, she realized what she had missed, not having a father around to ask for advice.

"He promises me a family. My family, with my children."

"That sounds like a pretty good offer. One that would be hard to refuse."

"Why aren't you freaking out right now?"

He let go of her hand.

"And what good would it do? Freaking out? You've already made so many sacrifices for our family and our coven."

"You're giving me your blessing?"

He put his hand up. "Let's not get crazy now."

Devlin sat, scanning her face. She had the sense he was trying to gather his thoughts and choose his words carefully.

"Our world is complex with the power we hold; there are no easy answers and our mistakes—our mistakes come with a heavy price tag. As you well know."

She waited for him to continue.

"But I also believe for us to navigate our power, we must have free will; otherwise, what's the point?"

"You're saying to me, if I decided to marry Samuel and run off, you'd be okay with it?"

"What I am saying is it doesn't matter what I or anyone else thinks about it. What matters is do you believe Samuel loves you, or wants the ring?"

Delilah pushed her chair away from the table and got a glass of water. She drank it down.

"You're trying to lead me to make the right choice instead of telling me what to do."

"You are too smart for your good," Devlin said, standing up and walking over to her.

"Isn't it possible he might love me for me?"

"Of course, it's possible," he said, kissing the top of her head.

Later that night, when Delilah was getting into bed, there was a tap at her door.

"Come in," Delilah said.

The door opened, and Jonathan's head peeked through.

"Hey, do you have a minute?" he asked.

She stood back and let him enter. Slowly she shut the door behind him.

"Have a seat," she said, pointing to her bed.

She got under the covers and yawned. Jonathan stood near the bed and rocked back and forth on his feet.

"What's going on?"

"You can't marry him."

"Excuse me?"

"I overheard you and Devlin," he said, pacing around her room. "He's using you for the ring."

"I'm not sure I want to discuss this with you."

"Delilah, our weddings aren't like human weddings. It's not all I love you for better or for worse till death do us part. It's a blood wedding. He owns your soul for an eternity," he said, sitting on the edge of her bed.

"He owns me. I don't own him back? That sounds very sexist and unwitch-like."

"This is serious."

"What you're saying is Samuel has been playing a long game with me spanning centuries only to steal the ring."

"Exactly."

"But when we met, I wasn't the guardian of the ring. I

didn't even know it existed."

"He did."

"And you can prove this how?"

"I can't. But I can tell you, Samuel wanted immortality and killed you to gain it."

"Jonathan, are you using again?"

"I found a mortality spell. A witch has to murder the one person they love to obtain it. It's the darkest of dark magics."

"I'm tired. And I don't want to argue with you."

"He doesn't truly love you."

"And you know this because you truly love me."

His face crumpled. It was as though Delilah had slapped him.

"Goodnight," Jonathan said, leaning over and kissing her forehead. "Before making a decision, just consider what I've told you."

Thirty-Six

"A second precaution is to be observed by the Judge and all his assessors; namely, that they must not allow themselves to be touched physically by the witch."

A few days later, Faye left an urgent message for Delilah to meet her at a coffee house in Logan's Square. Driving into the city gave her some time to think about her life and what was at stake. When Delilah arrived at the coffee house, Faye wasn't there. She ordered a latte and sat down to wait. It was a neighborhood place with exposed brick walls featuring graffiti artwork from local artists, along with mismatched plastic chairs and tables.

The spot was perfect for people watching, Delilah thought as she sipped her coffee. A man walked in. Surrounded by hipster gig-workers hunched over their laptops, with his like Thor meets the Incredible Hulk vibe, he stood out. She observed him as he ordered a coffee and made small talk with the barista. *Was he a regular?* Delilah wondered, watching him as he filled his coffee with milk and sugar. When he caught Delilah watching him, she quickly examined her phone.

"Hello."

Delilah glanced up. Thor-Hulk was standing at her table, holding a cup of coffee and a massive croissant.

"Mind if I have a seat?"

"I'm waiting for someone," she said, dragging the chair away from him with her foot.

He set his hand on the chair. "I'm the someone," he replied, sitting down.

Delilah scanned the room, searching for Faye.

"I asked Faye to set this up."

"You're the witch hunter?" she said, recognizing him.

He nodded. Delilah shot up, almost knocking over her coffee.

"I'm Wolf. Just give me five minutes. Please," he said, placing his hand on Delilah's arm.

"You tried to kill me, not once, but twice," she said between gritted teeth.

"If I wanted you dead, you'd be dead," Wolf said softly. "You're perfectly safe."

Delilah slowly sunk back into her chair.

"I can't believe Faye would do this to me."

Wolf pulled out the page from the D'Arc grimoire.

"We found something in the translation."

"You mean the witch hunters who were, or are, still trying to kill me," she interrupted.

"I'm on another mission now. For this to work, we'll need to work together," Wolf said, taking a bite out of his chocolate croissant.

"Why on earth should I trust you?"

"This is bigger than our former beef."

Delilah stared at him. He had this boy-next-door quality to him, which gave her the sense that maybe Wolf could be trusted.

"Show me what you found."

He unfolded the page. His massive fingers pressed down on the wrinkled page smoothing it out.

"To penetrate the power of hidden things, we conjure to find the knowledge to walk through the tower door of good and of evil. This knowledge was given to King Solomon for his humility to stand before the heavens. The power to open, to conquer, to subdue, to reprove the Spirits. These Mysteries of Mysteries will draw the Spirits from the four quarters of the Heavens." As Delilah read out loud from the translation, the winds picked up and shot ice and snow at the windows of the coffee house.

Wolf placed his hand over the paper. "You may want to read that to yourself."

Delilah looked up and saw people on the street trying to walk against the wild winds. Once she was finished reading the page quietly to herself, she looked up at Wolf.

"There's mention of a door. A door in which good and evil shall pass through. If the door is destroyed, it will render the ring useless," Wolf said.

"Are you sure it's not a metaphysical door?"

"No, because, if you see here," he said, pointing to the next line. "There's a distinction between door and doorway, leading us to believe it's a physical door to a tower."

"And if it is the case, why wouldn't one of our ancestors have figured this out and destroyed it?"

"Maybe they tried and failed."

Wolf leaned back and studied her. His gaze made her fidget. She found herself drumming her fingers on the table.

"You don't have a clue," he said.

"Enlighten me, please."

"Solomon has the door. He has the spell. All he needs now is the ring, and it's lights out, and game over. He controls heaven, hell, and everything in between."

"And you're keeping me alive because—" Her voice trailed off.

"You're the only one who can get close enough to end this thing once and for all."

The tone in his voice had changed from confident and cocky to unsure and shaken. This entire scheme was now squarely placed on Delilah's shoulders.

"It's all down to me."

He leaned toward her and placed his hand on hers. "It's all down to you," he repeated.

They sat with his hand on hers for a good long time. During the time, Delilah had a series of visions, of Wolf as a baby. Her mother, Maria, speaking to a court about him. Wolf, as a child, receiving a beating.

"It's you. You're the half-breed, witch slash witch hunter."

Wolf swiftly pulled his hand away.

"What did they do to you?" she asked, placing her hand on Wolf's shoulder.

"My father tried real hard to make me a bloodthirsty witch hunter."

"You don't have the appetite for it."

He sighed. "No, I really don't. You're the first person, I mean witch, to notice. I hate being a witch hunter," he said, as he smiled at her. "Wow, feels so good to say out loud. Like a weight off my shoulders. Thank you."

Delilah shook her head. "You're welcome," she replied, unsure what else to say.

Wolf glanced at his watch. "I gotta motor. So, are we good?"

"Um, what do you mean are we good?"

"You need to get close to Solomon. Find the door and

destroy it. Easy peasy," he said, draining the rest of his coffee and stuffing the last bite of croissant in his mouth.

"And how am I supposed to do that?"

"That's way above my pay grade. But I am here to tell you you'll have the full support of the witch hunters to help you execute your plan," he said, handing her his business card.

The card read, "Wolf Zandt, Security Specialist."

He stood up and bowed. "My lady, we'll await your marching orders."

She watched him wave at the barista, stuff a five-dollar bill in the tip jar, and disappear into the crowded street. Moments later, Faye entered.

"What's up?" Faye asked, sitting down.

"You tricked me into meeting with a witch hunter?" Delilah said, barely able to contain her rising anger.

"Now, you know the truth. And it's a good thing."

"Is it, though?"

"Yes, it is. Now, you know without a doubt Solomon is off the table."

Delilah gathered her purse, coffee cup and stood up.

Faye glanced up at her. "He's no longer an option. Right?"

She didn't answer Faye's question. Instead, Delilah set her cup in the bin and walked toward the door with Faye on her heels.

"What's the plan? How are we going to take him down?" Faye shot a stream of questions at her as they walked down the street.

Delilah stopped in the middle of the sidewalk. She could feel her temper rising.

"Why do you always follow me around like a little lost puppy? Searching for answers I don't have."

Faye took a step toward her and leaned into her. "We're a team. And, together, me and you, we'll make a plan."

"I'm not sure what you think"—Delilah waved her hand

back and forth between them—"is going to happen here, but it's not. Ever."

Faye stepped back. Her face changed from her normal I'm bored with the world expression to a hurt child.

"I'm so over it. You're on your own," Faye said, then turned around and walked away from her.

Delilah was left alone standing on the sidewalk. The weight of it all came crashing down on her. She instantly regretted what she had said to Faye. She had been nothing but a good friend to her through all this. The one person Delilah could genuinely count on. And she pushed her away. The strong coffee, her conversation with Wolf, along with her cruelty to Faye, caused her body to buzz and twitch. She zipped up her coat and began walking, street after street, the cold wind burning her cheeks, but she didn't stop. Before she realized it, Delilah found herself standing in front of Mahai's antique shop, The Golden Triangle.

She entered to find Mahai standing near a painting, talking to a couple. Delilah waited for him to finish. Once he saw her, he excused himself and greeted her.

Kissing her cheek, her right first, then her left, he said, "My darling, so good to see you. I can see you require an old friend, come, tell me your troubles."

Delilah followed Mahai to his office. Once inside, he helped her remove her coat and invited her to sit down.

"Would you care for a drink?" he asked.

"No, thank you."

"How can I be of service?" Mahai asked, sitting down behind his desk.

"Will I owe you for this help?" she asked, remembering the last time he offered his help.

"No, my darling. This is a freebie."

She unwrapped her scarf. "I think I'll take a drink now."

Mahai walked over to the cart and poured brandy into two

large round crystal glasses etched in gold. He handed her a drink. She took a sip of the amber liquid. It instantly warmed her and settled her frayed nerves. Then she laid out the entire problem to Mahai. He listened attentively, only interrupting her to ask a clarifying question. By the time she had finished, her glass of brandy was empty. He sat with his hands steepled under his chin.

"I have found the most efficient way to conquer an adversary is mastering the fine art of deception," Mahai said, emptying his glass. "To have your opponent believe that you're both on the same side."

"Like keep your friends close and your enemies closer?"

He stood up, walked around his desk, and sat down next to Delilah.

"I will now ask for my offering. There is an ancient tablet; it is in Mr. Solomon's possession. I wish to have it and require you to retrieve it for me."

"His entire home is a museum. You'll need to be a bit more specific."

"It's made of clay. From what I understand, it resides in his library on his desk."

"And you need me to retrieve it because?"

"The forty-nine seals on his front door cast an impenetrable ward, which makes it impossible for me to get in."

Delilah felt like Mahai had not only wrapped her in his web but had now administered his venom.

"I'll add it to my 'to do' list," Delilah said, wrapping her scarf around her neck.

Mahai reached out and seized her wrist in his hand. His grip was iron; with a bit more pressure, he could crack her bone in two.

"My darling, you mustn't fail. If you do, it's your life I will take," he said, releasing her.

After leaving Mahai, there was one person Delilah knew she needed to talk to—Maria. All she had to do was find a quiet spot and a cardinal. Her inner compass led her back to Graceland Cemetery. The trees were barren. Walking through the cemetery, the only birds she encountered were black crows. They were flying behind her, following her as she continued her journey along the winding path. It was nightfall, and the cold was leaching onto her bones, chilling her from the inside out. She was ready to give up when a majestic bright red cardinal swooped past her.

"Hey, you, Mr. Cardinal, bring me my mother, Maria," Delilah shouted. "Please."

The cardinal made an energetic loop around her. Then shot away from her, disappearing into the air. Unsure what to do next, she waited, afraid to move or breathe. A red light shot out of the sky, like a bolt of lightning, and Maria appeared. Delilah ran into her arms, nearly knocking Maria over.

"We don't have much time," Maria said.

"Samuel proposed to get back the ring. The witch hunters want to work with us to take him down. They think they found a door which, if destroyed, will make the ring useless. Oh, and Mahai wants me to steal a tablet from Samuel."

"Is that all?"

"Mahai will kill me if I don't."

Maria, dressed in her signature head-to-toe black, paced around in a small circle with her hands on her hips.

"First things first, how did you feel about Samuel's proposal?"

"It felt like he was handing me everything I ever wanted on a silver platter."

"A family to call your own," Maria said, nodding.

"Yes," Delilah replied softly.

"Samuel and his coven, they're powerful witches. I don't think you'll be able to take him down but destroying the ring would be a significant achievement. With the ring no longer in play, it would bring a new order to our world," Maria explained.

"How?"

"The spell requires Samuel's blood."

"Okay, am I supposed to like ask for a vile to wear around my neck or something?"

"In our weddings, like in all our ceremonies, we share our blood. If you were to go through with his proposal, you would have Samuel's blood for the spell."

"You want me to marry him?"

"No, I want you to start the marriage ceremony; once his blood is drawn, cast the spell."

Delilah started to feel dizzy. She could see how this plan could go all kinds of wrong.

Maria took hold of Delilah's shoulders. "You mustn't kiss him. If you kiss him, you are bound to him for eternity. Your soul and all your possessions, everything—including the ring."

"I'm feeling nauseous," Delilah said.

"And the power locked in the ring, it will try to fight the spell," Maria added.

"Super."

"I have all the faith you'll succeed. The blood that runs through your veins will carry you through," Maria said, hugging Delilah.

"What's the spell, then?"

"It's on page twenty in the grimoire."

"Then what?" Delilah asked, the panic rising inside her.

"Smear Samuel's blood on the ring, then say the spell. You must believe with every bit of your being when you say the words. Not one drop of doubt."

"I need to have unwavering faith, like Joan of Arc."

"Yes, exactly."

"Mom, I don't have that kind of faith."

Maria pulled her into a hug. She kissed the top of her head.

"You were born to do this. And believe me, your father and I tried to pull you away from your destiny, but here you are."

The cardinal returned; he circled them once.

"My time is just about up."

"What about Mahai?" Delilah asked.

"Leave him to me," Maria said, kissing Delilah on her cheek. "Remember, you were born to do this."

When the cardinal landed on Delilah's shoulder, Maria vanished into the ether.

Thirty-Seven

"I am my beloved's, and his desire is toward me."

Once Delilah finished devising her plan, she sent word to Wolf. She hadn't discussed it with Tabitha Anthea or Devlin because she knew they'd try and talk her out of it. She only shared with Wolf the details, and asked to work with the witches, angels, fairies, and anyone else he could convince. If anyone could talk Sage back into the game off the sidelines, it would be her son. Or so Delilah hoped. For her plan to work, they would need everyone back on the field to help win this battle.

With sweaty palms and shaky hands, she felt exactly like she did on her first visit to Samuel's mansion for her job interview. Mrs. Fairfax welcomed her like a long-lost old friend. After taking her coat, she directed her to the stairs to Samuel's private quarters. It didn't register until she was standing there waiting for Samuel—she was in his bedroom.

The walls were painted a milk-chocolate brown with a large wooden sleigh bed as the room's centerpiece. She saw open half-full suitcases scattered around the room.   .

"Samuel?"

He entered wearing a white undershirt tucked into his pants with a towel wrapped around his neck. There was a trace of shaving cream on his chin. Taking notice of her, he stopped abruptly.

"It's you."

"Yes."

"What are you doing here? I thought you were arriving in an hour," he said, glancing at his watch.

"You texted me to come earlier," she said, showing Samuel her phone.

"It wasn't me," he said, tossing the towel on the bed.

"I can go and come back. Where are you going?" Delilah asked, pointing to Samuel's luggage.

"Back to London, my plane leaves tonight," he replied. "Here, please sit." He directed her to a chair near the fireplace. "And let me finish getting dressed."

He came back moments later in a light blue dress shirt with large gold cufflinks with the letters "S," and "D" intertwined. He sat in the chair across from her and crossed his legs.

"You have come to give me your answer."

"I have," she said. Her voice sounded hollow, like it didn't belong to her. Her mouth was dry.

"A glass of water?"

She nodded. Her eyes trained on Samuel as he stood up and poured her a glass of water in a paper-thin crystal glass.

"Here you go," he said, handing it to her.

She raised the glass to her lips and drank down the water. She held the delicate stem tightly in her hand.

"My answer is..." she said, squeezing the glass so hard she

caused it to shatter in her hand. Time went in slow motion; when she looked down, she saw glass shards sticking out of her palm with blood flowing out.

Samuel shot up out of his chair. He pulled her up and led her into the bathroom. Before she realized what was happening, he had removed the pieces from her hand, throwing them into the sink. She watched as her blood stained the porcelain sink from white to pink. Wrapping her hand in a towel, he told her to apply pressure with the other hand. He went to work, pulling out the first-aid kit from under the sink.

Her blood quickly seeped through the white towel. Samuel gave up on performing first-aid and instead used magic.

"Blood flows out, blood flows in, bring it back to where it belongs," he chanted, then blew on her bloody hands.

She watched as her blood was drawn back into her body and her skin repaired itself in seconds. Her hands were still shaking from the adrenaline spike.

"Come," he said, helping her back to the chair by the fireplace.

He placed a gentle kiss on her cheek. "I had decades to figure out how to sweep you off your feet, and alas, I have failed. Pushed into the arms of another. Now go and be well."

She took two swift steps to the door with her back to him and with her hand on the doorknob. "Don't you want my answer?" she asked.

"I already know what you will say."

Delilah turned around. "Do you?"

"I do."

"You've got it all kinds of wrong," she said, running into his arms.

She slammed into him, throwing her arms around his neck. He froze. Then wrapped her in his firm embrace.

"Is this a yes, then?" he asked, touching her nose with his.

She nodded and kissed him. Leading him to the bed, she

began unbuttoning his shirt. His hand flew to hers, stopping her.

"Tell me, are you my beloved?"

Delilah ignored him and pressed her hand against him, feeling him get hard. He pushed her away and stood up. Their chests were heaving up and down as they faced one another.

"Turn around," he demanded.

She turned away from him. He pulled off her clothes and left her standing only in her bra. Slowly he slid the straps off her shoulders as his fingers shot currents through her skin.

He reached for her and began rolling her nipple between his fingers, "Tell me."

Delilah looked into his eyes. They were wild.

"Who is your beloved?" asked Samuel, his eyes changing into Jonathan's clear blue eyes.

Samuel leaned in to kiss her. His lips pressed roughly into hers. But they felt different. When he pulled away from her, it was Jonathan's face staring back at her.

"You belong to me," said Jonathan.

Samuel led her back to the bed. She sat down as he knelt on the ground before her. "Tell the truth."

Delilah peered around the room. She felt woozy. She could hear her heart pounding in her ears. Even though her head was motionless, the entire room began to rock back and forth. The bed was like a boat in the middle of an angry gale.

Samuel stood up. He took her face in his hands and kissed her. When he released her, she opened her eyes—it was Jonathan.

"Who is your beloved? Him? Or me?" Jonathan asked.

Jonathan gently pushed her down on top of the bed. His naked, lithe body pressed against hers. She could feel him hard against her sex.

"You're so wet," Jonathan said.

Delilah opened her eyes, and this time, it was Samuel

gazing down at her. He pushed her legs open, and as he was about to enter her, he stopped.

"Who is your true beloved?" Samuel demanded.

Frustrated with lust and longing, Delilah started to grind against him. She needed to feel him inside of her.

As Samuel pulled away from her, his face morphed into Jonathan's.

"You have to choose," Jonathan said.

The room pitched to one side and the walls spun around her as his face morphed back and forth between Samuel and Jonathan. It felt like the bed was going to lift off and fly away. She squeezed her eyes shut while willing the room to stop spinning. Delilah opened her eyes. Now it was Samuel peering down at her, his body pressed against hers. She lifted her head and tried to kiss him. He pulled away from her, and she bit his bottom lip.

"Am I your beloved?" he asked.

She was on the edge, and Samuel stopped.

"Say it," Samuel demanded. Delilah pushed her body against his. With his hands, Samuel pinned her down.

Jonathan was gazing down at her, yelling, "Answer the question."

"Him?" Samuel asked.

"Or me?" Jonathan said.

"You have to choose," they said in unison.

Delilah was on the edge of desire, on the edge of madness, with his cock pulsating against her wet and swollen sex.

"Samuel," she screamed. Finally, he sunk himself deep inside of her as her body exploded over and over.

—————————————————————————

December 19 @ 11:11 am - My New Home
State of Mind - Elated
I'm happier than I even could've imagined!

I'm marrying my beloved. I'll have my children there right beside me. It's everything I've ever wanted.

A family.

My family.

It's a dream come true. I'm walking... no I'm gliding on air. I feel dizzy and happy and so certain this is the right thing. I've never felt so certain of anything or anyone—EVER!

I wonder if this is what doing drugs feels like? If so, I totally get it now. Who wouldn't want to feel like this? ALL THE TIME!!!!!! It's amazing. I'm getting married TOMORROW!

All the doubt, all the fear. Like that, it's just gone. I love Samuel and I'm gonna marry him and live happily ever after! I get my happily ever after.

Finally!!!!!!!!!!

I deserve this. We deserve this. All of us. We've been separated for much too long. I can't wait to give myself, my body, my soul to Samuel for eternity.

Thirty-Eight

"For while they were in the flesh, the sinful passions, which were aroused by the Law, were at work in her body to bear fruit for death."

From the moment Delilah had declared Samuel was her beloved, there was a shift within her. She felt like she was in a dream watching as the events unfolded around her. It reminded her of the time she went on a road trip with Tabitha Anthea, and she used the cruise control on the highway. Delilah remembered the feeling the car was speeding along without her foot on the gas pedal. It frightened her and she quickly turned it off. That's how Delilah felt, like her body had shifted into cruise control. This time she couldn't flip a switch and turn it off.

The next evening, dressed in a gold lamé sleeveless gown with a deep V-neck, Delilah waited in the formal living room.

Samuel told her he had a big surprise planned for her. The lamé itched and dug into her armpits. The dress wasn't something she would've ever chosen for herself, but Samuel insisted. Sipping champagne next to a massive Christmas tree, she had a gnawing feeling she was forgetting something important. But for the life of her, Delilah couldn't remember what it was. Instead, she focused on spending her first holiday together with her family, Samuel, Aaron, and Evie.

The sound of music playing rocked her out of her dream-like state. She turned around to find Samuel dressed in a slim-cut tuxedo. With his hair slicked back, he looked like he had stepped out of a black-and-white movie. He held out his hand and pulled her up. Placing her hand on Samuel's shoulder, he swept her into a box step around the room. It felt like the two of them were gliding on the wind. When the music stopped, the sound of clapping broke the spell they were under. Standing in the archway, was Aaron and Evie decked out in their finest.

"Don't you two clean up nicely," Aaron teased.

Evie slapped Aaron on the arm. "Leave your sarcasm at the door," she said, leaning in to hug Delilah, then Samuel.

Samuel poured the champagne.

He tapped on his champagne flute. "It was important to me that you both be present for this," Samuel said, setting down his glass.

Delilah watched as Samuel unbuttoned his jacket, got down on one knee, and fished a jewelry box out of his pocket.

"Delilah Johanne D'Arc, I've spent centuries searching for you. I can't live another second without you by my side," he said, opening the velvet box. "Will you do me the honor of being my wife?"

The ring left her speechless. It was an enormous cushion cut diamond with a halo of small diamonds around it.

"Delilah, love, will you marry me?" he repeated.

She sank down on the floor, took his face in her hands. "Yes. My answer is yes," she said, pulling him into a kiss.

Crying and laughing, they touched foreheads.

"Let's open another bottle and celebrate," Aaron said.

Samuel pulled Delilah up off the floor. This time, they were in a circle, the four of them hugging.

"This is all I ever wanted," Delilah said with tears in her eyes. "Thank you, Samuel."

"When's the wedding then?" Evie asked.

"The solstice," Samuel replied, stepping away and breaking their cozy circle.

Evie poured more champagne for them. "That's tomorrow."

"And it's a full moon," Aaron added.

"Tomorrow?" Delilah repeated.

"I have waited for many lifetimes to be with you, and I cannot wait; I will not wait, one moment more," Samuel said, taking her hand in his and kissing the tips of her fingers.

Delilah smiled up at him. A feeling hit her again, like a gentle tap at the door; she knew for sure, there was something she was supposed to do.

Later that night, Delilah and Samuel snuggled on the couch, sipping tea in front of the fireplace. She took in Samuel's office. It was a short time ago; she sat in this very room meeting Samuel for the first time. Now, they were getting married.

"A penny for your thoughts," he said.

"I'm happy, more than happy; I'm ecstatic. I can't wait to be your wife. Would you like some more tea, husband?"

"Yes, wife."

She kissed his cheek and stood up to pour more tea. The tray was sitting on his desk. Delilah set their cups down next to a round tablet. She ran her fingers over the smooth grain. Memories hit her fast like a hard rain. She was on a mission.

Her breath hitched as her plan to destroy the ring, once and for all, came bolting back to her.

"Everything all right, love?"

She lifted her hand, pretending to look at her ring. "It's my ring. It's so dazzling, and I can't take my eyes off of it."

Samuel stood up and slowly began to remove his bow tie.

"I'm no longer in the mood for tea," he said, taking her by the hand and leading her out of the library.

After Samuel had fallen asleep, Delilah grabbed her phone and snuck up to the cupola. It was so cold, and dressed only in a flimsy lace and silk nightgown, she regretted not taking a robe or blanket with her. She texted Wolf and waited. Finally, her phone buzzed.

"It's on," she said.

"When?"

"Tomorrow night."

"Wow, that was fast," he replied, blowing air out of his cheeks into the phone.

"I'll text you the coordinates. Is the team ready?"

"Yes, we have full co-operation from everyone."

"I should go before Samuel wakes up and realizes I'm gone."

"Hey, is everything good on your end?"

"Yeah."

"I was worried when I didn't hear from you. You were supposed to text me."

"I think he cast a spell on me."

"Should we abort, private?" Wolf asked.

"No, we'll never get a chance like this again."

"You need to be in tip-top shape for this mission to work."

"I'll see you at the chapel."

"We'll be there before the blood kiss. And whatever you do, don't kiss Samuel."

"I know, I know, if I kiss him, he owns my soul along with

all my possessions, including the ring. I got it."

"Are you sure?"

"He still thinks I'm under his spell."

"Be careful."

"Says the guy who tried to kill me," she said, teasing him.

"You gotta let it go," he said before hanging up the phone.

Thirty-Nine

"My love, our winter has finally passed.
And our love has endured through the ages.
Now we enter our eternal summer."

The winter solstice brought the shortest daylight of the year and longest night of the year. For Delilah, when she was an accountant, the solstice held no significance. It was a day like any other. Now, as a witch, it called her to go into the obscurity of the night to uncover her inner strength. She spent her wedding day preparing for the ceremony, which included taking a saltwater bath. After which, she had to rub an anointed oil that carried a mixture of scents like cinnamon, vanilla, nutmeg, and cedarwood.

Throughout the morning, to double-check it was still there, her hand would land on the necklace, and she found herself praying to Joan of Arc. As the day wore on, she begged her ancestor for the conviction to believe in the words, to believe in the spell. When Delilah pictured a barely of age girl in a bloodied battlefield, she saw vulnerability, not courage. *Maybe that's what real courage is: the ability to be completely vulnerable, protected only by your faith,* Delilah thought. She wondered if she could access a conviction like that within herself.

"Hey, Mum," Evie said, snapping her fingers. "Where'd you go?"

Delilah smiled at her. She wasn't convinced, when the moment would come, she could turn her back on her children. Evie looked mercurial, dressed in a blush chiffon A-line dress with a delicate headband framing her face made out of diamonds and pearls.

"Are you ready to get this show on the road?" she asked, pointing at the garment bag.

Delilah nodded. Evie unzipped the bag. Inside was a simple, champagne-colored lace dress with a boat-neck collar, a large cut-out in the back, and a pearly pink silk sash, along with a matching fur shrug. Simple and elegant, her wedding dress was exactly what she would've selected.

"Do you like it?" Evie asked, her brow furrowed.

"I love it."

Afterward, they were whisked away in a shiny black, classic Rolls Royce. Delilah's entire body was vibrating. She visualized the spell while they drove into the night. Evie wouldn't tell her where they were headed. Soon they pulled up to Lincoln Park; Samuel and Aaron were waiting for them to arrive at the edge of the park. Samuel was dashing. Wearing a navy suit with a vest underneath, he seemed the part of the fairytale prince. No detail too small, his light-pink tie matched the sash on Delilah's dress. He opened the door and helped them out of the car.

He kissed the top of Delilah's hand. "I've waited so long for this moment."

With a wave of his arm, Samuel transformed the grassy field into a snow white-domed temple. The pillars had a delicate lace pattern engraved in them. Each massive arched window was lit up with giant golden candles.

Samuel led Delilah up the stairs. The door was made of pressed gold, and set into the middle of it was a shield with a serpent. Slowly the door opened for them. Delilah could feel her knees buckling.

"Steady on," Samuel said, softly.

As they entered, the dome opened to reveal the luminous moon hanging in the sky, the color of pen ink with layers of colors seeping through from hues of dark blues to magenta to black. He took her hand in his, and together they glided down a long, narrow mirrored aisle that reflected the stars in the sky.

A woman's voice sang in a clear tone, ringing like a fine-tuned bell. "Rise up, my love, and come away with me. For you are my beloved, and I am your beloved. For our love will soon be even stronger than death."

Leading up to the altar, under the dome, were six marble steps flanked with lion statues with their mouths frozen open mid-roar revealing a set of large violent teeth. Samuel helped her up the glossy steps, with Evie and Aaron following behind. Once they reached the top of the altar, the sky rained shooting stars. Delilah gazed up at the magic and wonder of it all. Her heart was bursting—half of her wanted nothing more than to kiss Samuel and seal her fate as his wife and mother to their children. The other half of her heart was breaking, knowing she had a duty to her coven to honor.

Samuel reached out and touched her cheek. "Are you ready?" he asked.

Their eyes met. In Samuel's eyes, Delilah saw a chance at a future. The two of them, together, for all time.

He embraced her. "My love, our winter has finally passed.

And our love has endured through the ages. Now we enter our eternal summer."

On a narrow table sat a series of sacred items for their wedding ceremony: a goblet, a piece of red silk cloth, and a curved dagger with a sharp point at the tip and a serpent-shaped handle.

Samuel lifted the goblet and took a drink. "My beloved is beside me to quench my longing."

He held the goblet to Delilah's mouth, and she took a sip. The concoction was so bitter; she had to force it down.

Aaron and Evie stepped forward. Aaron removed the red silk cloth from the table. Samuel took Delilah's right hand in his left as Aaron bound their hands together.

"Repeat after me," Samuel said. "My beloved is mine."

Delilah glanced at the table and realized the blood kiss was next. She knew what she had to do. Her heart thundered against her ribs.

"Mum?" Evie asked, concerned.

"My beloved is mine," Delilah repeated.

"I am hers," Samuel said.

"I am hers," she said.

Aaron and Evie let out a giggle.

Samuel shook his head. "I am his."

Delilah realizing her mistake, repeated, "And I am his."

Samuel presented his wrist to Evie. She picked up the dagger and ran it across it. Samuel's blood was seeping from his body. Evie handed the knife to Aaron. Samuel nodded at Delilah to do the same. Delilah presented her wrist to Aaron, and in one swift motion, he cut Delilah's wrist. The blade felt hot against her skin. She watched as her blood oozed out. Then Aaron placed the dagger on the table and stepped back.

"I am a seal upon your heart," Samuel said, raising his wrist and rubbing his blood on her lips.

Delilah placed her blood wrist on Samuel's lips. When she

touched his lips, they were frigid. This sent a current of fear through her body. His lips, instead of warm and inviting, were cold and dead.

His tongue shaped like a serpent shot out and tasted her blood. "You will be a seal upon my heart," Samuel said, leaning toward her, closing the distance between them.

It was now, or it was never. Their lips were centimeters from touching. Delilah could feel Samuel's breath on her cheek. It would be so easy to kiss him. He would protect her. They could all be a family. She parted her lips, ready to seal her fate; then she saw Joan of Arc riding through a bloody field on a white horse with arrows and cannons flying around her.

In one determined motion, Delilah, with all her might, tore herself away from Samuel. She yanked off her necklace and rubbed Samuel's blood on it.

"Earth to heaven, heaven to dust, demolish these angels and these demons we must," Delilah shouted out.

The ground underneath them began to quake. Then suddenly, the fairies and angels flew in through the open dome. They were followed by the witch hunters and witches descending into the temple from the windows and doors, shouting out indecipherable battle cries. The walls of the temple began to rock, crumbling around them.

"Delilah!" Jonathan yelled from the bottom of the stairs.

The moment his foot touched the stairs, the lions sprang to life, releasing guttural roars, shaking the building's foundation.

Samuel lunged at Delilah. He seized her by her shoulders. "Kiss me," Samuel demanded as he pulled her into his body. His arms were two vices crushing into her, still trying to land the blood kiss to seal their souls. She managed to break one hand free and slapped it over his mouth, wiping some of her blood off his lips. He released her, and she lost her footing and went tumbling down the stairs. She landed at Jonathan's feet.

Jonathan pulled her up. "Do you still have it?"

She glanced down and pressed into her palm was the necklace. With every ounce of faith she had in her, she chanted at the top of her lungs the spell.

"Earth to heaven, heaven to dust, demolish these angels and these demons we must," Delilah repeated.

And with each word, a wind howled through the chapel carrying her words up into the heavens. In her hand, the necklace scorched her skin, and without thinking, she dropped it on the ground. The necklace turned into the ring and unleashed apparitions of demons and angels. The demons were lost souls from hell; their ghoulish faces were all fixed in mid-scream. By contrast, the angels were saved souls from heaven; their exquisite faces were serenity.

Once released from the ring, they all scattered like a mist into the air. When the witch hunters breathed in the demon mist, they instantly turned on the witches. Possessed by the demons, the witch hunters were no longer able to stand by their oath to stand with the witches against Samuel and the OB coven.

Samuel strolled down the stairs with the lions behind him. "Oh, what have you done, Delilah? I offer you the entire universe, heaven, and hell, and you betray me?"

Jonathan grabbed Delilah's hand; together, they turned and started to run.

"Stay!" Samuel bellowed. He lifted his hand, and the ring flew into it.

Like children playing the game *Simon Says*, Delilah and Jonathan froze in place. They were at Samuel's command, unable to move.

"Face me," Samuel said.

Their bodies turned around like puppets.

"It is almost laughable—you thought you could outwit me. I've been devising this scheme since the day we met at

Versailles," Samuel continued.

"Now what?" Delilah asked.

"You will kiss me and seal our souls," he replied, edging closer to her. "And you will rule with me, at my side."

Delilah closed her eyes, and with every ounce of her being, she harnessed not blind faith but anger. She was apoplectic for all the lost years, all the decisions made for her, all the fear that had tormented her, and all the time lost with her family.

"No!" she screamed as her words became a howling wind blowing Samuel off his feet.

"You will never own my soul or me," she continued, and as the words left her mouth, the ring soared through the air toward her. Samuel tried to catch it as it shot away from him. In mid-flight, the ring turned back into the necklace and wrapped around Delilah's neck. When the necklace landed in her skin, it fused into her body, becoming a tattoo. Delilah and Solomon's ring were now one.

Samuel was now at Delilah's side. Jonathan seized her arm and Samuel the other. Jonathan pulled her toward him and kissed her, removing the last remaining traces of Samuel's blood from her lips.

Together, they turned and ran to the door, through the fighting surrounding them. The building was pitching and turning.

With one foot out the door, dressed in head-to-toe leather, Melia appeared.

"Mi Amore. You can't begin to know how it breaks my heart to find you here," Melia said, raising her arms, knocking them off their feet back into the sanctuary.

Samuel flew over the fray, landing on Jonathan's back. Samuel's eyes had become haunting and savage. Samuel snapped Jonathan's neck in one swift motion, and with a sickly pop and crack, his lifeless body slumped to the ground. Melia screeched and knocked Samuel over. They were fighting, and their movements were so fast, it was impossible to decipher who was winning or who was losing.

Delilah fell to her knees and gathered Jonathan's limp body in her lap. She held onto him.

"Please come back to me," she said through her tears.

Samuel raised his hands in the air, and time around them stopped.

"On your feet, we have business to sort out," Samuel demanded.

Delilah didn't move. With a wave of his hand, he yanked her body up.

"What about our children?" Delilah asked.

"Ah yes," he said, snapping his fingers.

Aaron and Evie appeared before them. Samuel circled them.

"You two are a massive disappointment to me," Samuel said.

"Daddy, please, we can't go back there," Evie begged.

"We made a deal. Did we not?" Samuel said.

"Father," Aaron pleaded. "Send me back, but let Evie stay."

"How chivalrous of you, my son. But I am afraid a deal is a deal," Samuel replied, and with a clap of his hands, an old television set appeared.

It was the same one they had used to send the Twins back. Samuel nodded his head, and Aaron and Evie disappeared, only to reappear in the television. Delilah watched as they both mutated back into the two gaunt children who tried to trap her in her memory. They pressed their faces on the screen and began pounding on it with their fists. Before Delilah could move, Samuel turned the television off, and it vanished.

"What have you done to our children?" she asked, horrified.

"They failed me. There are consequences for failing me, as you will soon find out. It almost doesn't seem fair to fight you,"

Samuel said, sauntering around her sizing her up. "You're so weak."

"Was any of it real? All this for the ring?"

"I'm a powerful witch, but I cannot control your true desires. Everything that took place between us happened because deep down, you wished it."

"Now, I wish for you to be dead."

"Do you really? It's still not too late for us," he said, as he gently brushed his hand along her chin.

"It's way too fucking late for us," she yelled, grabbing his arm and pulling it behind his back. "Time's up."

With a flash of lightning, time began again, in slow motion. Delilah watched as the battle commenced like they were all underwater. Samuel summoned the lions, and they surrounded Delilah, bloodthirsty, at the ready to tear her apart.

"Halt," Tabitha Anthea ordered, and the lions sat down like trained dogs.

It was Tabitha Anthea, dressed in her best crimson wool suit, and following behind her was Devlin. Delilah was so relieved to see them both.

Devlin walked over to the lions. He placed his hand on top of the lion's head. "Good little puppies," he said, and one by one, the lions turned into puppies.

"Time to retrieve your charge, Mrs. Fairfax," Tabitha Anthea said.

Mrs. Fairfax appeared. She rolled up her sleeves. "How many times do I have to tell you that the bloody ring is not meant for you?" she yelled at Samuel.

Samuel ignored Mrs. Fairfax, and he reached out his hands and pointed them at Tabitha Anthea.

"Delilah, I'm going to need some assistance containing Master Samuel," Mrs. Fairfax said.

"I'm nowhere near as powerful a witch as he is," Delilah shrieked.

"What is his greatest fear?" Devlin asked.

Samuel flexed his fingers, pointing them at Tabitha Anthea; he was using his powers to strangle her. Her hand flew to her neck as she tried to gasp for air.

"Delilah, we need to act fast," Devlin warned.

Darkness, Samuel feared darkness, Delilah remembered. She visualized a closet opening into a void, pitch-black nothingness. It would leave Samuel with nothing but himself and his thoughts. Delilah snapped her fingers, and a large, glossy black door with a serpent engraved on it appeared. Mrs. Fairfax waved her hand, and the door opened.

Tabitha Anthea struggled for her life. Delilah, Devlin, and Mrs. Fairfax stood shoulder to shoulder with their hands extending out in front of their bodies, willing Samuel into the darkness. He continued to press the life out of Tabitha Anthea as his feet slid toward the door. Faye appeared, her wings out, and tackled him. She threw him into the Closet.

With a wave of her hand, Mrs. Fairfax slammed the door shut, and it flew away into the night. "That child will be the death of me," Mrs. Fairfax said, falling to her knees.

Tabitha Anthea was on the ground. Her body was so still with all the life drained out of her luminous dark skin. Maria was standing next to her body.

Devlin ran over to her and took her pulse. He started CPR, then thought better of it. Devlin placed his hands on her chest and closed his eyes. He was trying with all his might, using his magics to bring her back.

Delilah heard a hissing sound and gazed up. The demons and angels hovered above her. She reached her arms up to the sky and summoned them back into the ring and into her body. Once they were back inside, she fell to the ground. They took over her mind and body. She had no control as they fought, trying to seize the power of her soul. One moment she felt a profound inner peace, the next a despair so profound she wanted to hurl herself off a building to end the suffering.

Amid it all Joan of Arc appeared. She offered Delilah her hand and pulled her out of her body. Delilah watched her body seizing and convulsing. Faye heaved herself on top of Delilah's body. Now, the two of them were bucking wildly.

"Aros, can I get a hand over here?" Faye yelled out.

Joan of Arc pointed at Faye and smiled. Aros appeared and placed his hands on Delilah's temples. Her body was thrashing back and forth.

"Aros, we'll see you in Hell," Delilah seethed.

Delilah was back inside her body, and slowly it stopped shaking until finally, it stopped altogether. She came to with Faye laying on top of her and Aros holding her head.

"Are you back?" Faye asked.

"Yep. Faye, you saved me once again."

"Hey guys, I don't mean to break up a tender moment, but we need to get Delilah somewhere safe," Wolf said, offering his hand.

"Tabitha Anthea?" she asked.

"Devlin got her out of here," he replied.

"Is she dead?"

"I don't know for certain."

Faye ran back into the fray. Delilah took in the battle before her. It was grisly.

"I can't leave," Delilah said, pointing to the fighting around them, "until this is over."

Aros pointed at Delilah.

"Me?"

Delilah felt helpless. Unsure what to do, she put her index finger and thumb in her mouth and whistled. To her surprise, the fighting ceased as everyone turned to face her. Wolf picked her up and placed her on a base of a broken column.

"Speech." Wolf cheered and clapped his hands.

Soon the entire temple was shouting "speech" at Delilah.

Public speaking gave her hives.

She surveyed the battlefield. Her heart stopped seeing the dead witches and witch hunters.

"Today, it didn't matter if you were a witch, a witch hunter, a fairy, or an angel when you heard the call you answered. Lives were lost today. And no matter what I say to you about honor, about sacrifice, about preserving the balance in our world, it won't replace the fallen. But know the ring is safe because of your efforts here today. Now, I ask you to lay down your arms, lay down your magics."

The temple was silent. Delilah glanced at Wolf, and he gave her a thumbs up. Then cheering and clapping broke out. Delilah jumped off her pedestal.

"I need to find my dad and Thea," she said.

Forty

"I do not know if they believe it;
I leave that to their hearts."

Delilah and Wolf ran to the entrance. Delilah glanced back. The sanctuary walls had completely crumbled. When she turned around, they were met with a crowd of humans with their phones up in front of their faces taking pictures and videos. Wolf and Delilah, blinded by the flash, held their hands up in front of their eyes.

A reporter holding a microphone with a camera behind her, jumped in front of them. She jammed the mic in Delilah's face.

"We've had reports of supernatural activity happening in Lincoln Park. Can you confirm this for us?" the reporter asked.

There was a commotion in the crowd.

"No comment," a voice called out.

It was Sage walking toward them, holding a staff.

"Yes, we're witches bitches," Sage said, then snapped her fingers at the crowd. "Now, scram."

In a daze, the spectators, including the reporter, put down their cameras and walked away like zombies searching for brains to eat.

"It's time for you to come home, son," Sage said, placing her hand on Wolf's shoulder.

"Not so fast," Gart said, walking up behind her.

"Miss me, lover?" Sage teased.

"Hunters don't miss their whores," he replied, sticking a cigar in his mouth and lighting it. "Wolf, the mission is over. It's time to wrap this up and head back to HQ."

Wolf crossed his arms over his chest. He stared for a long time at his father, Gart.

"Come on, boy, time to rally our troops and head back to HQ," said Gart.

Wolf pulled out his knife and his gun and set them down at Gart's feet. He saluted Delilah. Then turned around and walked away from them into the darkness.

Gart pointed at Sage. "Woman, this is your fault."

"You're blaming the wrong witch," Sage said, smiling at Delilah.

Gart stalked away back to the temple.

"The prophecy has come true," Mahai said, appearing from thin air. "A descendant of Joan of Arc has led the witches out of the darkness."

"Mahai, what are you talking about?" Sage asked.

Mahai pulled out his cell phone and showed them Twitter. "You see here the hashtag witches are real is trending."

Delilah took the phone from his hands. She scrolled through images of the witches fighting each other. There was even a YouTube video of the speech Delilah just gave. She handed him the phone.

"Where's Jonathan's—?" Delilah asked, unable to finish the question.

Aros appeared, holding his lifeless body.

Delilah touched his hair. "It's my fault he's dead," she said with tears streaming down her face.

"Let me take care of him," Sage said, placing her hand on Delilah's back.

"I need to find Devlin and Thea."

Faye appeared. "Let me take you home."

"Home?" Delilah asked. The word struck a chord. She didn't know where her home was anymore.

Faye pulled Delilah into a bear hug, and the two of them dematerialized. They reappeared on the lawn of Tabitha Anthea's house. There was a single light on in Thea's bedroom window. Delilah ran through the front door.

"Dad! Thea!" she called out, barely able to make it up the steps. She threw open the door to the bedroom. Laying on the bed was Thea, with Devlin sitting next to the bed, holding her hand and praying.

Delilah rushed to her side, taking her other hand. The room was so still and so silent. *Was Thea dead or alive?* She wiped the tears cascading down her face, too scared to say a word.

"I was lucky to find love not only once in this lifetime, but twice," Devlin said, placing his hand on Thea's chest.

"She always showed me love and acceptance," Delilah said.

Devlin reached over and took Delilah's hand.

"You lost two mothers in one lifetime," he said.

"Who died?"

They both glanced down and peering up at them was Tabitha Anthea. Devlin placed a kiss on her lips.

"For a moment there we thought we'd lost you," he said.

"You should know better; it takes more than some sorry excuse for a witch to take me down. And besides, I have the best ER doc with magic hands in the city taking care of me," Tabitha Anthea teased.

"So glad you didn't die on us," Delilah said, hugging her.

Devlin wrapped his arms around them both. "Thank God you're both safe and sound," he said, his voice cracking.

"I wasn't sure if I could do it," Delilah said, squeezing them both.

"I knew you could do it," Tabitha Anthea said.

The next morning, Delilah woke up in her bed in her childhood bedroom to the smell of coffee and pancakes. For one delicious moment, she felt tranquil before she remembered what had happened the night before. Then it was pure heartache. She stared at the crack in the ceiling, trying to reconcile the profound loss with the fact they did manage to keep Samuel from obtaining the ring. Her hand flew to her neck as she traced the tattoo of the necklace on her skin. It was raised like a brand. When she couldn't stand her thoughts any longer, she forced herself out of bed.

Sitting at the kitchen table was Faye and Wolf sharing blueberry pancakes and coffee like two old friends. Devlin was flipping pancakes at the stove, wearing one of Tabitha Anthea's frilly aprons.

"Are there any pancakes left?" Delilah asked, pouring herself a cup of coffee.

Devlin made a plate for her and set it down at the table before returning to the stove. Delilah wrapped her arms around him, hugging him with all her might.

"Thank you, Dad," she said softly in his ear.

He patted her hand. "I love you, kiddo," he replied, kissing the top of her head.

She sat down, and they ate their breakfast in a comfortable silence. Afterward, Wolf asked if he could have a moment alone with Delilah. She led him outside to the backyard, and he built a small bonfire. Delilah filled up a thermos with coffee and grabbed two thick plaid wool blankets.

"Look, I'm not so great with words," Wolf said, staring at his hands, "but I wanted you to know I'm sorry for trying to kill you."

Delilah took a sip of coffee.

"For which time? The first? Or the second?" she teased.

His head shot up like a bullet. He met her gaze.

"I'm sincerely trying to apologize to you."

"Bygones and all that," she replied with a wave of her hand.

"You've probably put two and two together by now, but the hunters are no longer working with you."

"They're on a new mission," she said, pouring more coffee into Wolf's cup.

"Especially now that the humans have proof witches exist."

"Now you have to exterminate us for good."

"Not me. I'm done with the Sect."

"Where will you go?"

"Maybe off the grid, get my head together, then re-enlist," he said, formulating his plans in real time.

"Would you ever consider working with me? We make a good team."

He sat back in the Adirondack, the wood wheezing, trying to accommodate his size. "I don't know. What's the 401K package like?"

"Don't you want to know what the job is first?"

He spat into his palm and extended his hand out to her.

"It doesn't matter. I'm in."

Sealing the deal, Delilah shook his hand. They sat around the fire, telling stories until the twilight descended. For the first time in her life, Delilah felt calm as her fears and anxiety had receded into the background. With popcorn and a bottle of Irish Cream, Tabitha Anthea, Devlin, and Faye joined them. Studying their unlikely circle, Delilah realized she finally had the family she had always wanted.

The End

Let's Stay Connected!

Sign up to receive my newsletter for more information on upcoming books in the *Delilah* series (*Delilah Forsaken* and *Delilah Saved*), deleted scenes, short stories, and more.

Website
AmeliaTellsStories.com

Instagram
@aedellos

Twitter
@DelilahD'Arc

Facebook
@AmeliaTellsStories

LinkedIn
@AmeliaDellos

Acknowledgements

My parents, George and Mary were voracious readers and at an early age took me to our small neighborhood library. I soon discovered my love for books and for reading. And a big thank you to all the librarians who run our public libraries. And to the small independent bookstores too, especially The Book Table.

Delilah came to me as a fever dream, and I had to write this story to find out what happened to her. She kept haunting me through the many years it took to complete and publish her story. My husband, Eric, saying thank you doesn't seem to be enough. I will say this – I couldn't have written this story or completed it without you and your support. And to my daughter Alena, you make me want to be a better mother, woman, teacher, writer, and human. You are our bright one. And to my loving familiars, Teddy, and Bo, I can't imagine life without you.

To my coven, Dena, Kathrine, and Gretchen, you are and will always be my sisters. Thank you for always believing in me and having my back in good times and in bad.

I have had the humbling honor to be in a community with some amazing women in circles and in writing groups. To my head witches, writer extraordinaire Barbara Demarco Barrett, for guiding me back to writing, and to the goddess extraordinaire Elena Vassallo Crossman, thank you for guiding me back to myself.

To all the readers on Wattpad that took the time to read various iterations of this story, and to take the time to comment, I owe you for encouraging me to complete this book. Although, it might look a lot different than the story you read. And to writer and teacher A.X. Ahmad for telling me to start with a blank page, because I am a better writer than I was when a started the book. I will be forever in gratitude.

And last but not least, to team Atmosphere Press, Trista Edwards, Alex Kale, Erin Larson, Kevin Stone, and Ronaldo Alves for helping me to launch Delilah out into the world.

About Atmosphere Press

Atmosphere Press is an independent, full-service publisher for excellent books in all genres and for all audiences. Learn more about what we do at atmospherepress.com.

We encourage you to check out some of Atmosphere's latest releases, which are available at Amazon.com and via order from your local bookstore:

Twisted Silver Spoons, a novel by Karen M. Wicks

Queen of Crows, a novel by S.L. Wilton

The Summer Festival is Murder, a novel by Jill M. Lyon

The Past We Step Into, stories by Richard Scharine

The Museum of an Extinct Race, a novel by Jonathan Hale Rosen

Swimming with the Angels, a novel by Colin Kersey

Island of Dead Gods, a novel by Verena Mahlow

Cloakers, a novel by Alexandra Lapointe

Twins Daze, a novel by Jerry Petersen

Embargo on Hope, a novel by Justin Doyle

Abaddon Illusion, a novel by Lindsey Bakken

Blackland: A Utopian Novel, by Richard A. Jones

The Jesus Nut, a novel by John Prather

The Embers of Tradition, a novel by Chukwudum Okeke

Saints and Martyrs: A Novel, by Aaron Roe

When I Am Ashes, a novel by Amber Rose

Melancholy Vision: A Revolution Series Novel, by L.C. Hamilton

The Recoleta Stories, by Bryon Esmond Butler

About the Author

Amelia Estelle Dellos is a writer and filmmaker. She is an MFA candidate and professor at Columbia College Chicago. Her novel, Delilah Recovered, won 2017 Watty on the international platform Wattpad and has found a home at Atmosphere Press. The novel will be published in Fall 2022.

Her short story "Psychopomp" was published in Writing in Place: Stories from the Pandemic, and she will have another short story, "It's About Time" published in Grand Dame Literary Journal. Writing in Place debuted on Amazon at number four in Essays and number nineteen in Short Stories. As a screenwriter and director, Amelia's films have appeared on PBS and Amazon Prime. Her films received the following accolades: Sundance International Writer's Lab finalist, Chicago International Film Festival Pitch Winner, and the Women's International Film Festival finalist.

She lives outside of Chicago with her husband, teenage daughter, and two feisty little dogs who video bomb her Zoom meetings. For more info, follow her on Instagram at @aedellos or visit her website ameliatellsstories.com.

Made in the USA
Monee, IL
01 September 2022

12036495R00163